ALEXIS BUXTON

ALSO BY ALEXIS BUXTON

<u>CTU Eagles Series</u>

The Late Hit

The Christmas Scramble

The Change Up

The Pass Protection

The Game Plan

To the girlies looking for someone who crawls to you and worships at your feet. May you find your own Tristan Nelson.

Reader Note

This book contains **adult content, including sexually explicit scenes**, and a **brief mention of the past death of a loved one**. Please read with care and at your own discretion.

Paradise in Progress
A Rivals to Lovers Romantic Comedy

Alexis Buxton

CHAPTER ONE

KENNEDY

TRISTAN NELSON IS THE *bane* of my existence, and now he's my new boss.

What have I done in life to deserve this torture?

For years, he's always been right there with his perfect smile and his perfect clothes, even his hair, which is supposed to look messy, always looks perfect.

In college, he was my enemy. Although I don't think he ever realized I dubbed him my nemesis, that would require him to pay attention to anyone else but himself.

I mean, how could I not hate him when he constantly beat me out of everything? He'd outscore tests by the smallest points, causing his paper to be used as the class example. When professors needed to call on students, they'd choose him every time, even though *my* hand was always raised. And don't even get me started on his blase frat boy attitude. He walked around like he was God's gift to New York University's campus.

Senior year is when things became really heated.

For our final project, the university organized a huge design fair where the architectural majors had to compete. The guidelines were to design a new community space that incorporated social events, art exhibits, and community gatherings, with a focus on fostering connections and love. The award for winning was a ten-thousand-dollar prize and an internship at one of the top real estate developers in the country.

Somehow, he beat me.

Of course he did.

Here I was, a nobody who worked her tail off to make it from a small, rural town in the Midwest to NYU, and the boy born with the silver spoon kept beating me out of opportunities.

Two years ago, after graduation, I thought my problems with Tristan Nelson were over. I landed a job at a decent architectural firm in Chelsea, designing smaller real estate developments, usually strip malls.

Was it my dream job? No, but it paid the bills, and I enjoyed the company I worked for.

Until a month ago, I thought Tristan was out of my life for good, leaving me to focus on myself and my career ambitions.

Now I'm sitting in a wrap-around glass conference room overlooking Midtown, staring down at a folder labeled *Nelson Signature Hotel & Resorts*, and if I dare to look across the table, my eyes will land on my arch nemesis.

Who is now apparently my boss?

Oh life, she has a funny way of throwing a wrench in your plans when you least expect them. A month ago, I was on the fast track to becoming the head of my department, but the owners decided they were ready for retirement, and instead of finding a new CEO to take over the company, they sold it to the highest bidder.

Nelson Signature was the highest bidder, owned by none other than Dennis Nelson, Tristan's father.

Most of my co-workers jumped ship when they realized who they would be working for. If I were smarter, I would've done the same thing, but along the way, I grew to love the company and what it stands for. My clients have all been amazing and I really enjoy my co-workers.

And a part of me wanted to beat Tristan. Why I thought I could beat him for a position in his father's company was beyond me. After days of interviewing with human resources and the Vice President of Development, I pleaded my case that I deserved to fill the position of development manager, only to find out the next day that Tristan Nelson would be taking over that position and I would be a member of the architectural team.

If it were at any other company, I would have swallowed my pride and gotten over it, but the fact that I thought I could win the battle of office politics at his dad's firm left me feeling naive and insecure.

Do I *really* want to work at this firm?

Do I *really* want to pick back up our competition?

The last two years have been a breeze. I've been able to focus on my dreams, accomplishments, and designs without needing to be the best. But staring at his devastatingly perfect hazel eyes and coiffed brown hair, a fire burns deep inside my soul.

One of these days, I'll beat him.

One of these days, it'll be my designs featured in Architectural Digest.

My eyes find his, only to discover that he's already watching me. His dark eyebrow quirks, as if he's reading my mind.

Damn him.

My attention is back to his brother, Alexander, who happens to be the Vice President of Development, making him my boss too. That is, until Tristan takes over that position when their father steps down. Supposedly, all the office positions will be shuffled around in the next three to five years.

Yay for instability.

Alexander ends our meeting, and I quickly gather my items before dashing out of the conference room, making a beeline for the elevator. Nelson Signature owns the top five floors of the Eisenhower building, each floor designated for specific levels inside the company.

The top floor consists of the higher positioned offices, while the second floor is the main entrance for guests. A large desk sits with four receptionists and conference rooms of various sizes.

Teams of architects and interior designers are located on the third floor, where my cubicle is. The remainder of the floors house human resources, sales and marketing, property management teams, and everything in between.

"Hold up, Firecracker."

That voice. I stumble in my heels and hope it's not enough for Tristan to notice as I do the opposite of what he demanded.

Spotting the line gathering at the elevator, I head straight for the door leading to the stairwell. I'm not against descending steps and breaking a sweat in these goddamn heels to get away from him. Shoving through the door, the wood hits my elbow, causing me to drop my notepad, and loose papers spill onto the ground.

"Shit," I hiss, bending down to gather them up. I'm quick, but not quick enough.

The sound of the door opening has me glaring over my shoulder. "Damn, Firecracker. Who knew you could move that fast?"

Unable to fight the urge, I roll my eyes. "Not now, Tristan."

"Ah, come on, I only wanted to let you know that I can't wait to hear what your proposal will be for the new location we acquired."

Pausing with my hands outstretched, I turn to stare up at the man leaning against the doorway, arms crossed, as a cocky grin spreads across his perfectly symmetrical full lips. The jerk couldn't even offer to help pick up my papers. Not that I would've accepted his help; it just would've been nice to tell him no. But Prince Nelson must not have wanted to wrinkle his Armani suit.

I narrow my eyes. "What are you talking about? What acquisition? And why would you need to hear it? Won't you design your own?"

His signature smirk shines back at me, which has his dimple appearing. "Oh, this is great. You didn't hear the news?"

"What news?" I grit out and crinkle the paper I'm holding.

"The St. Lucia project is mine."

Color drains from my face, but I fight to keep my facial expression relaxed so he doesn't see how much that bothers me. I have only heard a rumor that Nelson Signature acquired a resort in St. Lucia, making it their first international resort. Since it was a rumor, I didn't think too much about it. I've never been one to fully believe anything that comes out of the gossip mill. The only thing I knew for sure was that if this was true, the design project would be my first opportunity to give a full presentation since I was hired at Nelson Signature. Now I'm finding out he's going to be overseeing it. No matter how much time, effort, and energy I put into my design pitch, I'm never going to get accepted, especially if Tristan has any say.

I avert my gaze from his, gathering up the rest of my papers before standing and smoothing down my pencil skirt. As he tracked my movements, I feel his eyes blaze over my body.

"Oh yeah, Tristan? It's going to be me on top. Just wait." My cheeks flame as I watch his face morph into a lopsided grin, almost sinister, and it's clear he took it the wrong way. "I-I didn't mean for that to sound so-so sexual."

His chuckle fills the space between us. "Firecracker, are you finally admitting you want me in bed?"

"In your dreams." With a scoff, I turn on my heels and let my feet carry me down the stairs. His husky chuckle is the last thing I hear as I open the door to the floor we share.

Yeah, I loathe Tristan Lawrence Nelson.

• • • • • • • • • • •

The rest of the afternoon seemed to drag on. Not only have Tristan's words been muddling my brain, but I've had to go over someone else's designs for the resort in Aspen, Colorado. Nelson Signature wants to conduct a forty-million-dollar facelift at their resort, including upgrading the rooms to include a more apartment-like feel, new dining options, and a state-of-the-art spa with top-of-the-line wellness treatments.

It's going to be a stunning remodel, but going over the plans and budget for someone else is a bit tedious. I have five years of experience in this field, but I feel like I'm back in the training process, like I'm a newbie again. I have to familiarize myself with the type of accommodations and materials that Nelson Signature is known for.

Resting my elbows on my desk, I rub my temples. I'm so glad it's Thursday, which is the night my friends and I meet up at a local bar for happy hour. It's been a long week, and I'm desperate to blow off some steam.

"Ready?" Zoe, my co-worker and friend, asks as she pops her head over the wall separating our spaces.

A small gasp escapes my lips as her voice startles me. "Seriously, Zoe. You scared me."

She laughs, and I shake my head. Zoe and I hit it off right away. She's a few years older than I am and has been working here since she graduated from college. Our personalities meshed, and she swiftly took me under her wing.

"Come on, babe, let's go get our drink on."

I reach for my lower desk drawer, sliding the compartment open and pulling out my purse, where I make quick work at unzipping and pulling out my small makeup bag. Most people have to dig for their items, but I'm not one of those people. I'm as organized as they come. I could totally be the kind of girl on social media who films her life and everyone would comment that no one's lives are that organized. I believe everything has a place, and if it doesn't, it doesn't belong.

Using my compact mirror, I swipe a layer of blush on before pulling out my go-to Charlotte Tilbury Pillow Talk lipstick. With a fluff of my curled copper red hair, I'm ready to hit the town.

"I'm so jealous of your hair, Ken," Zoe compliments as I lock up my desk for the night.

"Thanks, girl. It's all fun until someone calls you 'Red' or —"

"Firecracker!" Tristan calls out, just as Zoe and I pass his office. My blood heats instantly with annoyance.

"Or *Firecracker*," I mutter under my breath, and Zoe lets out a chuckle.

Turning my attention to his office, I watch as Tristan rounds his desk and flicks off his light. "Heading out already?"

I glance at my watch to check the time, then scan the room, realizing we are one of the last ones left in the office. "As a matter of fact, I am."

He tsks, freaking *tsks*. "I thought for sure you'd be pulling the midnight oil for your big presentation next week."

He's just getting under your skin, Kennedy. Ignore the pest and go have drinks.

Deciding he's not worth my time, I resume my walk to the elevator, with Zoe in line beside me. Only that doesn't stop Tristan, as he steps up right behind us. Pushing the button to call the elevator, I choose immaturity and give him the silent treatment.

"So where are you two off to?"

"We're heading to Rumors." Zoe's reply is out of her mouth in the next second. My head whips in her direction as my eyes narrow, shooting daggers at her for telling the enemy where we're going.

"Of course you're going there." His arrogant tone drips with disdain as we step into the elevator.

"What's the matter, Tristan? Rumors not good enough for you?" I stare at my rival and watch as Zoe's eyes ping-pong back and forth between us.

How am I supposed to work here with him? Is this really the type of workplace atmosphere I want to have?

"It's not beneath me." He shrugs. "I assumed you'd be going to Whiskey Barrel."

My mouth flounders at his attempt at an insult. "Are you making fun of me because I'm a country girl from the Midwest?"

Raising his hands in defense, he eyes me with a quirked eyebrow. "Hey, you said it."

I fight the growl that is so desperate to escape. He's infuriating. Absolutely impossible. But somehow his charm has women eating out of the palm of his hand. Hell, Zoe is happily married, and her eyes are doing that whole googly, dreamlike stare.

Saved by the bell, the elevator doors open. This man is insufferable with his constant need to torment me. Rushing ahead of him, I tug Zoe's arm so we can haul ass away from the insufferable man as the security guard wishes us a good evening.

"It'll be a good evening once he's gone," I mutter under my breath, but not quietly enough as a chuckle comes from the gnat in front of me.

We exit the spinning doors, and I stop dead in my tracks when I see the black town car waiting there. Tristan brushes past me, our shoulders making contact, and a slight shock stings my shoulder from where our bodies connect.

"Would you ladies like a ride?" Tristan interrupts my thoughts before I have a chance to dwell on what just happened.

"No," I blurt, turning on my heel and guiding Zoe down the sidewalk.

He leaves us with a wave and a laugh.

"Oh my god, will you two please have sex already?" Zoe asks as she hails a cab.

I can't help gagging at her question. "Are you for real right now? You know I can't stand the man."

A yellow cab pulls over, interrupting our conversation. Climbing in, I politely instruct the driver to take us to Rumors. The ride is fairly quick, but it allows both of us time to check our notifications. There's an alert notifying me of a new money transfer from my share payment app. Assuming it's from my parents, I don't think too much of it. Not until I open it and find a hundred dollars from @Just-TrisNelson with a note that says, *drinks on me ;)*

How am I going to survive this man?

CHAPTER TWO

TRISTAN

"WHAT THE HELL ARE we doing slumming it with the commoners?" my friend, Rafe, asks as he sits down across from me.

We're seated in a black high-top six-seater with matching full-back bar stools in the back corner of the dimly lit bar. Rumors is known for their dimly lit space and hot pink neon lights, where associates from local high rises congregate to bitch about their jobs and the executives running their companies. The name wasn't just a fluke. It's the place where all the gossip spreads.

"Little brother wanted to spy on his co-worker," Alexander—or Xander, as everyone but my parents call him—says as he takes a sip of his whiskey.

"I didn't come to spy on her."

Rafe turns in his seat and tries to figure out what woman my brother is talking about. No doubt he spots her immediately. Her copper hair stands out amongst the bottle blondes and brunettes. And if that doesn't give her away, the smattering of freckles across her face will surely pull you in. Kennedy is too good for the hustle and bustle of New York City. It's not because she's not strong enough; she's the most headstrong woman I've ever come across. But it's because her heart is too pure. New York City will chew her up and spit her out before she even realizes it.

And she has named me the bane of her existence, but she couldn't be further from the truth. There's nothing I love more than toying with her. Somewhere along the way, our communication went from jabs to a flirty banter filled with all kinds of sexual innuendos. We're a human resource department's wet dream with the amount of workplace rules we've no doubt broken a time or fifty.

While I love pushing her buttons, I'm waiting for the day when she throws her Midwestern politeness to the side and gives me a piece of her mind.

"Damn, the redhead?" Rafe asks, hunger deepening his voice as he turns back to face me.

I glare at him over the brim of my glass. "Don't even think about it," I say before taking a pull of my beer.

"It's not like you're going to make a move," Xander muses and leans back in his seat, as if he's getting comfortable for a show.

Ignoring them both, I keep my eyes focused on her. Since she's left the office, Kennedy has relaxed. Her hair still hangs down her back, curls bouncing with every move. But she's managed to unclasp the first few buttons on her black blouse, allowing the top of her lacy red bra to peek out. She's stunning and completely off-limits. Especially with my recent move from the architectural team to being named design manager, a steppingstone for me as I work my way up the corporate ladder.

I tried to look away, but just as I was about to, she laughs at something funny her friends say. The sound causes a group of frat boys standing near their table to grow some courage and walk over to them.

A polo-wearing guy places his arm around the back of her chair, and she leans closer to Zoe.

"Oh no, man, looks like one of those fraternity douchebags is making a move on your girl," Rafe chides.

"First of all"—I snap my head toward Rafe—"she's not my girl. And secondly, you were one of those douchebags at the University of Southern California."

Xander chuckles from beside me. Like me, Xander stayed in state and chose Cornell instead of going to NYU with me.

As much as she hates me, and as much as I instigate our antics, I could never sit back and watch something bad happen to her. I watch intently as she scans the bar, and that's when she finally sees me. Our gazes lock as her green eyes latch onto mine, and I watch her eyebrow lift with curiosity. Then something that looks a lot like relief flashes briefly across her features. I flash her a wink. Her cheeks pinken before her signature scowl she reserves only for me returns. It's almost as if she remembered who she was playing a staring contest with. She turns her attention back to the guy who has moved even closer to her. If I hadn't spent the last four or so years learning her tics, I would have missed the blush completely.

Standing from my chair, my feet carry me to her without a second thought. Groups of people scurry out of my way as my gaze lasers in on the girl who will turn me gray before I'm thirty.

"Firecracker. Fancy seeing you here." My words are husky as I clear my throat while never breaking eye contact.

"What are you doing here?" Kennedy looks up, the corners of her eyes crinkling as she scowls up at me. The guy standing next to her puffs out his chest. *Ha, as if this is going to be a battle.*

"Please," I scoff. "Even I deserve a break from the office. Spending all my time outdoing you is getting exhausting."

Her jaw drops, and I can imagine the steam building in that pretty head of hers, waiting to combust. "Outdoing me?"

"Yeah, outdoing you. It doesn't even seem to be a competition anymore with you constantly playing catch up."

Zoe shakes her head, hiding a smile behind her drink and attempting to look anywhere but at us during this interaction. She's been witness to our antics since Kennedy started with our company a month ago.

It was a shock to see Kennedy sitting in the conference room meeting with HR when I walked down the hall. As discreetly as I could, I paused to observe her for a few brief seconds. Kennedy was poised and flawless. Confidence oozed from her as she held her head high, shoulders back in the grueling interviews with the hiring committees.

After college, I heard she found a job at a small firm in Chelsea, and I assumed we'd never see each other again.

Fate's a funny one.

Another girl is sitting with them tonight, and based on the pictures Kennedy has decorating her cubicle, I think I'm safe to assume she's the roommate.

"Hey, man, the girls are with us," one of the polo wearing guys complains to interrupt our banter.

"Nah, I think they're here on their own," I retort, knowing it's the age where women don't need to be claimed by men. "But if you'd ladies like any company, we've got a table in the corner."

Zoe and the roommate—I think her name is Laura or Lana, or something like that—turn in the direction I'm pointing as Xander gestures to the girls with his glass. My attention slides to Kennedy, who's staring at me, eyes narrowed and her perfectly manicured eyebrows pinched. She's no doubt wondering about my motives.

"We'd love to join," Lana says, jumping from her chair.

"Lana," Kennedy hisses, eyes widening at her friend as she flicks her eyes toward me. No doubt, she's scolding her friend. Both girls continue having a silent conversation as their looks bounce all around the table, implying which person they are talking about.

Zoe stands from her seat and, with a smile, heads toward the table. "I guess she's spoken for the both of us," Lana says.

Moving to the side, I step in front of the frat boy who isn't budging to let Kennedy out of her seat.

"Listen, asshole, I don't know who you think you are—"

"You're right," I cut him off. "You have no idea who I am, which means you should move and let this pretty woman out of her seat and go back to minding your own business."

Kennedy slides from her seat, grabbing her purse and smoothing down her skirt. The guy's eyes land down her shirt and my blood boils.

"Fuck you, man. You have no idea who my dad is."

"And I don't care." I take a step closer to the prick, but soft fingers curl against my hand, causing my head to whip to the side.

"He's not worth it," Kennedy whispers. Using the hand not clutched in mine, she flips her long locks off her shoulder in a sexy move that causes her tendrils to whip the other guy in the face. She pulls me away, and I wait until she's in front of me before I turn and follow her.

The few spectators who have gathered around us move to the side, and as quickly as she grabs my hand, she drops it. Her shoulders steel, and she storms ahead of me. When she reaches the table, she takes the empty seat next to Rafe, the one directly in front of me.

Sitting down, I flag down the waitress as she's passing by.

"What can I get you guys?" she asks, scanning the table.

Rafe and Xander both order another whiskey, while Zoe and Lana order margaritas. I order another bottle of domestic beer and, with much surprise, Kennedy orders the same. "We'll also take a round of green tea shots."

When the waitress leaves, I stare at Kennedy. I'm waiting for her to burst the tense bubble we have somehow found ourselves in.

"How are you liking Nelson?" Xander asks Kennedy. He's been privy to our squabbles a time or two. The first time he heard us bicker, he prepared a long conversation between me and him about how unprofessional it was. I reassured him that it was just a part of our dynamic. Now he plays mediator when he thinks it's going to take a turn for the worse. He could always read a room and find a way to bypass the swirling tension. It's why he's going to make an excellent CEO when Dear Old Dad decides to step down.

"Oh, what Nelson are you referring to?" She pauses, head tilted. "Nelson Signature is fantastic, but this Nelson," she says, hiking her thumb in my direction. "Well, this Nelson is kind of an ass."

Rafe chokes around his sip of whiskey as he breaks out in a laugh. "Damn, she got you."

"She's been busting my balls for years."

"Oh, please, Golden Boy. You've brought this on yourself."

I guffaw. "Golden Boy? That's a new one for you. How long have you been waiting to call me that?"

"Too long," she admits, and I smirk.

Our drinks arrive with the shots Kennedy ordered. Reaching our shot glasses in the center of the table, we clink them before downing the whiskey, peach schnapps, and sweet and sour concoction. I'm not even going to lie; that was a pretty damn good shot. I'm actually impressed with her choice of drinks. I guess you can take the girl out of the small town, but not the small town out of the girl.

"I've got a little wager for you," she muses, taking a long pull of her beer.

"What's that?"

"The last one to finish their beer buys the next round?" She shrugs as if it's no big deal.

Little does she know, I spent most of college at the bars. If I wasn't in class, the guys and I were at a party. I might look like a prep boy, but pretty boys can drink her tiny ass under the table.

"You're on." I reach my hand across the table. Her delicate hand slides right in mine, and I fight the shock that zaps me as our skin meets. She goes to pull away, but I hold her tighter. "Be prepared to lose again...Firecracker."

With a huff, she rips her hand from my grip, and I instantly miss the connection. "Don't choke on your words, Golden Boy, especially when you're buying the next round."

"I'm not taking care of you tonight," Xander groans from beside me.

I shoot him a grin. "Nah, there's no way I'm losing to her. Never have before, why start now?"

Two hours and a deep buzz later, the four of us are making our way out of the bar. One beer chug turned into a night of friendly competition. The rest of the table joined in, and I have to say that, even though I hate going to Rumors, it turned into a fun night. Zoe left an hour ago when her husband stopped in with some friends, while Rafe decided to stay back and enjoy some more drinks.

Kennedy will have one hell of a hangover tomorrow, but she impressed me. For once, she let her guard down and laughed in my company. She still felt the need to compete against me, but it was done in jest rather than hatred.

"Let us drive you home." With my arm wrapped around her shoulders, I guide her out of the packed bar and onto the street. Lana and Kennedy live in Brooklyn, which isn't on my way home, but I'd feel more comfortable having my driver take them than a stranger in a cab. Especially when we've consumed as much alcohol as we did tonight.

She stumbles over a crack in the sidewalk, and I'm quick to steady her. Her head whips around, mouth hanging open, breaths uneven from the near fall. "You called me pretty tonight."

Emerald eyes render me speechless for a moment. Of course, I called her pretty. Does she not see how gorgeous she is? "I don't hate you, Kennedy."

"No, you just steal every opportunity that I work my ass off for out from underneath me. No one can say no to their precious Tristan Nelson." Her comment freezes me, and she slips from my grasp. I can only watch as she climbs into a waiting cab with Lana, realizing we're back to this rivalry she created during our sophomore year of college.

What did she mean by that? I haven't stolen anything from her.

CHAPTER THREE

KENNEDY

My head pounds as the queasiness in my stomach takes hold. What got into me last night? I never drink like that, let alone on a work night. I don't usually allow myself to let my hair down and act like the twenty-five-year-old I am.

Growing up in a small town, it wasn't uncommon for my classmates to have parties in barns or even in fields. I never attended them. Instead, I stayed in reading, studying, or taking practice ACT and SATs. As much as I loved growing up in my town, I knew there was more to life than corn fields and two-lane highways. I knew deep down I was destined for more. Or at least that's what my parents and teachers told me.

My parents were hard workers—my dad was a factory worker and my mom stayed home with me and my sister, Olivia. It's crazy that somewhere along the way, we both got the itch to travel. She graduated high school a couple of years after me and headed to Arizona to live with my grandparents, while I headed east to New York.

Popping a few migraine relief pills, I chug the bottle of water with electrolytes I had waiting on my nightstand in hopes this hangover ends fast. The only positive so far this morning is that I'm going to a doctor's appointment instead of heading into the office early.

Shoot, did I set my out-of-office email?

As I stare at my dresser, I'm wracking my brain, trying to remember how I left the office last night. Hopefully, nothing important pops up between now and when I get in around lunch.

I got to my appointment on time but, of course, they were running behind, no surprise there. They tell you to arrive fifteen minutes early whenever they schedule your appointment. I'll never understand why they ask that when they're constantly running thirty minutes late. I'm a punctual person. If you ask me to be somewhere at ten, I'll arrive by nine forty-five at the latest.

Now here I am, exiting the cab outside of Nelson Signature an hour and a half later than I expected. I learned while I was in the waiting room that I, in fact, didn't turn on my out-of-office notification, because emails were pouring in.

Stepping inside the lobby, I greet the security guard as I reach inside my bag for my badge to show him. As I'm walking away, my phone dings, alerting me of a new message, and I can't help but groan in frustration. Swapping my badge for my phone, I step inside the elevator as I read the new text message.

> **Zoe: Where are you?**

> **Zoe: Tristan called for an urgent meeting in five minutes.**

> **Zoe: You need to be here.**

Shit, shit, shit. I wait impatiently for the doors to open, foot tapping on the marble floor, praying no one else calls the elevator. Today, of all days, to run behind. As soon as I step off at my floor, I beeline to my desk. Dropping off my purse, I quickly grab my laptop and open it as I make my way to the stairs. I'm typing in my login information as I make it to the floor above us.

Looking up, I notice all the seats are occupied around the large conference room table. Furious hazel eyes find mine as our gazes lock on each other. Long gone is the fun we had over beers last night. He's back to being a prick. His chiseled jaw hardens and a fire flames inside me. Walking into the room, everyone's heads whip in my direction and the dread of being the center of attention rachets my nerves.

"Nice of you to finally join us." Tristan's deep voice silences the murmurs around the room, and I feel like the size of an ant.

I realize as I scan the room that the only empty seat is next to him, which isn't a surprise, considering most people avoid him due to his brooding, self-confident swagger. And maybe he is a little self-centered and above all of us. This is his family's company, after all; he's only slumming it with us peasants until he takes his rightful place as department head.

With my head held high and a false sense of confidence, I round the table until I'm sitting in the seat next to him. Our legs brush against, and I fight the sensation that forms in my stomach at that brief touch. Out of the corner of my eye, I take in his features, which seem completely unfazed by our contact. His dark, chocolate-brown suit is layered over the top of a cream dress shirt and matching brown tie. I've never been one for that color when it comes to suits, but there's just something about the way he wears it that hugs his strong-muscled body and brings out the darker elements in his hazel eyes.

My phone buzzes against the table, and heads turn in my direction again. Quickly grabbing the distraction, I bring it to my lap to avoid more stares as I glance at the screen.

Zoe: Quit eye-fucking the enemy.

Heat spreads across my cheeks as I flip the phone face down to obscure it from the man on my right, hoping and praying he didn't look over my shoulder to see the message. But based on the hard set in his jaw, I think it's safe to say, he's more annoyed by the interruption. Fumbling with the phone, I bring my hands to the table, folding them, and focusing back on the reason we're gathered here.

"If everyone is finally ready, we'll get this meeting started," Xander says, startling me. I didn't even realize he was sitting in this room when I walked in.

Get it together, Ken. Stop thinking about him.

Xander stands from his seat and strides over to a screen, where he clicks a few buttons on his laptop. A PowerPoint presentation appears before us, and I open a blank document on my computer to take notes.

"Being hungover isn't an excuse to be late," Tristan whisper-hisses for only me to hear.

My jaw drops, but I snap it closed. "I had a doctor's appointment, not that it's any of your business," I say, but keep my gaze on my computer, refusing to give him the time of day.

"Is that really the excuse you want to go with?" He scoffs before leaning closer. His shoulder touches mine, and I fight the urge to pull away. I'm standing tall, because I will not let him affect me. "Who knew you were so sloppy on weeknights? No wonder you always come in second place."

Hatred courses through my veins with every word. I don't know why I thought one night of us hanging out after work would instantly change my opinion of him. He's still the same arrogant, entitled jerk.

"As some of you may know, Nelson Signature has recently acquired a failing resort," Xander says, causing my full attention to bounce back to him, where a slide includes photos of a tropical destination. "It's an all-inclusive resort in St. Lucia. By acquiring the property, we have unfortunately gained its poor reputation."

He flips to the next slide on the PowerPoint, and comments litter the screen with one negative review after another. My eyes scan words like *dirty, outdated, rude staff, unsafe, and below luxury standards* all over the screen.

Yikes, this is not what someone wants to read when they spend thousands of dollars to vacation at a luxury resort.

Xander paces in front of the projector. "As you can see, the reviews are not good. Along with an entire facelift of the property, including a new layout, design to match our company's luxurious elements, and upgrading the technology, we'll need to work on completely rebranding the image of this resort, not only with tourists, but locals as well." Xander pauses and stares at each one of us.

"Emails will be sent after this meeting to break up the architectural and interior design teams. You'll be working with each other to brainstorm ideas on how to elevate this resort. You have one week to come up with a complete design pitch. Once it's approved, the St. Lucia resort will be your only priority. By shutting down this resort for an entire year to do this remodel, we're losing a lot of money. Making this a top priority project, we expect to be completed within eighteen months."

People begin scurrying around the room, no doubt rushing to their desks to get started. But I can't find it in me to move. I stare straight ahead as thoughts invade my mind about how I can win this competition–*pitch*. A mix of anxiety and excitement has me frozen. After all those years I spent doodling in my sketchbook of different buildings and landscapes, it's finally the moment I've been waiting for to put my work out there.

"Good luck, Firecracker," Tristian says. I turn to face him and that stupid, smug grin. "You're going to need it." And then he shoots me a wink.

Holding back a huff, I lean back in my chair, crossing my arms over my chest and letting confidence take over. "I'm not competing against *you*."

"No, sweetheart," he says, leaning into my space, his cedar and citrus scent flooding my senses. When the hell did we get so close? "But I'll be one of the deciding votes, remember? This is my project." With a light, condescending pat on the table, he stands from his chair and makes his way over to his brother and Xander's assistant.

That motherfu–

"Kenny!" Zoe whisper-shouts from across the room. She gestures to the door, and I grab my electronics before I'm up off my chair and hustling out of the room. I refuse to spare Tristan any more of my attention, but that doesn't mean I don't feel his eyes on me as I walk away.

"Is it safe to assume you won't be coming out for dinner tonight?" Zoe questions as she pushes open the door to the stairwell.

"Are you kidding me? I won't be leaving the office until I have a solid plan. Takeout for one, please."

Zoe shakes her head as the sound of heels clicking against the metal stairs fills the space. "Girl, it's not that deep."

"Would you stop?" I laugh at Zoe's constant need to incorporate one phrase the "kids are saying these days." Her words, not mine. She said that one day she was standing in a coffee shop surrounded by teenagers and she had no clue what they were saying, so in her vow not to seem too old, she's going to learn their language. Zoe is barely thirty; it's not like she's old by any means.

Once we step onto our floor, it's mayhem. People are running around, trying to figure out where to start with this project, but it looks like Wall Street and the stocks just dropped. One thing I like about working here is that the company isn't afraid of a little friendly competition. I've been competing my whole life in some aspect or another, so it feels like just another day.

"I'm running to pick up lunches at Green Goddess if you ladies want anything," Jill, an intern, calls to us from her cubicle. Stopping at her desk, I reach for a sticky note before jotting down my go-to Green Goddess order—a simple grilled chicken Cobb salad without the bleu cheese.

We thank her before going our separate ways.

• • • • ❋ • ❋ • • • •

Running my fingers through my hair, I let out an exasperated sigh. For hours, I've been glued to my computer, researching the country of St. Lucia. When it comes to a new project, it's important for me to not only look at what design style speaks to the location while fitting into our company's branding, but also look at what would make this location stand out from its competitors.

Since this is an acquisition, we have to rebrand the image of the resort, which Xander stressed in the meeting. There's a negative connotation associated with the resort, which means our property management team and marketing team need to do a great job at recreating the location's image.

The issue Nelson's is facing is that locals are against the new buyout, and without the support of the locals, things could go south quickly.

Stretching my hands out in front of me, I tip my neck up, working out the kinks. I notice the outside of my right hand is smeared with lead from where I've been sketching all afternoon. Which I'm not complaining about. Despite new technology making things easy, I'd prefer my pencil and sketchbook to draw out the first concept. It's more freeing.

Somewhere, the sun drifted from the warm winter light and cascaded the city in darkness. Lights from neighboring buildings highlight the city that never sleeps. The small lamp on my cubicle is the only light illuminating my workspace. It's Friday evening and my co-workers started leaving when the clock struck four-thirty, staggering out until I was the last one left at six o'clock.

That was an hour ago.

Tonight, as I sit here in this empty, quiet office, I can't help but realize this is it. After all these years, I still find it hard to believe that New York is home. There was a time when I thought my dreams wouldn't come true. No matter how much I studied and how many practice tests I took, life might not have allowed the chance to see everything I worked so hard for to come to fruition.

"Burning the midnight oil?" *His* voice causes me to jump. I guess I'm not alone here, after all. Has Tristian been here the whole time?

Spinning around to face him, I immediately regret the decision. Sometime during the day, Tristan shed his suit jacket and rolled up the sleeves of his dress shirt. The cream color perfectly contrasts with his tan skin. Even in the dead of New York's winter, Tristan Nelson looks like a bronzed god who just stepped foot off the plane from paradise. Why have I never noticed how strong his forearms are? Ugh, why am I checking him out? Snapping my face up to meet his as he leans against the wall of my cubicle, I recognize his famous smirk. It's like he has a glimpse inside my head.

"Someone has to set the bar around here." Crossing my arms across my chest, I watch his eyes follow my movement. A small smile toys at the end of my lips as I lean back in my seat.

"And you think that someone should be you?"

Eyeing him up and down, I fight to show how much his standing here affects me. "Why not? Not all of us can rely on their title and daddy's money to get them everything in life."

"Ouch," he mocks. "You know he pays your paychecks, right?"

"I don't have an issue with him."

Pointing a finger toward himself, he retorts, "So you have a problem with me. What, are you gunning for my job?"

"You know damn well I want the seat you're sitting in."

"Please." He rolls his eyes. "You know I set the bar and you're always under it."

I scoff. "I'm the one pushing it higher."

He glances around my space, as if he's looking for something, before his eyes lock back on me. "I don't see *Director* next to your name anywhere. You'll never get anywhere if you keep doodling like you're still in elementary school."

I follow the path to where he's staring at my sketchbook and colored pencils. Quickly, I slam the cover shut on my sketchbook, not wanting to show him any of my cards right now. Closing the top on the colored pencil box, I rip open my desk drawer and place my sketchbook and pencils into my bag. I've had enough of this. I'm exhausted and don't have the energy to sit here and take his insults anymore.

Grabbing my things, I stand to leave but stop in front of him. Making myself level with him to make sure he hears me clearly. "Keep my seat warm, Tristan."

I shove past him, but he's immediately on my heels

"C'mon, Firecracker."

"No, Tristan," I spit out, jamming my finger into the elevator call button before whipping around to face him to say more. But my chest brushes against his and we both suck in a breath at our proximity. Staring up into his eyes, I can't find the words I wanted to say just seconds ago. His eyes bore into mine and darken at the same time he takes a deep swallow. I track the movement, unable to control the tension swirling around us.

When the elevator chimes behind me, I force myself away from him, keeping my eyes on his for one more blink before averting my gaze to hit the button to close the door. My hand darts out to stop the door, because this isn't another thing Tristian is going to win.

"Like I said, keep my seat warm, Golden Boy."

With that, I press the button again to close the door, leaving him on the other side.

Chapter Four

Tristan

It's been a week since Kennedy and I were alone on this same floor. She's been constantly in my thoughts ever since. Watching her get on that elevator nearly destroyed me. I fought with every ounce of my willpower to keep my feet grounded and not race down the stairs to finally claim her lips with mine.

But I couldn't do that.

She hates me, and I don't blame her. Admittedly, for the most part, I mess with her because it gives me a chance to get a few minutes of her time. It's not something I'll say to her face, but her design will win. I have no doubt that whatever she presents to the team will be exactly what they are looking for because she knows her stuff. She's a damn hard worker too. There hasn't been a night this week that she hasn't been the last one left on the floor. I've done my best to avoid her, but my conscience wouldn't allow me to leave her here alone in this building. I know it's safe, but my protectiveness flared.

A knock sounds on my door, pulling my attention to my sister standing there. "What can I do for you, little sis?"

Her nose scrunches and she groans. "What have I told you about calling me that?"

"You're a Nelson," I start, waving my hand to gesture to the floor of people. "They all know you're my sister."

"That doesn't mean I want to be called that. I'm in my twenties, Trist. It'd be nice to be seen as Victoria and not as the *little sister*." She enters my office and plops on the chair across from me.

A chuckle leaves my lips. "You want to be treated like an adult, then stop flopping around like a petulant child, Victoria."

She rolls her eyes. "No wonder Kennedy can't stand you," she mutters under her breath.

"I heard that."

"I wasn't hiding it." Giving me the attitude we've had to deal with since she was born, she squints pointedly. I swear she came into the world with a scowl and enough sass to solve the energy crisis.

"Is there a reason you're here and not getting ready for our meeting we have in"—I glance down at my watch—"fifteen minutes?"

"As a matter of fact, I did come in here for a reason." She aims her finger at me, seriousness morphing her expression. "Don't fuck with Kennedy. Her idea is brilliant, and I know how you are with her. She's worked endlessly on this idea, and it's good, Tristan. Really freaking good."

Leaning forward on my elbows, I keep my poker face in the way that us Nelsons were taught in this business. "I won't fuck with her, but I'm not just going to give this project to her. If she wants it, she needs to earn it in her presentation."

"You're seriously such an ass. When did you become a corporate douche?" She stands from her seat and marches toward the door, just in time for our oldest brother to enter.

"Woah, hey there, little sis!" Xander stops Victoria from strolling out of the room.

Flailing her arms in the air, she stomps her foot, letting out another boisterous groan. "I should've gone to work at Clinghams."

Clingham Property Group is one of our biggest rivals. Our two companies are constantly fighting for the same land to develop. There's no way she would have gone to work there, and she knows it. This has been her go-to remark whenever she feels she isn't getting treated properly in our company or when Dad decided she'd have to work from the bottom of the company and slowly make her way to the top, like the rest of us.

She glares at Xander before turning that look onto me and storming past him.

"Whatever, Tori. See you in the meeting."

Xander places his hands in his pockets as he crosses the room, then says to me, "She's still a lot."

"Yeah, and now we have to work with her. There's no escape."

"At least we don't live with her anymore," he adds.

Gathering my notepad and pen, I stand and make my way around my large desk. "Until she decides to take my other guest room like a certain big brother of mine."

"You like the company." He pauses, fixing the sleeve of his dress shirt. It's a nervous habit he's picked up since he joined corporate America, telling me there's more he wants to add. I stand and wait for whatever he's about to say. "Listen, are you sure you're ready for this? I don't have a problem leading the project."

I take a deep breath, jaw clenched. I'm so tired of everyone in my family—hell, in this company—thinking I can't handle this job. Never have I given anyone a reason to doubt me. Have I always taken it as seriously as my brother? No. But that doesn't mean I don't show up when I'm supposed to and stay until I'm one of the last ones working. It's like everyone is waiting for the day I make a mistake so they can shout "I told you so."

Sliding my gaze out of the glass walls that make up my office, I scan the faces of my co-workers until I find my favorite shade of red.

She's standing with my sister and Zoe, with her laptop tucked under her arm. Dressed to kill in a pair of black pleated pants, a tight matching shirt tucked in, and an olive-green blazer that accents her rich copper locks that fall gracefully over her shoulders, she turns her head to face me like she can feel me watching her. Her eyes level me as if she were warning me to watch my back. No doubt she'll charm everyone in that room today.

"I can handle it." I grit out the words meant for my brother, but I can't take my eyes off Kennedy. "I'm more than capable of running the entire design department."

He nods. "I was just letting you know that the offer stands."

"Thanks," I grunt, brushing past him. He follows as I make my way to the elevator where Kennedy, Victoria, and Zoe wait for the car.

"Ladies." Xander greets them with a smile. Victoria turns her back to us, rolling her eyes in the process. *Brat.*

"Mr. Nelson." Kennedy greets my brother with a handshake before snapping her attention back to me. She's likely waiting for me to greet her first, but I surprise her by putting my hands in my pockets. I give her a nod at the same time the elevator doors open, then step inside with everyone filing behind me.

I hear Zoe whisper "good luck" to Kennedy and Victoria as we all step off and head to the largest conference room. This one is set up to resemble more of a university auditorium rather than a traditional conference space. Tables are set facing the front, with chairs behind them. A large whiteboard is situated on the main wall with a screen that drops down for presentations.

"Break a leg, Firecracker." My shoulder brushes Kennedy's as I move past her, my sister right behind me.

"You're only supposed to say that to performers," Victoria says.

A grin spreads across my face as I look at my sister. "Well, are we not about to see how well Kennedy performs under pressure?"

"Asshole," she mutters, shaking her head.

A few associates have already arrived, taking their seats.

There's a renewed energy in the room that comes with every project meeting. Between the nerves and excitement, the room is buzzing with anticipation of members ready to share their pitches.

Pulling open my notepad, I write down the date and what meeting this is about so it doesn't get lost. I've learned the hard way, when it comes to management, it's important to ensure the notes are detailed. During my first month on the job, I had so many meetings but never labeled what notes were from which one, if I took any at all. I was pulling out the wrong sheet for follow-ups and looking like I had no right to be in the same room as some of these people.

The first group begins their presentation and I'm instantly bored. Their design lacks creativity and, somehow, they manage to clash with the entire Nelson brand. Scribbling down notes, I try to keep my mind focused, but I can't help but find a nervous Kennedy sitting stiff as a board in her chair as she chews her bottom lip.

I reach inside my pocket and pull out my phone discreetly. Clicking on the messaging app, I scroll until I find her name. It's office policy that everyone shares their numbers with department employees in case of emergency or work-related issues. Selecting her name, I quickly thumb out a text.

> **Me: Relax.**

> **Firecracker: New phone, who dis?**

> **Me: Funny, girl.**

Glancing over, I watch her as a— Wait, is that a smile?

> **Firecracker: You might want to pay attention. Maybe you'll learn something.**

> **Me: You're up next. Show me what you got, Firecracker.**

When she reads the text, her breath stutters. She's nervous, but she has no reason to be. I've snuck a few glimpses at her project, and I know it'll be the one we pick. All we need is for her to sell it to us, which might be where she struggles.

"Miss Reed, please present your project," Xander calls from his seat beside me as everyone shuffles papers around in front of them.

Kennedy is quick to take the front of the room, and with the help of my sister, the two have the slides pulled up in no time. While a group worked on the design, Kennedy was the lead architect and Victoria was the lead interior designer, which means only those two needed to present.

Running her hands down her pants, Kennedy steels her shoulders. As her eyes find mine in a fleeting moment, I don't miss the opportunity to wink at her. A slight blush covers her high cheekbones and my brother's head turns toward me. With a shake, his attention turns back to the ladies commandeering our attention.

"Good morning," she chokes out, clearing her throat. "I'm really excited to pitch our concept for the St. Lucia location. My team has worked diligently to bring you what we feel is the best option for a full facelift on the property while not only enhancing the luxurious feel but also benefiting your pockets and increasing revenue for the local economy. Our proposal focuses more on creating an exclusive feel for any guest, no matter if they are honeymooners who will never spend this much money on a trip again or the top one percent who experience lavish vacations regularly. Our goal is to make sure everyone feels affluent for their time on our property."

Pausing, she nods to Victoria, who switches the slide to showcase their first rendering of the property. This slide displays a modernized version of the preexisting property to save time on construction.

She crosses the whiteboard, where the presentation is displayed, and extends her arm to the slide. "As you can see through this rendering, we've updated the outside of the resort in order to keep on a fast-paced remodel by replacing the existing exterior with a soft beige stucco and similar soft neutral travertine tiles mixed with rich brown teakwood accents to allow a modern, but warm, welcoming feel. Cream and light beige travertine and limestone pathways would invite guests to explore the property while taking in the lush landscaping."

Victoria switches to the next slide, which is the first interior photo.

"As the resort is shaped now, you can see a giant wall takes away the immediate ocean views. By installing fifteen-foot-tall glass accordion doors, guests will immediately see the bright blue ocean of St. Lucia. This also allows the ocean breeze to greet our guests, along with our diligent staff."

"Interesting," one of the members of the development team says. I nod in agreement as I tap the ink pen against my chin, soaking in her every word.

Kennedy takes a brief second to look at my sister, the two of them engaging in a silent conversation before Victoria flips to the next slide, which is a rendering of the lobby.

"Now this might feel a bit bold, but I think it's best to remove some of these large columns and install support beams across the ceiling. This might be a costly expense; however, opening up this space creates a more inviting feel to the lobby," she explains, using her pen to show the space she's discussing. "Instantly, guests can see every inch of the expansive space. In the center, it's important to incorporate chairs and couches which you can see in these images. Victoria and her design team felt we should stick to warmer sunset shades such as corals and orange hues mixed with the reclaimed wood tables."

"These are great design ideas, but we aren't focused on those items at this time," Harry Stewart, our Chief Development Officer, rudely interrupts. Kennedy's cheeks redden with embarrassment.

Before he has a chance to berate her, I jump in. "While we are definitely interested in the design aspect. We know those items will come. What's important right now in *this* meeting is that we finalize your views on more of the design concept and elevating the resort."

Her eyes meet mine, and I give her an encouraging nod and mouth, *Keep going.*

"Right, of course. I'm sorry to have wasted your time," she starts again, flipping through her slides.

"No time has been wasted. These are important details as well, but let's get to the bigger picture first," Xander adds, calming the situation further.

When Victoria lands on the slide Kennedy's been searching for, Kennedy picks up where she left off with a quick throat clear. The slide illustrates newly redesigned public spaces, including larger walkways, more cabanas, and shaded benches.

"With newly designed public spaces, this will quickly improve the flow of guests while enhancing the overall experience. This allows for each area of the resort to feel intimate and exclusive. Moving on to the technological integrations to bring the property to the same technology age as the mainland..." she trails off as she points out new items on the next slide.

"Inside each room, I've allowed integrations such as smart room controls and a virtual concierge, which allows our guests to order anything they need while not having to call the front desk for each request. As you know, our staff are busy either attending to or checking in or out guests. This elevates the guest experience because most people prefer having things at the touch of a button rather than speaking to someone over the phone."

"But wouldn't locals fear you're taking away their jobs with *robots*?" Harry interrupts, condescension dripping from his tone.

I cannot wait until Xander or I take over his position. It's clear as day he doesn't think a young woman, much less a woman as brilliant as

Kennedy, can handle this job. He's stuck in the nineteen-fifties where he believes women should be at home birthing half a dozen children.

Kennedy doesn't fluster at his interruption. Instead, she smiles and nods politely. The slide flips to photos of locals. "I'm glad you brought that point up, Mr. Stewart. To reassure locals that their jobs are safe and not being fazed out, by— What did you call them? Robots? We'll implement job retention strategies and provide workshops to enhance their skills. Eventually, we'll establish long-term contracts with local suppliers and support business initiatives, ensuring our property boosts the local economy without compromising the resort's profitability."

There's my Firecracker.

Choking on my breath, I garner the attention of everyone in the room. Shit, *my* Firecracker? Where the hell did that come from? She isn't mine; she doesn't even like me.

With a slap on the back, my brother stares at me with a raised eyebrow. Breathing slowly, I'm able to stop the coughing attack.

Good grief. Get it together, Tristan.

"This is a great proposal, Kennedy," Xander says, leaning back in his chair as he tilts his head to side, deep in thought as he stares at the final slide.

The rendering includes the entire property with all the upgrades Kennedy and her team pitched, down to the luscious jungle views, guests lounging in and around the infinity pool, and couples strolling hand in hand along where the clear blue water meets the white sand, while people mill about the property. The landscape is exotic, the design neutral and clean with pops of turquoise and shades of the sunset.

It captures the essence of paradise. Which is fitting, considering their pitch included the name: Paradise at Piton Peaks.

"There's just something missing. I can't quite put my finger on it," he adds, bringing his hand to his chin. Confidence melts off Kennedy's face, doubt and insecurity taking over.

"What if..." I stand and make my way over to the screen before looking at Victoria. "May I?"

Victoria slides the laptop toward me, and I quickly backtrack to the first rendering, where she added the accordion doors. I stare at the drawing and feel her gaze bore a hole in the side of my head. I can only imagine that she's cursing me out in her mind.

"That's it."

"What's it?" Kennedy stands, arms folded across her chest.

"Right here." I grab a black marker and point to the entryway that leads to the lobby. "You're right, the view is immediately blocked by a wall of smaller windows. That definitely needs to go. But what if we shifted the entryway of the resort? Instead of keeping it where it has always been, let's move it," I say, drawing on the whiteboard, "over a few feet and clear out this deck and landscaping."

Chairs rustle from behind me, where I'm pointing out my ideas on the whiteboard, her presentation reflected.

"If you look closely, you'll see that these palm trees"—I circle them—"and walls are blocking the view from the upper level, but if we shift the walkway, close off the existing entrance, and funnel guests to this wall, which will become the new entrance. They will be greeted the whole way with the ocean view. They won't need to wait to walk inside the lobby before saltwater blowing off the bright blue water greets them."

Peering over, I watch Kennedy react to my idea. Steam is without a doubt building inside that pretty head of hers. What she has is a good idea, but by shifting the entire entrance, now that makes this entire project—

"Brilliant!" shouts Harry from behind me. "Mr. Nelson, that is exactly what this property needed. I knew having you included in this project would pay off."

"It was an easy fix; anybody could have found this idea." My words come out modestly, as I don't want to rock the boat I'm finding myself in with Kennedy. This wasn't my proposal, and I don't want the accolades.

"Of course," Harry says. "Miss Reed, please be sure to email Tristan your entire proposal with the new modifications he pointed out."

"Yes, sir." Her voice is meek, and I hate this for her. No matter what she believes, I'm not the enemy.

Xander stands at the front of the room and thanks everyone for joining us today. The meeting is dismissed, and before I have a chance to gather my things, Kennedy flies out of the door.

Dammit.

CHAPTER FIVE

KENNEDY

From: alexandernelson@nelsonsignature.com
To: kennedyReed@nelsonsignature.com
CC: tristannelson@nelsonsignature.com
Date: January 18, 2024
Subject: St. Lucia Proposal

Kennedy,
Congratulations! We are thrilled to announce that your proposal on the St. Lucia project has been accepted. Please see Tristan to sort out the details.

The company values how hard and attentive you worked on this project. Please know that you're a valued member of Nelson Signature. Keep up the great work, Kennedy.

Regards,
Xander

PS- Try not to kill each other.
PPS- Feel free to kick his ass if needed. He's a stubborn one.

Alexander Nelson, Development Manager
Nelson Signature Hotels & Resorts
New York, New York

Squealing, I reread the email for the third time. I can hear Lana running up the stairs seconds before my bedroom door flies open.

"What? What's going on?" Her question is full of concern as she holds the toothbrush away from her mouth. White bubbles outline her lips as her hair pours out from her claw clip.

I throw myself back in bed, kicking my arms and legs in celebration before sitting up and bringing myself to my knees.

"Tell me right now!" Lana shrieks, her voice a mixture of worry and excitement.

"They want my design for the St. Lucia property!"

Lana jumps on the bed, toothbrush still in hand and foam now dripping down her chin, but it doesn't stop her from sharing the joy. "I told you, you would crush it, babe!"

Only the words are mushed together and sound like "I tollf you, youf woulf crusf if, bafe!"

"Oh my gosh, Lana." I laugh when I realize my best friend is jumping on the bed with me while toothpaste hangs from her mouth. "Go finish brushing your teeth, you dork."

In an instant, she's off the bed and running into my en suite bathroom, and I lie back again with a sigh.

I can't believe my design was picked. I knew it was good, but there has been this niggling feeling inside that told me I wasn't good enough. After the Chief Development Officer reacted to the fact that I was a—*gasp*—woman, I thought he would demand the first group's designs be selected, since they were all men. Even though their project was horrible and clashed with the Nelson brand, he seemed to love their pitch.

"So how are we celebrating?" she asks, voice cheerful, as she jumps back on the bed next to me.

"Rumors for happy hour?"

"You got it, babe."

Turning to face Lana, we both squeal and kick our legs. Cheesy smiles spread across our faces as the realization of how important winning the pitch competition was. Rolling over, Lana smacks my butt playfully. The thwack echoes off our walls and causes us to laugh.

· · · ● · ● · · · ·

Me: I GOT THE ST. LUCIA PROJECT

Olivia: Go, big sis!

Me: I'm heading into the office now. I still can't believe it.

Olivia: Did you dress your best to rub it in Golden Boy's face?

Me: *Smirking emoji* oh little sis, you know I did.

Olivia: *three laughing emojis* I love you! Go crush it, sis! I'm going back to sleep for a few.

Me: OMG I totally forgot how early it was in Arizona. Love you! Miss your face.

Pulling up outside Nelson Signature, I splurged this morning and took an Uber instead of the train. I didn't want to risk anyone spilling something on my dress. After thanking the driver, I send him a tip and rating as I exit the silver sedan. The streets bustle with people rushing to their jobs. Sounds of horns honking and sirens fill the air while a cold, winter breeze can be felt even through my wool trench coat.

I'm greeted by one of the security guards as I walk through the revolving doors, and I raise my badge like I do every morning. The sun's rays cascade through the pristine lobby, reflecting off the shiny, white marble floors, where my black stilettos click and the silk fabric of my dress kisses my ankles with every step. Rolling my shoulders backward, I hold my head high, emitting the pride I'm feeling. It helps that I'm wearing my favorite dress, the dress I wear when I'm feeling my most confident.

I still cannot believe *my* pitch won. Giddiness seeps through my veins, and I can't fight the grin that has been so desperate to break free.

There's a line waiting at the elevator, and I step behind the last gentleman who I've seen before. I think he's in finance on the sixteenth floor. He watches my approach, trailing his gaze from my feet to my face in a slow perusal. The metal doors slide open and Mr. Finance steps to the side, holding the door open as I enter the crammed car as people make room for us.

"Which floor?" his deep voice asks from beside me.

"Fifty-third, please."

With a nod, he clicks the button for my floor and his, which I was right in assuming he was one of the finance guys.

He turns his attention back to me, his navy-sleeved arm brushing against mine, and I take in his chiseled jaw and fine-line wrinkles around his eyes that crinkle when he smiles. "Ah, you're one of Nelson's. How is it on top?"

I quirk an eyebrow and feel my cheeks flame at the innuendo. "Well, I'm on their third floor, so not quite the top."

"With legs like that, I thought you'd be one of Nelson's girls. He always has the prettiest assistants." I cringe at his backhanded compliment and his implication that I could only be an assistant.

"You're looking at one of our top architects, Baldwin," a voice I instantly recognize calls from the back.

Looking over my shoulder, I find none other than Tristan Nelson standing in the back of the car. His jaw is set tight as he eyes the gentleman—if I could even call him that—to my right.

Mr. Finance chuckles as a smarmy grin quirks the corner of his mouth. Onlookers watch the showdown between the two beefy suits. "Oh look, if it *isn't* a Nelson. Say, how is it slumming it with the commoners instead of sitting in royalty like the rest of the men in your family?"

Energy shifts in the tight space as I shift on my heels uncomfortably. "Jealousy looks bad on you, Baldwin. Still upset we didn't want your moronic ass on our finance team?"

Thankfully, the doors chime on the sixteenth floor, and a few people disperse out of the crowded car, including Mr. Finance. Heat blazes in his glare as he gives Tristan one final stare-down before the doors close.

I tilt my head, risking a peek, and am met with swirling amber staring back at me. Snapping my head forward, I won't let Tristan Nelson ruin this monumental day for me.

It's not long before we are the final two on the car as it arrives on our floor. I refuse to acknowledge he's here. I didn't need his help with the douche from finance, and I certainly don't want to deal with his cruel jokes.

Rolling my shoulders back, I step onto the shiny marble floor. The ding of the elevator has heads turning in our direction from where they are gathered at our small reception desk.

"Congratulations!" Zoe greets from where she's leaning her hip against the desk, a white and green to-go cup in her hands. A few of our colleagues clap their hands. I guess the word spread quicker than I thought.

A blush creeps onto my cheeks, thanks to my insecurity of being the center of attention, but I can't help but smile. My strides quicken as I walk in the direction of Zoe and the coffee that is waiting for me. She hands me the cup, which warms my chilled hands immediately. Bringing the cup to my lips, I savor the cozy flavors of sweet pistachio and brown buttery toppings as the flavors burst on my tongue.

"This is delicious," I moan. "Thank you."

"Celebratory coffee is a must when you deserve it." Zoe smiles, and I'm so thankful for the friendship I have with her. Even in this competitive work environment, she never lets it affect our friendship. We are constantly working together to lift each other up and not beat the other out.

"You look stunning," someone else says, approaching the group. "And congratulations, by the way."

I smile at Victoria before pulling her in for a celebratory hug. "Congratulations to you too, Victoria."

A throat clears before *his* rich tone commands the gathered group. "It's after nine. Don't you all have work to do?"

Shaking my head, I ignore him and let his sister send him a glare. Zoe, Victoria, and I move in the direction of our cubicles without another word. Lighting from the office mixed with the golden cast of the New York morning causes my dress to shimmer subtly and bring out the deep emerald hue complimenting my copper-red hair.

A long slit slices up my leg, showing off my lightly bronzed tan—from a bottle, of course—while still being office appropriate. Sleeves meet my wrist in a tight button band while allowing a soft balloon effect up my arms, where it meets the high neckline and trails down the tight-fitting bodice. Everything about this dress screams chic while allowing me to feel like I'm wearing armor gearing up for a long battle in the professional space.

I feel strong. Powerful. Sexy.

Which is why heads turn as we stroll by.

"My brother can't keep his eyes off of you," Victoria whispers as we walk around the backside of the section of cubicles where my desk sits.

"He's probably just contemplating how he's going to make my life miserable for the next twelve-to-eighteen months since he's now my *boss* on this project—or my death."

Zoe slides across the floor in her desk chair to my side. "Or how he's going to strip you out of your dress and ravish you on his desk, glass windows, and everything."

"Ew, that's my brother," Victoria says, wrinkling her face in disgust as her body shivers.

"That's never going to happen," Victoria and I say at the same time, though my stomach does a weird flip at the visual of that ravishing.

Zoe laughs and replies, "You just wait," she sing-songs as she rolls back to her desk. Victoria congratulates me again, and before I know it, I'm left alone with my celebratory coffee, still thinking about Zoe's comment.

Once upon a time, I thought Tristan Nelson was attractive. Who wouldn't? A small-town girl moves to the big city, finding herself in the same lecture hall as a perfectly polished guy with trendy clothes that look like they were made for him. He's kept the trimmed beard that frames his chiseled jaw, and his rich brown hair is still styled in his intentionally messy way. Only now he uses more hair products and has upgraded to tailored suits.

Too bad his personality is the complete opposite of his appearance.

The day flew by in a blur of meetings, brainstorming, and sketching. At a quarter to five, Victoria traipses up to my desk, a brimming smile taking over her face. "I've got a surprise for you," she coos.

Spinning in my seat to face her, I get the suspicion that Zoe and Victoria have been up to something all day. They have been eerily quiet, both in person and through our instant messenger chat.

"I still have another hour of work to put in."

"Nope." She shakes her head and turns me around to face my computer. "As the owner's daughter, I'm demanding you shut down, gather your things, and leave the office with me without asking any questions."

I chuckle. "Oh my gosh, Victoria, you did not just pull the owner's daughter's card."

She raises her finger in a matter-of-fact way. "I most certainly did. Now do as I say, or I'll have Tristan write you a warning."

I narrow my eyes. "You're cruel, Victoria Nelson. So cruel."

She folds her arms across her chest as Zoe laughs from the cube next to me. Victoria is vibrating with giddy energy, and I have a feeling that whatever they have concocted will be quite a delight.

Chapter Six

Tristan

We're four weeks into the St. Lucia project now. That means, I've spent four awkward, tension-filled weeks working closely with Kennedy and her simmering hatred. I still haven't got a clue why she hates me, but it's driving me a little crazy. I find myself thinking back to our college days more and more, sifting through memories and trying to find a reason that might explain it. So far, I've got nothing.

I mean, was I a preppy asshole in college?

Definitely, but so were all the other guys in our major. It's not my fault that professors used me and not her. It always seemed like she was trying to make herself invisible, though I have no idea why. It wasn't my problem then, but it sure feels like my problem now.

"Are you meeting with Kennedy today?" Xander asks as he barges into my office, derailing my train of thought.

Looking up from my computer, where I should have been reviewing the specs for the resort instead of thinking about Kennedy, I watch as he leans against the doorway, tucking a hand into his pocket. "You already know the answer to that."

"I'm just making sure you're taking this seriously."

That makes my anger flare. "Of course I am," I snap, glaring at my brother's retreating back.

I've never given him a reason to doubt me at work. Yes, there was a time when I confided in my brother that I wasn't sure if I was cut out for Nelson Signature. But I put my dreams aside to work for my father's company, just as he always wanted. Since making that decision, I've been putting my all into my dad's company. I started interning for him during school and kept at it, working my way up to Project Manager from the entry level position I took right after college. There has never been a question about my dedication to our family's company and the path I'd take that was laid out for me as soon as I showed an interest in being an architect.

Or at least there wasn't one out loud, but I can be honest enough with myself to admit that. Though I'm grateful I had a job the second I graduated, and I didn't have to compete for a position at another firm, sometimes I wish I could have started out somewhere else. Just for a year or two to see what it's like to leave New York. I'd always come back, as this is home, but the chance to live in another city, be on my own, it might have been great. Hell, I didn't even get to try going to college somewhere else. NYU was it for me. And as much as I wanted to become an architect, a part of me wonders how long that was instilled in me. Did I always want to be like my dad, or was that the seed he planted?

As soon as I step foot in the conference room, I'm greeted by the smell of vanilla and lavender. My eyes immediately find hers as she brings a mug up to those perfect heart-shaped lips I've thought about way too many times since meeting Kennedy Reed.

Narrowing my eyes, I watch as she takes a long sip from— Wait? "Did you steal my mug?"

The corners of her lips twitch as I follow her swallow down her long, slender neck. She pulls the mug from her mouth, spinning it as if she's just now realizing which one she's holding. The white ceramic mug has '~~I'm An Arcateck Arckatect Architech~~ I Draw Stuff' written on one side. Victoria bought it for me for Christmas one year as a gag gift. It was the perfect edition to my coffee mug collection since I could not spell "architect" to save my life. Hell, there're still some days when I struggle with spelling that damn word.

Lips pursing in a tiny smirk, those deep emerald eyes glimmer with mischief. "Hmm, borrowed. I wouldn't dare think to steal from Mr. Golden Boy." Her little nickname for me has always flustered me, but after the way my brother insinuated I wasn't taking this project seriously this morning, it really strikes a match inside of me, causing my jaw to clamp tight. "Besides, you left it in the kitchen."

Grinding my teeth together, I stare her down. Two can play this game, Kennedy. "I can't even trust you with my mug."

"But you trust me with this project?" Her eyebrow quirks as the slightest bit of insecurity flashes across her face. If I didn't know her cues as well as I do, I would have missed her moment of vulnerability.

"Barely," I snark, taking my seat across from her. "You do have your moments when you know what you're talking about."

"That's high praise coming from you."

"I'm not the bad guy you think I am, Ken."

She sucks in a small breath as she digests my words. Clearing her throat, she shuffles her papers around, changing the subject. "Let's get this started?"

"We're just waiting on Xander. Apparently, he thinks he needs to sit in on all our meetings."

Her eyes narrow. "Why?"

"He seems to think we'll rip each other apart and never finish this project." She cringes, because she knows full well that she's the reason why there are trust issues between us, and that's why it feels like there are issues with the project.

"Ready?" Xander muses. I turn and find him pausing in the doorway. The tension is palpable in the small space, but it's not with the same animosity as it normally is. There's something else mixed in, causing him to squint his eyes as he observes the two of us.

Kennedy nods and pulls up her renderings on the screen. "Ready."

I can feel Xander's eyes boring into the side of my face, but I refuse to look at him, so I turn my attention back to Kennedy. After basically admitting no one in the company trusts my judgement and now this, I don't have the energy for either of them. I'm looking forward to the end of this meeting when I can cut out early and hit a cycling class.

"We are a month into the project, and while we've sent all the specs to our construction team, there are a few items we need to work through," I say, standing from my seat and making my way to the screen, which has an aerial view of the property. "As you can see, there's an empty parking lot on the northwest side. Currently, it's considered wasted space since there are only a couple of local bars and public beach access that really use it. Not the best use of what's there. So we've purchased the property in our acquisition."

"You're taking more away from the locals?" Kennedy interrupts, her voice dripping with disdain.

"If you would let me finish," I grit out, and her face heats. "While we have purchased the property, we don't want to take anything away from the locals. However, the space needs a facelift. The concrete has deteriorated, and sand has blown in and started to take over. It's an eyesore for everyone with businesses around it and for all the locals trying to sell their goods to tourists and guests headed to hike the National Trust. What it needs is a refresh. Do you have a few ideas that might work both for us and the locals?"

A wide grin spreads across her face. "I've got the perfect idea."

"Of course you do," I mumble sarcastically.

Her eyes roll, and she turns attention from me to where my brother is sitting. "A farmer's market."

"A farmer's market," he repeats.

"Yes, locals are already trying to sell their goods, so why not make it more official."

Kennedy stands, and I can't stop my eyes from raking over her hourglass figure. It's hugged by fitted black slacks and a green blouse, my eyes catching at the hint of cleavage she's showing and up to the top of her head, where instead of the usual curls, it sits high and sleek in a ponytail. My fingers twitch to wrap it around my fist, preferably as she drops to her knees. Shit. I shake my head and turn my attention back to Kennedy, who's watching me, something unreadable in her eyes.

Does she know what I was thinking?

"Earth to Golden Boy?"

"I'm sorry, I was distracted at the fact you're proposing a Podunk farmer's market on a multi-million-dollar property."

"Yes, that's exactly what I'm proposing, you pompous ass." Slamming her hands down on the desk, if looks could kill, I'd be ash.

"Okay, okay." Xander stands, his voice calming but forceful as he tries to settle the air around the room. "Let's hear your idea, Kennedy, because I really don't hate it."

Her glare doesn't leave mine, and that's when my eyes slip down to her heaving chest. I need to get a fucking grip. This is Kennedy Reed, my off-limits co-worker and rival.

With one final deep breath, her head turns to my brother, and she proceeds to direct her words to only him as if she's removed me from the room. "After repairing the pavement, we could build a few covered pergolas that fit the island style with picnic tables set up underneath them. Local vendors could purchase an inexpensive permit which allows the company to make a little while ensuring our rules and guidelines are followed when selling their goods and services. This would allow guests to feel comfortable roaming the outside of the property since they are in an unfamiliar country. Safety to our guests and to locals should be at the forefront of everyone's minds. By having a farmer's market, it would allow those local bars to gain even more business."

"By pulling tourist businesses away from the resort?" I question.

"No," she answers, but doesn't spare me a glance before continuing. "The resort is all-inclusive; therefore, we don't lose anything since we already have the guests money. This would be the extra money they want to spend on the island."

"Interesting," Xander muses, nodding repeatedly like he's considering this right now. "Can you come up with a few renderings for how you would design the extra space? I'll pitch it to our CDO."

"Absolutely." She beams with satisfaction. "I'll have it to you by the end of the day."

Kennedy jots down a few notes in her notepad, and before I have a chance to think of it, words are spilling from my lips. "The end of tomorrow is fine, Kennedy. The business day is almost over, and there's no need to stay late."

With a terse nod, she goes back to writing down a few things. "I have one more suggestion."

"Of course." Xander nods.

Kennedy risks a slight glance in my direction. Reluctance has her gnawing on her plush lower lip. "As you know, we are the farthest resort from the airport, which might be a deterrent for some guests. What if we provided a drive there that was more fun?"

"We will continue with the private driver options," I answer for Xander. For the most part, we are continuing the business model the previous resort had, with a few tweaks, to make it more successful. One of the options is that instead of riding a shuttle with up to ten passengers, guests can select their own private cars. It makes sense to offer an exclusive option for those who want a more secluded stay.

"Yes," she bites out before taking a deep breath, still refusing to look at me. "But why not make all guests feel special? Our shuttles are nice, but guests have more than likely been traveling all day. They're exhausted, hungry, and ready to start their vacation. Why not have the driver and one other resort staff on the shuttle, which would provide drinks and small snacks to our guests. We could also work with a local bar to allow us a stop for quick drinks. Guests can grab a local brew or cocktail to enjoy on their scenic route to the resort. The driver would pay for the drinks from our funds, which would encourage guests to join in. The shuttle would play music with island vibes, like a party bus. Party buses are huge in my hometown, and there's such a unique energy when you're on one."

"So once again, we are incorporating your small-time lifestyle into our luxury resort." My eyes roll of their own accord. This is ridiculous.

"That's exactly what I'm suggesting," she snaps, turning to face me. Clearly aggravated, her finger jabs my chest. "If you want to stand out from the others, this is how you do it."

Our eyes lock in a stare-off. Secretly, I don't hate the idea, but I can't let her know that right away.

"Send me over all your suggestions with the renderings, Kennedy. I think you're on to something," Xander interrupts, standing from his seat. "If that's all, I've got a hot date tonight."

"With your right hand," I mumble, and Kennedy's lip twitch.

"No, that's you," Xander adds as he leaves the room, and now I'm the one blushing, because he's not wrong. It's been months since I've gone out with a woman, much less slept with someone. Every time I go out to the bar to meet someone, copper-red hair and green eyes take over my subconscious. Kennedy Reed has ruined me.

Kennedy leaves right after my brother, and I'm not far behind them. I need a screaming cycle instructor to kick my ass and get my head on straight.

CHAPTER SEVEN

KENNEDY

"HE'S THE ABSOLUTE WORST. I don't know how I'm going to be able to finish this project. He called me Podunk. Basically, I'm completely insignificant because I grew up in a small town," I whine to my sister as I walk down the busy Manhattan sidewalks.

"You have two options," my sister, Olivia, suggests from the other end of the phone.

"And what are those options, Liv?"

"You can either hike up your big girl panties and show him that being from a small town doesn't make you less than him. Sure, we didn't have luxury cars and designer clothes, but that doesn't mean we aren't as smart as him." She pauses, and I'm waiting for what could be her other suggestion, since that one sounds like the right choice. "Or you could bang his brains out."

"Olivia!" I practically scream, garnering looks from passersby. "I am *not* going to '*bang his brains out.*'"

"Why not?" She barks out a laugh on the other end of the line. "It might do you some good. Plus, all that tension and animosity between the two of you would lead to some explosive sex."

"He's the enemy, Liv. I'm not secretly pining for him." I pull open the door to my gym, and I'm hit with the sound of clinking weights and the smell of bleach cleaners. "I'm at the gym. Talk to you later?"

"I'm not saying you're pining for him, by the way. I'm just saying, a little romp in the sheets might not be a bad thing," she says. "But we can discuss this later. Have a good workout class."

She ends the call before I have a chance to argue. Staring down at the blank screen, I shake my head in disbelief. I make my way to the women's locker room, where I quickly change into an asymmetrical navy longline sports bra and matching leggings. Strapping my shoes on my feet, I grab my water bottle before I lock my locker and head to the workout studio.

The lights are dim as I walk in, and a popular pop song plays through the speakers. Making my way down the line of cycling bikes, I find an empty one in the middle of the room. I'm not a fan of being in the front, but I also don't enjoy being in the back. Others funnel in, and bikes are quickly occupied, leaving only a few empty. I'm in the middle of doing a few breathing exercises when a familiar tingle rolls over my spine and my senses are consumed with cedar and citrus.

Glancing to my left, I'm met with amber eyes and a familiar smirk that shows off that damn dimple. "Firecracker," his deep voice rumbles through my body.

"What the hell are you doing here?" I hiss. As much as I need this workout, I need to be away from Tristan more.

My phone call and cycle class were supposed to be enough to get the stunt Tristan pulled out of my mind. During our meeting, I tried like hell to avoid looking at him and letting him affect me. I kept my focus on Xander, but Tristan wouldn't shut the fuck up. He kept interrupting my ideas and trying to shut down everything I suggested with his passive-aggressive banter. It's like it's in his job description to make my life a living hell. And here he is, after office hours, when it's *my time*.

He turns his head, looking to his left and behind him, before turning back to me. "I thought this was a cycling studio."

Clenching my jaw, I mentally cross my fingers that the scream threatening to explode from me stays in until I'm home and my face is buried in a pillow. I lean forward to unclip my feet from the pedals, but before I can even touch them, the music changes, and the instructor comes running in.

"What's up, Cycle Craze?" Her loud, energetic voice comes through the speakers, and I realize that I'm too late to leave the class. Besides, Kenzie is my favorite instructor, and I really don't want to miss out on a chance to take her class. She's become popular over the last couple of weeks, and while I'm excited for her, it means her classes book up quicker.

With one last drink, I toss my water bottle down and focus on Kenzie. She's chugging an iced coffee as she adjusts her headset.

"Try to keep up, Firecracker."

Glaring at my nemesis on the bike beside me, Tristan tilts his head back and forth, cracking the muscles in his neck. Kenzie switches her music on, and a hip-hop song plays through the speakers, instantly putting me in the mood to climb these hills she'll no doubt force us to endure in tonight's class.

My legs are screaming at me as Kenzie encourages us to push our cadence from one hundred to one-hundred-ten while increasing our resistance by five. Sweat rolls down my face, down my cleavage and back, no doubt casting this navy workout set in a darker shade. Typically, I try to stay at the cadence and resistance the instructor calls out, but there are some days when my legs refuse to cooperate.

Today feels like one of those days, but I'll be damned if I let Tristan Nelson outride me. Peeking out of the corner of my eye, I see that he's just as saturated in sweat as I am. I'll never understand how these instructors can not only ride the hell out of their bikes, but they do it while freaking talking during the whole class. Kenzie has been belting out the lyrics to the rap songs she's selected on her playlist *while* dancing along. I'm barely able to breathe, and here she is, exerting even more energy. She's seriously such a badass.

"Keep crushing it, Craze!" she encourages from the front of the room. "Ten more seconds, and we'll start our descent."

Thank God!

Very slowly, Kenzie calls out for us to lower the resistance as we recover.

The music changes to a slower-paced song as Kenzie reaches for her water bottle and the rest of the class follows her lead. There's no question when I unclip from this bike that my legs are going to be Jell-O, and I'm going to have to try my hardest to stay upright. I knew coming to Cycle Craze would be the distraction I needed from Nelson's, even though Tristan is beside me. I used his presence as motivation, but at some point during our ride, I completely forgot he was there and let my mind escape. Kenzie's motivational stories and high energy led me on a journey and, suddenly, thoughts of designs and permits were no longer at the forefront of my mind.

"Before we end class, I want everyone up out of the saddle with their left leg in the back. Let's stretch out those muscles we worked.

Don't forget to head out to the main room, or even the small space between bikes, and do a longer stretch. Today's ride was tough, but we're tougher for it."

Following her lead, I lean forward, allowing the calf muscles down to my Achilles to stretch out. Switching sides, we all sigh in relief. "Great work today, everyone. Let's take a deep inhale and remember stronger rides today—exhale—lead to unstoppable victories tomorrow! Have a great rest of your night!"

And with those final remarks, we follow her instructions on how to unclip our shoes and dismount our bikes.

"Nice work, Firecracker," Tristan's exasperated voice says. He gathers a towel, swiping it down his face. His stupid, perfect face doesn't even look like he just spent the last forty-five minutes in a cycle class.

Reaching for my water bottle, I take a long pull as the cold liquid slides down my throat. "Keep up good enough for you?"

He smirks. "Surprisingly, yeah, you did."

With an eye roll and shake of the head, I take a step away from the bike and feel my body sway. Strong arms catch me. "You okay, Ken?"

My eyes blink rapidly as I focus on his voice. "Ye-yeah, I'm fine. Just a little light-headed."

"Have you eaten anything recently?" His deep tone is full of concern as I shake my head, and he steers me to the side of the room. "Here, sit down for a second."

My body feels too weak to protest, and I hate that he gets to witness my weakness, especially after how hard I worked in this class. People pass us, and I don't miss their curious glances.

Kenzie makes her way over to where I'm sitting, and I watch as she drops down until we are at eye level. "Hey, you doing okay?"

"Yeah," I answer weakly. "I think I overdid it."

"I'll grab you a power bar. That should help get your sugar levels back up. Do you have someone who can come get you? We'd hate to have you passing out on your way home."

"I'll be fine–"

I'm quickly cut off by the thorn in my side. "I've got her."

Huffing an exasperated sigh, I start to object, but his dark gaze slices through me. "Let me do this for you, Ken."

"Oh my gosh, you have the sweetest boyfriend," Kenzie coos as she stands.

"He's not my boyf…" My words trail off as I realize that Kenzie is no longer standing beside us in her mission to find me a power bar to eat.

My face heats, and I tuck my head, refusing to look at the all-encompassing, hypnotizing eyes. "Thank you."

"You're welcome, Firecracker."

Kenzie returns with a peanut butter and chocolate chip power bar, which I quickly scarf down. Turns out, working out when all you've eaten is a grilled chicken Caesar salad isn't enough nutrients for a high-intensity cycle class. Once Kenzie is reassured that I will be fine and I do have someone to help me get home, she leaves us sitting alone in a dark, quiet room. The animosity that normally swirls around us is gone, but in its wake is something I can't quite put my finger on.

Tristan straightens and his six-foot-three frame towers over me. Sparing him a glance, I look up at him from under my lashes and watch as his chest inflates with a deep breath. Heat glimmers in his eyes as he stares down at me. For a brief moment, my mind flashes, wondering if this is the same look he would give me if I were in front of him…on my knees…taking him in my mouth.

What?! This is Tristan. The bane of my existence.

Shaking my head, his eyes flicker back to his usual shade of hazel where his eyes look more green and gold, rather than the darkness which was staring down at me. Was he thinking the same thing I was?

He reaches for my hand, but I refuse to take it as I push up from the ground, slowly, with my water bottle and keys in my hand. "Let me grab my things, and I'll meet you out front."

With a terse nod, we funnel out of the room and go our separate ways. I need space and room to breathe.

A few minutes later, I'm walking out of the locker room and heading to the front when I hear his deep, throaty laugh. Turning my head, I watch as the receptionist shamelessly flirts with Tristan, and he returns the gestures. There's that ice-cold bucket of water I needed to remind myself that he's my rival, not my friend. And definitely not the guy I should be imagining dirty, hot, explosive sex with. I blame Olivia for putting the idea in my mind.

Deciding not to interrupt him, I push through the glass doors and start walking. To punish myself even more, I spare a glance back inside the building. The receptionist is passing a note to Tristan, no doubt with her number on it, but he's not looking at her. No, his face is marred in a scowl as he storms away from the desk, eating up the space between the desk and the front door. Turning on my toes, I move at a brisk pace and hope to get away from him. I'm feeling much better, so I don't need him anymore.

"Kennedy!" he calls, and the seriousness of his tone has my feet faltering. He's behind me in seconds, grabbing my elbow in a gentle but firm grip. Spinning me around, I'm met with a flurry of emotions. "Where the hell are you going?"

"Home," I snap, hands clutching the straps on my gym bag.

"Okay," he draws out, eyes searching mine. "My car is over here."

"I'm fine, Tristan. Thanks for everything back there, but I'm fine."

His hands fly to his hair, where he pushes them through dark locks. "Why are you so impossible? Get your ass in the car and let me make sure you're okay. For once in your life, just trust me and let me take you home."

I thought wrong, because the light-headedness comes back with full force as I nod reluctantly. His shoulders physically relax as he turns toward his car. Quickening my pace, I fall in line beside him. He mumbles something that sounds a lot like *"you're insufferable, woman,"* and I can't help my small chuckle.

If I'm insufferable, he's incorrigible.

Twenty minutes later, after giving his driver my address, the sleek black BMW parks in front of my hideous brown townhouse. The sight is ridiculous on this block. Pushing open the door, I thank Tristan's driver before exiting the vehicle and walking up the few steps to my front porch.

"Firecracker."

Clutching my chest, startled, I drop my keys as I turn around. "Shit, Tristan."

"You weren't even going to thank me?" He sounds hurt, and for some irrational reason, I hate that.

My eyes scan the street, and the unmistakable car is no longer there. "Where's your car?"

His feet carry him closer, and I watch on bated breath as he lowers himself to pick up my keys. "I sent him home."

"But why aren't you in the car?"

Is it hot out here? Why does my voice sound so breathy? What is happening right now?

"Because I'm not leaving you alone."

Chest heaving, I reach for the keys in his outstretched hand, jumping as our fingers brush. Did I fall and hit my head?

Hoping it was a weird fluke, I glimpse and find a small smirk on his face as he stares at his feet. Turning around, I insert my key and twist it to unlock the beat-up white door. I'm met with silence when I step across the threshold. Lana must be working late tonight, which means I'm alone with Tristan in our townhouse, my emotions all out of whack, with the lingering embarrassment and memory of his gentle touch muddling my mind even more.

The door clicks closed behind me and my heart races. "Dinner will be here in about ten minutes."

"What?"

"I ordered dinner in the car on our way here. I'm not leaving until I know you've eaten and you're not going to pass out."

"Tristan, this is ridiculous." I roll my eyes and feel my body sway, but keep it together so he can get the hell out of here. "I'm twenty-five years old. I can take care of myself." My hands land on my hips as my frustrations pour out.

His hands raise in defense. "I'm just making sure my competition doesn't croak on me. What's the fun in that?"

Clenching my hands into fists, I let out a very unattractive growl. "You drive me crazy."

"That makes two of us," he mutters as his gaze wanders, taking in the townhouse.

I found this townhouse on a whim.

Built in 1899, the 1,000 square foot two-story unit was newly remodeled with affordable rent. I couldn't pass it up and, luckily, Lana was looking for a place to live, which made the decision so much easier. While I could have afforded the rent on my own, there's an added sense of financial security by having a roommate–and it helps that your roommate is your bestie. Living in New York is expensive. I realized that real quick in college, but it's worth it when my dreams get to come true.

I watch in fascination as the man who has everything he could ever desire takes in my humble space. The front door opens into our kitchen with white shaker cabinets and gray granite countertops. A long, rustic farmhouse table runs the length of the cabinets where it sits atop a neutral oriental rug. The shades complement the distressed brown shade of our table and the gray hues on the counters.

The space is spotless, since my obsessive mind won't let me go to sleep or leave for work with anything out on the counters. Past the kitchen is a tiny living space with a cream-colored sectional and a few houseplants along the edge of the room. Across from the couch is a TV mounted on the wall with a skinny cabinet underneath it. Lana's door is a frosted glass sliding door on one of the walls in the living room.

"Nice place." There's an air of comfort around Tristan as he makes his way deeper into the house, as if he's been here a million times before plopping down on our couch.

"Make yourself at home...I guess." I gesture to the couch and watch as his large frame envelops the space. Tristan looks comical in our tiny townhouse.

Turning toward the refrigerator, I pull out a cold bottle of water and then reach for a packet of electrolytes. Hopefully, the added electrolytes will help with whatever issue caused me to get so light-headed after our workout.

Leaning against the counter, the lemon lime-flavored water slides down my throat as I stare at the man in the next room.

Is this what it's like to have a boyfriend?

A husband?

Someone to come home to at the end of a long workday?

Growing up, I was never one of those girls that wished for Prince Charming and their happily ever after. For me, life has always been about studying for the next big exam that will allow me the opportunity to fight for my dream. I've always wanted to put my career first. Even now that I'm living in New York with my dream job, there's always something else I'm striving for. The next big project or proving my worth in corporate America where so many still believe women should be at home raising their children.

And there's nothing wrong with that. Nothing at all. My mom left her job to stay home with us when Olivia was born. By having her home, she was able to spend more time with us to focus on our developmental needs while providing a stable and loving home. She worked hard, and anyone who thinks staying at home with children is easier has never done it. It's a lonely and thankless job that left her exhausted while rewarded at the same time.

As much as I admired my mom, I never wanted to end up in her shoes. A tiny seed was planted in my brain at a young age, telling me I was strong, brave, and could conquer the world. And that's exactly what I plan to do.

I take a seat opposite Tristan, tucking my legs underneath me, making sure I leave as much space between us as humanly possible. No accidental touches with the enemy, I remind myself, as I bring the water bottle to my lips and savor the taste of the lemon-lime mixture.

Hearing him chuckle, my head whips in his direction, casting him a long glare. "What's so funny?"

"Nothing...just that you're terrified to touch me. Afraid you'll fall in love with me with only one touch?"

"As if," I scoff, turning my attention back to the television. "You know, I could've just taken an Uber. Or, you know, you could leave now. I'm fine."

"And risk you dying and me being the prime suspect? Hell no."

"You're right."

His body twists in my direction as he stretches his arm across the back of the couch, fingertips nearly brushing my shoulder. I cower closer in my corner as he huffs a breath. "Right about what?"

"You'll be prime suspect. I have a hidden folder that says if I go missing, Tristan Nelson did it."

A booming roar of laughter explodes from him, vibrating off the walls. "You fucking would."

"I know I would because I did." I fold my arms across my chest, frustrated that he's invaded my space with no sign of leaving. He shakes his head as he turns his attention back to the television.

The food he ordered better arrive quickly because playing domestication with him is my worst nightmare.

CHAPTER EIGHT

TRISTAN

"TRISTAN, HONEY?" MY MOM muses from where she's sitting across from me. It's Sunday afternoon, and the family is gathered around for our weekly lunch. It's been a tradition for as long as I can remember. Growing up, we would all go to Grandma and Grandpa Nelson's house, and in the summer, we would all go to the beach house in the Hamptons.

Once my grandpa passed, my grandmother moved into a retirement home, which left my mother to pick up the hosting obligations. She didn't mind, though. Mother is a natural-born hostess with her collection of fine China and an elegant palette. Her joy is spending hours in the kitchen preparing a feast, even though it's just the five of us. It's always way too much food, leaving me stuffed beyond measure and craving a workout. This is why I found myself leaning back on the couch, relaxing after her lunch of a roasted rack of lamb, dauphinoise potatoes, roasted parmesan asparagus, and homemade dinner rolls.

I turn my attention back to my mother, whose warm hazel eyes, ones that match mine, are staring right back and analyzing me. "Sorry, Mom. What were you saying?"

"I asked if you've been seeing anyone?"

Absentmindedly, I move my hand holding the glass in a circular motion, causing the amber liquid to swish and the ice to clink against the sides. Images of bright red hair sprawled across my chest flash through my mind. Thursday night plays on repeat. I don't know what came over me, but there was no way I was sending Kennedy on her own when she almost passed out after our workout class. One thing led to another, and sometime after dinner, I found myself sitting opposite her as we watched HGTV. An HGTV show where they're looking for their new house and given three options to pick from quickly led to a heated debate over which to pick and then some rom-com Kennedy put on afterwards.

What felt like only minutes later, I heard a throat clearing, startling me from my spot on the couch, and when I looked up, Lana was staring at me, her eyebrow quirked. Glancing down, that's when I realized at some point during the movie I had drifted off to sleep with Kennedy's head on my chest. She looked peaceful. No stress, no competitiveness, just calm. There was no way I could stay the night—hell, I didn't plan to stay as long as I had. So I had reached for the pillow that was behind me and gently replaced my body with it. Lana watched with fascination in her eyes, but I couldn't risk the wrath of Kennedy if she woke up to me beneath her. Somehow, she would end up twisting the harmless, innocent moment with accusations that I was trying to sabotage her or some shit. And I was a little worried that not only had it been one of the better nights I'd had recently, but it had felt good having her weight on my chest, breathing her in, just having her so close.

"No, Mom, I'm not seeing anyone."

With a deep breath, she sighs. "Will one of my kids please settle down and give me grandbabies to spoil?"

"Jesus, Mom." Victoria sits in the empty spot next to me with a heavy pour of wine in her hand. "Kids are not in my forecast anytime soon."

"No, you'd have to settle down for that." Xander peers up from where he's been typing away on his phone.

Victoria scoffs. "As if either of you are any better."

"Please leave me out of this." Bringing the glass to my lips, I let the smooth, oaky liquid slide down my throat.

Victoria's body turns toward me, an evil smirk on her face as her eyes light up. "Oh right, we have to leave Tristan out of it since he's so desperately in love with Kennedy."

"Who's Kennedy?" Amusement and curiosity lace Mom's voice.

"She's no one," I say, just as Xander says, "She's his nemesis."

"Ooo, tell me more." Mom claps, actually *claps* her hands in excitement.

I can't fight the groan and glare at my annoying little sister. "There's nothing going on between Kennedy and I. She can't stand me, and I'm not ready to settle down."

"If there's nothing going on, then why did you spend the night at her house?" Victoria mumbles behind her wineglass.

Xander chokes on his drink, and through his coughs, he asks, "You did what?"

Leaning forward, I rest my elbows on my knees and shake my head. "First, I did not spend the night at her place, and second," I pause, turning my attention back to Tori. "who told you that?"

She shrugs, taking a long gulp of the red liquid.

"I've missed this," Mom says wistfully.

"Missed what? The three of us bickering?" Xander shakes his head.

Mom's smile lights up her face and meets her eyes where they crinkle. "Yes, Alexander. I miss having my kids at home. I miss the pranks you three used to pull. But above all, I miss the love that was shown within these walls. It's quiet and lonely now."

My heart warms at her admission.

The hum of laughter and the clinking of glasses fill the parlor, my siblings tossing banter back and forth like they've done every Sunday for as long as I can remember. I lean back in my chair, the leather creaking beneath me, and swirl the bourbon in my glass, letting its rich aroma rise with each slow turn. My family's voices fade into the background as my mind drifts to thoughts of her—the bright-eyed, red-haired beauty with a sharp mind and a fire to match. She's working under me now, forcing us even closer than we already are. I can already see the sparks that her confidence and boldness will strike. A smirk curves my lips as I stare into the amber liquid, the thought settling in my head: *Let's see how the next few months go with this project.*

NINE MONTHS LATER

CHAPTER NINE

KENNEDY

STEADY POUNDING OF THE rain hits the windows as a cloud of gray surrounds the outside. The weather is fitting for Thanksgiving in the late Ohio fall. This is my first trip back home in nearly two years. Last year, I was too busy sorting out where I would be working that I didn't want to risk leaving the city in case I was contacted for a job interview. It was a good thing I didn't leave, since Nelson Signature contacted me the Friday after Thanksgiving to meet the following Monday.

It's crazy how much life can change in a year. Not only my job, but as I glance around at the long dining room table my mom has decorated for every holiday my entire life, I take in how much my parents have changed. With time comes aging, and with both of my parents retired, I notice how much older they appear. In my mind, they're both the same spry thirty-year-olds who taught me how to ride a bike or how to make perfect chocolate chip cookies.

"Sweetie, how's the city?" Mom asks from where she's sitting across from me. She reaches for the bowl of sweet potatoes before passing them to her left, where my sister sits.

Scooping out a large portion of green bean casserole—my favorite—I pass the bowl to my grandpa, where he's eyeing the green bean and cream of mushroom concoction speculatively. "New York is still New York. Oh, but there's this new coffee shop that just opened down the street from the townhouse, and Lana and I did a coffee experience there. We got to go in and sample four different origins of coffee and brewing methods while they teach you about how to recognize the differences in flavors and aromas. It was a lot of fun!"

"Now that sounds right up my alley," Olivia chimes in. "What was your favorite?"

"The Puerto Rico coffee in the V-60 was my favorite."

"What's wrong with Maxwell House from a coffeepot?" Grandpa grumbles from his place at the head of the table. My dad and grandpa have always sat at the head of the table while my mom, sister, grandma, Aunt Julie, Uncle Ed, and myself sit in the middle.

"There's nothing wrong with it, Dad," Mom says with an eye roll. "You know how adults today enjoy the finer things in life."

I chuckle because, to everyone sitting around this table, except for Olivia, no one has left the county in years. And while it's a great county, that is slowly coming to times, it's still so behind on the happenings of the big city. The latest thing to come into town was a new automotive garage and a microbrewery.

"Olivia, I see you have some new designs on your body." Aunt Julie points to the start of my sister's sleeve. Tattoos of flowers and vines line her arms, with a new detailed monarch butterfly weaved from her wrist around her forearm and toward her bicep. The flowers aren't new, but the butterfly is, which is drawn beautifully and captures the eye immediately.

"My roommate moved to Texas, so we decided to get butterfly tattoos together."

"Why a butterfly?" Uncle Ed asks around a forkful of food. His manners have always been lacking.

Reaching for her glass of water, Olivia takes a long drink while I scoop another serving of green beans onto my plate. They're truly the superior Thanksgiving side dish. "Butterflies symbolize a lot of things in different cultures. They signify a powerful beacon of growth and new beginnings, which was perfect for Bret and myself since she was moving and I was starting a new job."

"At a tattoo parlor," Grandma adds with disapproval in her tone. No matter how wonderful her grandchildren are, Grandma can never get over the issues with tattoos. She doesn't understand the idea of marking yourself permanently.

Using her roll to mop up the rest of the food on her plate, Mom turns to Olivia, wearing a hopeful expression. "Do you think you'd ever move back home?"

Eyes widening, Olivia looks at me for help. With a shrug, I leave her to her own devices. Mom has been trying to get us girls to move back home every chance she gets. And while I understand her home feels empty without us, she did a good job of teaching us to spread our wings and fly.

"What would I do? Open a tattoo parlor on Main Street?"

"Yes!" I nearly shout, as my grandmother gasps.

Olivia sends me a wink as Dad interrupts the conversation. "Kenny, how's your resort project going?"

"Oh, what project is this?" Aunt Julie asks.

"Nelson Signature acquired a resort in St. Lucia, and in January, my design pitch was selected for the remodel."

"Sounds like a vacation to me," Uncle Ed chimes in, always looking for a way to get something handed to him for free.

"I'm not sure about that. There's a good chance I'll never have the opportunity to visit the resort. Everything is done through emails and virtual meetings."

"We're really proud of you, sweetie. Both of our girls." Mom's warm smile meets her eyes as she reaches over and squeezes Olivia's hand.

The rest of dinner flies by, and soon enough, plates are cleared, pies destroyed, and my dad's dropping Olivia and me off at the new microbrewery, Iron Horse Brewing Co. so we could have a little sister time.

• • • • • • • • • • •

The bar is packed with familiar faces, many home for the holiday, much like we were. Conversation flows as easily as the drinks and time seems to slip by as a local band plays music from our high school days. My phone vibrating on the table pulls my attention from where I'm watching Olivia flirt with the Blackwood brothers.

Tate and Gage have been in love with my sister for as long as I can remember. Tate graduated a year before me, while Gage was a year or two older than Olivia, falling in between the two of us in school. Liv looks like she fits in perfectly with their group, and I wonder if Tate will finally confess his love to my sister. Unlikely, but it's worth a shot. Glancing away from where the three of them are playing pool with a few others, I see the name "Golden Boy" flash across the screen.

Leave it to Tristan to ruin a perfectly good holiday.

"What could you possibly need?" I say by way of greeting.

"Hello to you too, Firecracker," Tristan says before letting out a long groan. "What is that awful noise?"

"That sound, Golden Boy, is the sound of a local band playing our town's anthem, Wagon Wheel."

"Sounds delightful."

"I'm glad you think so too. But seriously, what do you want, Tristan?"

"What's the matter? You haven't missed the sound of my voice?"

"I heard cats fighting in the barn earlier. Sounds about the same," I retort.

"I'm wounded, Kennedy, deeply wounded."

"Uh-huh." Reaching for the pint glass in front of me, I enjoy a long pull of the American IPA and savor the fruitiness of mango and pineapple.

"Promise not to kill the messenger?"

"There's never any promises in hate and war."

"We need to leave for St. Lucia. There's an issue with the resort."

Sounds fade out around me as my pulse thunders in my ears. "I'm sorry, what did you just say?"

He starts to explain, but I quickly cut him off, telling him I need to find a quiet place. Too bad the only quiet place is outside and I'm not disappearing without telling my sister where I'm going. Finishing the last couple of sips of my beer, I stand from my seat and weave through the crowd of people gathered around to listen to the band.

Gage Blackwood eyes me as I approach the group. "Damn, Kennedy, you look good. Liv, why didn't you tell us Kenny was here too?"

"Who the hell is that?" Tristan grits from his side of the phone.

I smother a laugh. "Friends of my sister's," I tell him before pulling the phone away from my mouth.

"I've got to take this outside."

Olivia nods, and I step around the group of bikers as I head for the back exit.

The patio is dimly lit, with only a few strands of bistro lights hanging from the poles. A couple of smokers are huddled together, and I find a table to sit away from the lingering smoke and glances.

"What's the problem?"

"Finally," he grumbles, and my eyes roll on instinct. "There is a problem in St. Lucia, and since we are the project leads, we need to be on location for at least a month."

"A month!" My jaw drops. A month in paradise sounds amazing, but not being stuck on an island smaller than the county I grew up in. "When do we leave?"

"We really should be settled for a meeting first thing Monday morning. I can have the jet ready by Saturday morning."

Nibbling on my lower lip, my mind spins with how I'm going to get to New York in time, when my flight home wasn't supposed to be until Sunday. "Okay, I'll see what I can do about getting my flight changed."

"I'll take care of it. Can you be at the Columbus Airport by nine tomorrow morning? Will that give you plenty of time to pack and get everything you need for a month or more in St. Lucia?"

Mulling over his words, I run through a list of all the things I'm going to need, like toiletries and island-appropriate business clothes. "Yeah, I'll make it work."

"I'll text you all the flight details."

And with that, he clicks off the call, and I'm stuck sitting in the cold forty-degree weather, wondering how the hell I'm going to survive a month with Tristan.

Willing my fingers to work in the colder weather, I tap on my messaging app and find Lana's name.

> **Me: Guess who is going to St. Lucia for at least a month.**

> **Lana: A hot redheaded bombshell?**

> **Me: Yes...**

> **Me: With Tristan.**

> **Lana: Lead with the juicy details next time!**

I groan to myself. My best friend and my office bestie see this undeniable chemistry between us, even after all the frustrations I've vented to them about.

> **Me: Lana, he's arranging a flight to come pick me up tomorrow and then we leave on Saturday.**

> **Lana: *Wide Eyes Emoji* Oh damn. Do you have island clothes?**

> **Lana: Wait, of course you do. What do you need from me?**

Me: I mean I have vacation clothes but not stuff I'd consider wearing for work.

Lana: Then stop texting me and order store pickups. I'm free tomorrow. I'll be your pretty little errand girl.

Lana: No, promote me to assistant. Look at you going to St. Lucia and hiring an assistant. Look ma you made it *wink emoji*

Me: You're delirious. But if you mean it, I think I might take you up on it.

Lana: Put that credit card to use and I'll see you tomorrow.

Me: *kiss emoji*

Closing out of the messaging app, I pull open my notes and start making a list of all the things I'm going to need and what sizes will meet TSA standards. Wait, do private jets have to follow TSA standards? After a quick search, I find we don't have to follow TSA requirements, which means I can order normal sizes of all of my things.

Light from the bar pours outside, and I hear "Kenny!" shouted. My cute little sister, with her silver hair shimmering in the night light, appears in the doorway of the bar and she has Tate Blackwood's arm wrapped around her shoulder, while hers is at his waist. They look friendly, all cozied up together. I knew something was going on between the two of them.

"You two look cute," I say, watching Olivia's eyes widen while Tate smirks at me.

"Who was on the phone?" Olivia asks me.

Groaning, I toss the phone on the table and wipe my hand down my face. "Tristan."

Her smile grows. "Aw, it's sweet that he missed you."

"He didn't miss me. He called to tell me that I have to fly to St. Lucia for the next month. Apparently, there's a problem with the resort."

Her eyes widen as she raises her eyebrows up and down. "Have fun sleeping with the enemy."

"Are you ready if I text Dad to come pick us up?" I ask her, ignoring her comment.

She nods as Tate tucks her closer to his chest. "C'mon, Livvy, head back to the house with us."

"Not tonight." She peers up at him. "I only have one more night with my sister."

Reaching into his pocket, he pulls out a cigarette. The two of them carry on while he has a smoke and we wait for our dad to show up, while I search for items I need for in-store pickup. Hopefully, by ordering tonight, I'll avoid the Black Friday rush of tomorrow, which should be fine since most of the items I need aren't the in-store specials but everyday essentials.

Tomorrow's problems are for tomorrow.

Tonight, I'm heading back to my childhood home with my little sister to have one of our Reed sister sleepovers with popcorn and a cheesy 2000s romantic comedy playing in the background while we gossip.

Chapter Ten

Tristan

The last forty-eight hours have been an absolute whirlwind. One minute, I was sitting at my parents' dining room table, enjoying a delicious spread my mom and sister spent hours preparing, and the next, my phone was blowing up with problem after problem on our St. Lucia project. Dad glared at me from across the table as if these issues were my fault.

Too bad for him, I filed all the paperwork correctly, and the zoning committee decided they had more issues than they previously let on. It's almost as if they want us to fail with this remodel.

I certainly don't want this project to fail. Not for my sake and certainly not for Kennedy's. For the past nine months, the two of us have worked diligently to make sure everything runs smoothly—well, as smoothly as possible when you're dealing with a renovation two thousand miles away.

I dreaded making the call to Kennedy while she was home with her family. She was so excited to finally be able to see everyone and, unlike what she might think, I didn't want to rain on her parade. These situations are not ideal for anyone, and based on the new timeline, she won't be going home for Christmas either. The two of us will be having Christmas on the island.

But it's fine. Or at least it will be.

Bringing the ceramic mug to my lips, I take a sip of the rich, dark roast coffee and find Kennedy curled up on the couch opposite me. She looks exhausted, but still gorgeous in her matching slate gray waffle loungewear set. When she climbed the steps to board the jet, I noticed the dark circles she tried to hide under her eyes. And after much convincing, I talked her into lying on the couch for a few more hours of sleep. She refused to go to the back of the jet and sleep in the private bed, but I'll take the couch as a win. The flight to St. Lucia will be around five hours, so she might as well make the most of it.

As we approach the island, there's a small bout of turbulence that has Kennedy jumping out of her skin. She quickly hops into the captain's chair across from me, fastening her seatbelt in record time.

Practically trembling, she squeezes her eyes shut. Her fingernails are going to leave half-moons in the leather from the death grip she has on the armrests. Reaching across the aisle, I place my palm on her thigh, unintentionally startling her, and her eyes bug out at the contact.

"We're okay, Firecracker."

Her eyes squeeze shut, and her head shakes, telling me she doesn't believe a word. Flying has never bothered me. Sure, the idea of plummeting to the ground thirty-thousand feet in the air is terrifying, but I've never given it much thought. I figure I have a better chance of getting hit by a cab in the city than crashing in a plane.

Clearly, Kennedy doesn't have that same mindset.

Without much thought, I'm unfastening my seatbelt and reaching for hers.

"What the hell are you doing, Tristan?" she hisses, her eyes wide and wild as pure panic takes over.

I don't answer. Instead, I unclip her belt and reach underneath her knees. Pulling her toward me as she panics, I carry her back to my seat, where I stretch the belt across both of our laps. Without hesitation, she curls into me, burying her face in my neck.

The movement causes growing farther south as she sits on my lap. I cannot have that kind of reaction to her, especially not right now, while she's in the midst of a panic attack.

Gritting my teeth, I try to think of anything else. Maybe I should think about us plummeting to the ground—that will no doubt cure any arousal. But then her nose nuzzles into my neck, and I fight the groan that wants to escape. It's been forever since I had a girl this close to me.

"You smell good."

A soft chuckle leaves my lips. "Thank you."

"That was supposed to be an inside thought."

"Of course, Firecracker. We can't have you giving me compliments." We hit another rough patch, and her fist tightens against my dress shirt as I pull her in tighter. "I've got you, Ken."

"I don't want to die in a fiery crash with you." Her words are mumbled against my skin, but I hear every one.

Trying to soothe her, I rub small circles on the inside of her thigh as I look for any way to keep her mind preoccupied. "God forbid you spend all of eternity with me."

"Exactly. I'm glad we're on the same page."

A few minutes later, the pilot comes across the speaker, letting us know that we should be clear of the turbulence as we make our descent into St. Lucia. Kennedy's head pops up from my shoulder and our eyes meet. There's something in her gaze I can't quite figure out. Is she relieved? Thankful for the distraction? Before I have a chance to analyze her more, her fingers work the clasp of the safety belt.

As quickly as I pulled her onto my lap, she's up and taking her place across from me as she snaps her belt into place.

"Are you feeling better?"

With a deep exhale, her eyes find mine again. A tight-lipped smile lines her pale pink lips, and she gives me a small nod as she fidgets with her pants. "I will be once we get wheels on the ground."

"I never pegged you as afraid of flying. I figured you'd be used to it since you live two states away from your family."

"I don't make it home that often. Between college and then work, my trips home got few and far between. Plus, I'm from the Midwest. We drive everywhere."

"I never understood that."

"It's because you have money, Golden Boy. Not all of us have the luxury of dropping a couple of thousand dollars on flights to go on vacation. If we wanted to go somewhere, we'd load up the minivan and drive to wherever we were going. Not like we went on many vacations."

There's a drop we feel in our stomachs, causing Kennedy to grip the armrest again as we start to land.

One skid.

Two skids.

And our wheels are on the ground.

I can hear her audible sigh as relief floods her system.

"We made it," she whispers.

Thirty minutes later, Kennedy and I are in the back seat of a black town car as we make the long drive to the resort from the airport.

I'm trying to read over files and emails as we go around hills and curves, making my focus a challenge. Kennedy has all but given up. She popped motion sickness medicine as soon as we landed. Her head has been on a swivel as we drive through various terrains of small towns and mountains.

She slides across her seat to the middle seat, our legs brushing, which she doesn't acknowledge as she leans forward and points out the window. "Sir, can you stop up there?" she asks our driver.

His eyes find hers in the rearview mirror, and he nods. I try to get a better look at what has caught her eyes when I spot a small wooden building with a red roof. Open-sided patios line the space with picnic tables underneath. It's a quaint local bar.

Our driver puts the car in park, and before he has a chance to shut off the ignition, Kennedy is jumping out of the backseat. I'm immediately opening my door and stepping out after her. The air is thick with humidity, and I feel the moisture gripping my dress shirt. With a glance over her shoulder, she winks before she's strutting inside the bar.

The inside is much like what you'd find inside an American bar. Pub tables litter the space, with beer logos and novelty signs on the walls. A dark-stained bar takes up most of one side, with fridges of bottled beers and an older, dark-skinned woman stands behind it, her long black hair braided and piled on top of her head.

"Good afternoon." A kind smile plasters across her face as she welcomes Kennedy into her bar.

"Hi," Kennedy greets, climbing onto a bar stool across from the woman. "I'm Kennedy."

"Nice to meet you, Kennedy. I'm Elysha. Welcome to my little slice of paradise."

"You have a lovely bar." I'm stuck, my feet barely inside the bar as the two women interact. Kennedy is all smiles with the stranger. A sudden pang of jealousy hits me as I observe the two, noting Kennedy has never given me the same warmth as she's giving this woman.

I want to change that. For the next month, I want to show her I'm not the enemy. I never wanted us to feel like we were constantly competing. There's more to me than this preconceived notion she's painted me with. Yes, I was born with a silver spoon, but it hasn't always been easy.

"Hey, Golden Boy." Her voice cuts off my thoughts. "Come meet Elysha and order something to drink. Lighten up a little bit."

Pointing to myself, I quirk an eyebrow at her. "Me, lighten up? You're the one wound so tight."

Her eyes roll as she turns her attention back to the woman. "See what I have to deal with. What's your local beer?"

"You must try a Piton. It's a pilsner lager beer that has a floral and hoppy aroma."

"Sounds perfect." Her smile is contagious as I make my way toward the woman. "Golden boy will have one too."

Elysha turns to the coolers and pulls out two bottles. The golden liquid shines through the glass bottle. "What brings you two to the island?"

The bottles are placed in front of us, condensation immediately surrounding the glass. Kennedy's smile drops a fraction. "We work for Nelson Signature."

Elysha's eyes widen and her demeanor immediately changes. "You sly, girl."

"Please, let me explain," Kennedy says, her hands going up in defense. Elysha's eyebrow raises, as if permitting Kennedy to keep going. "I'm a small-town girl. I grew up in a tiny town in Ohio and, believe me, I understand what big corporations can do to small businesses. But let me just say, I've done hours and hours of research on how the previous resort owners hurt local businesses. I've implemented policies to make sure that doesn't happen again. Nelson Signature doesn't want to hurt locals. In fact, we want to work with local businesses."

Elysha tsks. "That's what you all say. You get us to trust you, and then, bam, you find a way to screw us over."

"What if I told you that Nelson's wants to find a local bar where buses of tourists can stop on their way to the resort? The driver of the buses will be in charge of paying for the guests' drinks while giving you a twenty-five percent gratuity."

Her eyes widen, and I take a pull of the beer as Kennedy works her magic.

"We'd love to offer your bar the opportunity to work with us."

A door opening has us all turning to see who's entering. Our driver, Jayden, walks inside.

"Jayden!" Elysha exclaims. I turn to watch the woman take in the young man. "They have you working for them?"

He nods. "It's completely different than the last owners. They *actually* care about their employees. We've been doing extensive training for months to help us grow and feel more comfortable with our jobs."

"Do I have to decide today?"

"Absolutely not." Kennedy reaches inside her purse for an envelope. "Inside is the proposal, along with my direct business card. Feel free to call or email me anytime with any questions you may have. You really do have a lovely bar. I saw it as we were driving and asked Jayden to stop."

Elysha's gaze finds Jayden's, and he nods in agreement, assuring her Kennedy is telling the truth.

"Thank you. I've put years of hard work into this place. It's more than just a business; it's an extension of my home."

Another smile brightens Kennedy's face. Reaching into her cooler, Elysha slides two more bottles our way. "On the house."

Grabbing the bottles, I thank the nice woman who has shared a part of her story with us. Kennedy shakes Elysha's hand and reassures her that we aren't the enemy on the island and that the company is doing everything it can to make sure the locals feel the support.

I replay the interaction the rest of the way to the resort as I nurse my beers and take in the sights. Jayden gives us a history lesson as he drives us through the mountainside, pointing out things in nature and historical markers. He even pulls over on the side of the road to point out a few celebrities' houses.

Turning through the large wrought-iron gates, I hear a gasp to my left.

"Oh my gosh." Kennedy's voice is laced with awe as she admires the changes to the resort.

Much like Kennedy, I'm immediately impressed with the remodel. Long gone are the dark stone colors, but in its place are soft beige stucco and neutral travertine tiles. The teakwood accents give the space an inviting feel.

"How's it feel to see your designs in person?"

Her hand covers her mouth as she stares at the large building ahead of us. "It's surreal."

Jayden shifts the car into park before getting out and opening Kennedy's door first. She steps outside in wonder as I open my door, not waiting on Jayden. Reaching into my wallet, I pull out a large bill and slip it into Jayden's palm as I shake his hand. "Thank you for driving us and for the history lesson. You really do know your facts on the island."

He nods. "Thank you, sir. I appreciate the opportunity to work for your company. I'll bring yours and Miss Reed's bags into the lobby."

Speaking of Kennedy, she's no longer standing by the door. Instead, I catch a glimpse of her copper locks as she walks up the footpath. The warm, salty air mixes with the slight breeze as it swirls around us. With a hand in my pocket, I erase the space between us as we enter the lobby. A construction site greets us, as the entryway is still in the process of being switched to match the plans.

The exterior was the first phase, and now the construction team is busy making all the changes in the interior. We are approaching the eleventh month of the remodel, and the hope is to have the main location open in the next two months.

"Mr. Nelson." A petite woman comes scurrying across the tiled floor, causing me to pause and wait for her. She stands in front of me, reaching her hand out for me to shake, which I accept. "I'm Destiny, the general manager."

"It's great to meet you, Destiny. Please call me Tristan. And this is..." I turn, wanting to introduce Destiny to Kennedy. Only, she's gone. "I'm sorry, I was going to introduce you to our lead architect here with me, but I'm not sure where she's gone."

"No problem, sir. I'll let you take in everything, and then I'll show you both to your room." Destiny smiles and turns on her heels before I have a chance to correct her by encouraging her to call me Tristan. While I am a Nelson, I hate being referred to as sir or Mr. Nelson. It feels weird, and I can't explain why.

Glancing around the space, I don't see any trace of the woman I'm stuck on an island with for the next month or longer. I take in the view as I make my way toward the back of the lobby. It opens up to a patio off to the side, where lounge chairs and fire pits reside. Down below is a view that encompasses the entire backside of the property, where cabanas and lounge chairs surround the main pool.

Past the tower, which overlooks the pool, are palm trees swaying in the wind and the gorgeous ocean view, with white sand beaches and turquoise water. Scanning over the sand, a flash of red catches my attention. Standing with her toes where the water meets the sand is Kennedy.

How the hell did she make it down there so fast?

Moving through the lobby, I trot down the stairs and follow the tiled path past the expansive pool to where the walkway meets the sand.

I slip out of my dress shoes and thumb off my socks before stepping off the walkway. Instantly, I feel the soft, grainy sand as it moves around my toes. It's hot in the island sun, but after weeks of cold weather in New York, I welcome the searing heat on the bottoms of my feet. Kennedy hasn't seen me, or if she has, she isn't making my presence known. I watch her as she stares ahead at the passing boats. There's a grin on her lips as the water slides over her toes.

"It's beautiful," she says, keeping her eyes ahead.

"It is." And I'm sure the ocean is, but what's more beautiful is the woman standing in front of me as I watch a few tears slide down her cheeks. She brushes them away before sheepishly turning to look over her shoulder. Her cheeks heat, and I hope she realizes I wasn't talking about the water but the woman I can't keep out of my head.

I follow her gaze to where she's watching her feet disappear in the receding sand. "I've never seen the ocean before."

My head whips in her direction. "Never?"

"Never," she admits quietly as she shakes her head. "Dad worked hard, but we could never get away to go on a beach vacation. The closest we got was Lake Michigan for a long weekend. But this is nothing like the lake."

Words fail me. Growing up, we spent every weekend in the summer in the Hamptons, where my grandparents had a house. It wasn't uncommon for my mom to pack us all up and take us there for a week at a time during the long hot stretches in August.

Unsure of what to say, I change the subject. "Whenever you're ready, Destiny, the general manager, is going to show us our rooms."

She nods before walking back in the direction we came without another word.

I'm stuck in the sand as the flip switches from her moment of vulnerability to the Kennedy I've grown accustomed to.

One of these days, I'm going to break down the damn wall she's so desperate to keep impenetrable.

And when I do, she's going to see the real me.

Chapter Eleven

Kennedy

> Me: Hi everyone! We arrived a few hours ago. The drive from the airport was long but the ocean is breathtaking. I can't believe how much the resort has changed already. It's so surreal to see my designs come to life. Liv, there will be no making Tristan jealous. I'm here to work. Tomorrow we have a few meetings with the staff and then Monday it'll be nonstop meetings with the zoning and compliance departments as we try to sort out what's going on with the permit holdups.

> Olivia: Just try to have some fun! xx

Steeling my shoulders, I climb the steps back into the resort and forget the moment of vulnerability I shed on the shoreline. I cannot believe I actually cried in front of Tristan. I can't wait for him to hold that over my head.

Construction workers busy themselves in the Saturday afternoon heat. Thankfully, there's a refreshing breeze that makes its way through the open space. As much as I hate to admit it, Tristan's idea of shifting the entrance is the right call. It'll be magical to step foot off the shuttles and follow the pristine tiles to the incredible view of sparkling water.

A petite woman scurries through the space, but her feet come to an abrupt halt as soon as she sees me. "Miss Reed, it's a pleasure to meet you." She extends her hand in a polite greeting. "I'm Destiny, the general manager. If you need anything at all, please do not hesitate to ask."

Taking her hand in mine, I smile. "Hi, Destiny, please call me Kennedy."

"Or Firecracker," Tristan's voice interrupts us, and I roll my eyes.

Shaking my head, I ignore him. "Please don't call me that," I whisper, making sure my eyes relay how serious I am about not being called that. I want to punch him in the face every time he calls me that, because I can't stand it. There's nothing worse than someone giving you a nickname based on your hair color. It'd be like me calling him *Brownie* because he has dark hair.

How idiotic.

She smiles, her expression uncertain as to what she's supposed to do now.

Great job, Prince Nelson, you've gone and made her uncomfortable.

"Thank you, Destiny. If it's not too much trouble, would you mind pointing me in the direction of my room? I'm feeling a little beat from the day of travel."

"Of course." Destiny gives me a friendly smile as she nods, and her gaze bounces from mine to over my shoulder. "I'll show you both to your room."

And with that, we follow her across the lobby as she leads us to another section of the resort.

After a brief walk, which takes us to another building next to the main facility, Destiny escorts us into the waiting elevator car. It's almost as if she called ahead to make sure it was vacant and waiting for us.

Tristan's steps erase the space between us, and I hiss a small breath at the feel of his hand against my lower back. Goosebumps break free as a sensation rushes through me. I can't say I'm a fan of whatever reaction my body is feeling from our connection. Risking a glimpse, I peek over my shoulder in hopes he didn't feel the betrayal of my body, but I'm met with his annoying smirk.

Damn him.

With a special card, Destiny holds it against a sensor before she presses the button to the fourth floor, which happens to be the top floor. My heart is still pounding as the uncertainty creeps in because the top floor is the exclusive penthouse.

Maybe she's showing Tristan his room first before leading me to mine.

The ride is quick, and with a loud ding, the doors slide open, welcoming us directly into the suite.

"Welcome to the Presidential suite, Mr. Nelson and Miss Reed." Destiny gestures to the grand room in front of us.

Wait. No, this can't be right.

There's no way I'm sharing a room with Tristian. Not when I'm already going to be forced to spend the next month working in even closer proximity than before.

The breathtaking room distracts me from my thoughts for a moment. It's been updated to include the same modern designs as we are implementing around the resort.

Light gray luxury vinyl plank flooring runs throughout the entire space, inviting you to enter and enjoy the impeccable panoramic views of the property. Floor-to-ceiling windows take up the entire wall, which invite you outside to what appears to be an oversized balcony with couches and a fire pit.

A cream U-shaped sectional welcomes you to relax while getting lost in the oversized cushions as you watch a movie on the large flat screen, which is hung opposite. Sitting between the openings of the couch is a large square coffee table with a modern console table underneath the television.

Behind the couch is an expansive dining room, with a large rectangular glass table that seats eight with off-white leather chairs placed around the table. An oversized and unique shell chandelier hangs above. Behind the table and directly across from where we're standing is an oversized round mirror that bounces the natural light around the space. My reflection catching my eye, I realize the humidity has not done my red hair any favors, turning the beachy waves into frizzy curls, but it's not my hair that makes me pause. It's the six-three man behind me. While I'm busy taking everything in, Tristan is glued right inside the door. His arms are draped across his fit frame, his eyes on me. For some unknown reason, I don't hate the idea of him watching me. Clearly, the heat has gone straight to my head.

Opposite the dining room is a large galley-sized kitchen, where white cabinets line both sides of the room, providing ample storage. White and grey veined marble countertops are home to state-of-the-art appliances. The kitchen is luxurious and encourages people to take advantage of the private chef the resort offers those staying in the presidential suite.

"This room is breathtaking. I cannot believe how beautiful it turned out." Bewilderment lines my tone as I spin around and find Destiny and Tristan standing together.

I've never been in such an opulent space, and it catches me completely off guard. A blush spreads across my cheeks as I realize how childish I've been drooling over the interiors.

"I'm sorry about that." Clearing my throat, I step toward the door, mentally saying goodbye to the room I'll never get to stay in. "Destiny, if you wouldn't mind showing me to my room, I imagine Tristan would love to unpack."

"Miss Reed, I'm sorry if there was any confusion, but you and Tristan will be staying together." Destiny's eyes widen with alarm. "When the emails were sent, we specified we were working diligently to get the presidential space together as we wait for the other furniture for the other rooms to arrive."

Don't panic. Don't panic. Don't panic.

"Oh, right, of course." I nod, as if it was me who misunderstood an email I never received. An email Tristan never sent me. Flicking my gaze over to him, he meets my stare with a shrug.

A shrug?!

The asshole knew all along that we would be staying together.

Oh my gosh, what if there's only one bed?

"Please tell me we won't have to share a room!" I plead with the poor woman who has been nothing but helpful.

Tristan scoffs. "Heaven forbid, you have to share your space."

Squinting my eyes, I level him with a glare.

"Of course not, Miss Reed—"

"Kennedy," I interrupt.

"Right, Kennedy." Her smile is tighter and not as warm as it was before. I imagine she's starting to feel awkward, ready to be separated from the animosity constantly swirling between me and *him*. She points past the kitchen to a small hallway, where a smaller version of the living room console table sits. A decorative piece sits below another round mirror. "Your room is on this level to the right, and directly across from your room is the primary suite with unobstructed views of the ocean."

Okay, this is going to be fine, Kennedy. It's not like this is a vacation and we'll be lounging around in the common space. When I'm not working, I can hang out in my bedroom. And during working hours, I'll be busy anyway. It'll be like we aren't in the same space at all.

"If there isn't anything else you two need," she pauses, glancing down at her watch, "I'm going to call it a day and head home. Tomorrow is typically my day off along with the construction crew, but if you need anything at all, you both should have my contact number. I only live a few miles away."

"Thank you, Destiny. Please enjoy your day off."

"Thank you for all of your help," I say.

She nods. "My pleasure. There will be members of the hospitality team floating around. Please don't be afraid to ask for anything. Most of the restaurants will have kitchen staff practicing new recipes. I've also passed along their schedules in your email. While the resort is still closed to the public, there are still a lot of people milling around."

And with that, Destiny closes the door on the elevator car, leaving Tristan and I alone. Suddenly, the oversized presidential suite feels like the size of a bargain motel room.

"Does it feel surreal?"

His question causes my head to whip in his direction from where I was staring out the window. I still cannot believe the ocean is right in front of me. For years, growing up, I was jealous of all the kids who got to go on lavish vacations to the beach while I was stuck in our small town helping my grandparents' farm and burying my nose in book after book, studying as often as I could. "Does what feel surreal?"

"Seeing your design come to life. You did this." His voice sounds almost, dare I say, *proud*. Maybe a little envious. Ha, that'll be the day when Tristan is envious of *me*.

It doesn't stop the grin from breaking free as my chest warms. "I feel like I'm dreaming."

"Ouch!" I scream, rubbing the skin on the back of my arm. "Did you just pinch me?"

He chuckles. "You said you felt like you were dreaming, so I thought I'd show you that you aren't."

Groaning, I shake my head as I turn and walk toward my bedroom. What an asshole. This might be the longest month of my life, but I'm determined to make this work. These are my designs and I'm proud of the hard work I've accomplished. If everything goes well, this might be my chance to be featured in a magazine showcasing the luxurious remodel of a long-forgotten resort.

Rounding the corner to enter the hallway, my feet halt as my eyes widen. Oh my gosh. If I thought the main space was gorgeous, it has nothing on this bedroom, which is the guest room in this space.

My eyes immediately go past the silver metal framed four-poster bed to the glass windows with gray shutters. The far two walls are completely covered in floor-to-ceiling windows, which slide open to the same balcony off the main space. Palm trees float in the breeze while the turquoise waters below call to me. I can see myself sorting through emails on the lounge chairs and daybeds situated outside to provide endless views of paradise.

Soft white linens tempt me to collapse on the king-sized bed. And as heavenly as that sounds, I'm desperate for a shower. Reaching for my suitcase placed on the cream upholstered bench at the foot of the bed, I mentally thank the staff for bringing it to my room for me. Unzipping the case, I pull out everything I need for a shower, including skincare and a swimsuit. I'm in need of some vitamin D.

But as I rifle through my packing cubes, I can't find any of the swimsuits I packed.

I pull out my phone and find Lana's name.

Me: Lana Elizabeth where are my swim-suits?!

Continuing my perusal, I unpack some of the cubes into the dresser drawers while I wait for my friend to message me back. The little devil switched all my swimsuits with teeny-tiny bikinis.

When I step into the bathroom, my jaw hits the pristine marble floors. A mirror takes over the entire first wall that greets you, with two matching his and hers sinks. Windows with unobscured views take up the other two exterior walls. A large soaking tub sits below one wall of windows, while a glass shower rests opposite the tub. Between the bathtub and shower is another door that leads to the outdoor shower.

This is what bathroom dreams are made of.

Stripping out of my travel clothes, my phone chimes.

Lana: I have no idea what you're talking about.

Me: Liar.

Lana: Fine…you can blame your office besties.

Rolling my eyes, I put down my phone. I'm not mad. Am I surprised? Absolutely. But I'm not going to lie...I'm going to look delicious in that red bikini.

And a part of me really wants to watch Tristan squirm.

Chapter Twelve

Tristan

We've been in our room for thirty minutes and I already have no idea how I'm going to spend the next month with Kennedy. Was it mean of me not to tell her we would be sharing a suite? Probably. But what were we supposed to do? The furniture hasn't arrived yet for the other rooms. Since the presidential suite features unique pieces of furniture, it was ready first. There was no way of avoiding this situation, so why rock the boat before we even arrive?

Besides, seeing her flustered is my favorite part of the day. Her cheeks flame to a deep red that almost matches her hair, and her hands clench at her waist, as if she's debating on punching something. But she never overreacts. Nope, Kennedy always forces her reactions down and puts in place this polished version of herself.

One of these days, I'm going to get her true reaction, and it's going to be a day I celebrate. I know there's a firecracker waiting to detonate and the real Kennedy Reed will make her appearance.

I admire the design much like the main space as I stand inside the primary bedroom. A four-poster bed sits in the middle, with a clear view of the Caribbean in front of us. The neutral bedding looks soft and inviting, and I'm fighting the urge to take a nap. The stress of the last forty-eight hours is catching up with me. And there's nothing we can really do about it until Monday when offices open.

Knowing there's a perfectly good hot tub, I unzip my luggage and dig through the mess of clothes I hastily packed until I find teal swim trunks. After shucking off my dress pants, I slide into the mid-thigh shorts and let out a sigh of relief. Wearing slacks and dress shirts is a hazard to the job, but there's nothing I love more than a pair of athletic shorts and a fitted tee. Only now, I'm skipping the shirt and heading straight for the hot tub. My muscles could use the heat to relax, even though it feels like the devil's armpit.

I notice missed calls from my dad and my brother as I place my phone on the nightstand, but decide they both can wait until later. I've been in business mode for hours, answering their emails on the flight and giving updates as they come in, which have been few and far between. For the next hour, I need some time for myself. Sliding the glass door open, I'm met with the salty breeze, and I inhale deeply. Smells like serenity.

As I pad over to the hot tub, I catch movement out of the corner of my eye and freeze. Lounging in a chaise is Kennedy *fucking* Reed. My gaze locks on where she's sprawled out in the chair, one leg propped up while the other stretches in front of her, her flawless sun-kissed skin glowing in the late afternoon sun. My eyes trail up her oiled legs to the barely-there red string bikini that accentuates her slightly curvy hips, showcasing her toned stomach and her ample breasts that practically pour out of the nylon swimsuit top, if you can even call it that. The vibrant color contrasts beautifully with her copper red hair messily piled high on the top of her head.

The scene is straight out of an ad for the resort, and for a moment, I'm wondering if the heat and exhaustion have me hallucinating her presence. The way she lies there, exuding confidence that's as intoxicating as it is irresistible, while she's completely at ease and owning the space around her.

Frozen in time, I can't peel my eyes off her. My tongue is practically hanging out of my dry mouth.

"Take a picture and it'll last longer." She interrupts my blatant ogling, her sunglasses tilted down the bridge of her nose to stare at me.

"Can I?"

"Jesus, Tristan," she purrs, or at least that's how I imagine she says it, as she slides her glasses back to their rightful place. "Wait!"

My eyes pop up to where she's removing her glasses again as she leans forward, which gives me an even clearer view of her boobs. I'm praying she doesn't have a wardrobe malfunction, because I'm having a hard time fighting an erection as it is. And there's no way I'll be able to hide it in these tiny swim trunks.

"Did you reconsider your offer of letting me take a picture?"

Her eyes roll and, suddenly, I'm imagining myself standing over her, having her eyes roll for a whole other reason.

"Is that a thigh tattoo?"

Glancing down at my exposed leg, I look at the black ink as if I'm just remembering I have a tattoo. I find her gaze locked onto my leg as I smirk up at her, and if she keeps staring down there, something else is going to make an appearance. My brain goes to her on her knees, tracing the intricate lines inked into my skin.

"Does that surprise you?"

She flops back in her chair. "Yeah, it does. I never would've imagined that Prince Nelson has ink."

"Prince Nelson?" I've heard her call me by my full name, by Golden Boy—which I hate, and now Prince Nelson. Based on the number of nicknames she has for me, you'd think she's secretly in love with me, not busy hating me.

"Don't flatter yourself."

"Nah, Firecracker, I'll leave that to you."

I send her a wink as I walk past. Climbing up the single stair, I enter the hot tub—or what I thought was a hot tub. Turns out, it's just a private plunge pool, and I can't say I'm disappointed. Even though I was looking forward to relaxing against the hot tub jets, the water inside the pool felt incredible.

Dropping down into the water, I tip my head back to the cloudless sky and release a moan. "This feels incredible."

"Mind if I join?" she asks, startling me, and when I glance over, I find her standing on the step, waiting for me to answer. Biting my lip, I try to think of anything else besides Kennedy in that scrap of fabric.

Words won't form on my tongue. Instead, I gesture for her to join me and reach out my hand for her to hold. She slides her delicate hand into mine, and I swear I could combust from the connection. Every time this woman touches me, a shot of electricity slices through my body. How can she not feel this?

Once inside the pool, she moves to the opposite corner, where a moan escapes her lips as she sinks her shoulders lower into the water. "I don't know why I thought this was a hot tub."

A laugh escapes. "I thought the same thing. Didn't you design this, though?"

"Yeah, I did." A chuckle leaves her lips, and I decide that I want to hear it more often. "That's why I was so surprised. Clearly, I forgot about that suggestion."

Stretching my arms out to the sides, I rest them against the side of the pool and soak in the silence. It's weird being one of the only people on this property. Of course, workers and security guards are milling around the property, but there aren't any guests.

No one is splashing in the pool, no chatter down below us where lounge chairs line the property and, best of all, no street noise from cabs honking and endless sirens.

It's peaceful, with only the rustling of palms and birds chirping.

Hell, I could get used to this. Maybe I can just tell my dad running Nelson's Signature isn't for me and that I'd like to run the operations here on the island. He'd laugh in my face and tell me to grow up. That's always been his go-to. Whenever I wanted to feel like a normal kid and play sports or go out with my friends, he'd tell me I needed to grow up and focus on the bigger picture. It's Dennis Nelson's life and I'm stuck living in it.

A stream of water hits my face, and my eyes snap to the opposite corner, where a burst of laughter comes from. A wide grin stretches across Kennedy's face as I wipe the droplets from my eyes.

"Did you just splash me?"

With a cocky head nod, she shrugs. "Yeah, I did. What are you going to do about it?"

I shake my head and flash her a mischievous smirk. In seconds, I've pushed through the water and wrapped my arms around the curve of her hips. Without hesitation, her arms circle my neck as she holds on with all her might.

"Tristan Lawrence Nelson, don't you dare dunk me!" she squeals, her slick body rubbing against mine as she wraps her legs around my waist. The death grip she has on me has me laughing.

"Oh, I see how it is. It's okay for you to splash me in the face, but I can't return the favor?"

She pulls away until we find ourselves nearly brushing our noses. My eyes get lost in her emerald greens, the joking pushed aside as we realize how close we are to each other.

Sleep deprivation plus humidity isn't a good mix.

Clearing my throat, I snap us out of the trance. My hands snap away from her hips at the same time Kennedy releases her legs from around my waist. Pushing off my shoulders, she finds her spot in the corner again.

Heat blooms across her freckled face as I move back to my spot, needing a moment to tuck the erection, she no doubt felt, into the waistband of my shorts. Settling back on my side of the pool, my gaze can't help but land on her. She's staring off to the side, and I watch her watch the ships pass by.

The ringing of my phone interrupts our moment. Letting out a sigh, I shake my head. I thought I had put the stupid thing on silent but, apparently, I forgot.

"Do you need to get that?"

"No," I snap without meaning to. "Sorry—"

"It's fine." She stands from her spot and glides through the water toward the edge of the pool. "It's probably best we stop whatever that was between us and go back to being colleagues."

"Colleagues." I scoff, the words tasting bitter on my tongue. "After all these years, that's what we are to you?"

With her out of the pool, I can only see from her stomach up as her hands land on her hips. "Yes, Tristan. Colleagues, rivals, the competition. That's what we are. Nothing more, nothing less. In fact, for the next month, we are merely two people sharing the same space while working together to solve whatever problems we need to in order to get this resort up and running. Then we can both go back to New York, and I can try to find someplace else to work."

"Woah!" I stand, moving to the edge so that we're face to face. "What the hell do you mean 'find someplace else to work'?"

"Nothing," she replies, shaking her head. My phone ringing *again* interrupts our conversation. "You should probably get that."

And with that, she turns her back to me. Swim bottoms hug her curves, accentuating her toned ass. The firm contour is a testament to her cycling classes and has me unable to take my eyes off her.

While watching her walk away, I spot a tiny turtle tattoo below the string of her bikini, right on her ass cheek.

Fuck my life.

CHAPTER THIRTEEN

KENNEDY

"THANK YOU ALL FOR being here," I greet our IT Director. "Dave, we understand there seems to be an issue with the integration of high-speed internet and pairing it with the smart technology systems. As you know, with the resort closed, we're losing money every day that we're not up and running."

"That's right. We are losing quite a hefty amount every day, and since the smart technology integration is a major design element, we need things up and running now. What seems to be the exact issue?" Tristan interrupts from where we're gathered around a large table in one of the many conference rooms.

Monday morning is here after a day and a half of getting used to the resort. We should've called people in on Sunday to get these meetings over with, but Tristan felt we needed to acclimate to the location before our meetings. I think he wanted to lounge around in the sun since New York has been unseasonably cold for the last couple of weeks. *Slacker.*

Our lead IT man on the island, Dave, shuffles through paperwork. While he takes his time finding his notes, I bring a steaming mug of Jamaican Blue Mountain coffee to my lips. The smooth, sweet, rich flavor slides down my throat without leaving the bitterness most coffees have. It's an exceptional blend, and I'm already trying to figure out how I can ship this stuff to New York.

Dave slides Tristan and me a copy of a chart. "We've been monitoring the network traffic." He pauses, pointing out what he's noticed. "It appears certain parts of the resort are experiencing high latency. We need time to assess these dead zones and figure out why the access points aren't delivering consistent speeds. And then figure out what is disrupting the internet and the smart docking systems."

"Time is not on our side. And I don't understand why these problems weren't addressed earlier. Were there always internet issues at this resort?" Tristan's question is laced with frustration as he threads his hands through his dark locks.

With a deep inhale, I rack my brain with a solution. Tristan is clearly stressed out. His phone hasn't stopped ringing since we arrived on the island. "Is it an infrastructure issue? Cabling?"

"Jesus, we don't have time to run new cable throughout the entire property," Tristan tells me, leaning back in his chair and tossing his pen on the table.

"Don't." I shake my head. "I'm just throwing out ideas and trying to find a solution."

"Yeah, well, running cable is our absolute last option. Walls will need to be opened up and we don't have time for that bullshit."

Dave pulls out his phone and begins typing away. "I'll have my team start running more diagnostics and a comprehensive site survey right away, but it might take some time."

"That's the one thing we don't have. We need a temporary solution within the day, at the bare minimum. The longer we're closed, the more money we lose. Most of the resort is going to be ready for reopening by January."

"Dave, can you set up temporary hot spots at all the problem points?"

He scrunches his face, and it's an expression I don't care for. "It's not ideal, but I'll see what we can do."

"Great." My voice rises. I don't care if it's an ideal situation. We need a temporary solution before Tristan blows a gasket. "Let's prioritize the main areas, including the lobby for the kiosk check-ins, restaurants, and some of the larger suites that will require the butler services."

"Dave, we need this done today," Tristan adds.

"I'll have them get started right away. In the meantime, I'll keep working with the service provider to figure out if there are any external issues affecting the resort."

Gathering my paperwork, I glance at the time on my phone. I have another fire to put out in an hour. Before I have a chance to rise from my seat, Tristan speaks again. "Can you make sure that all smart systems have priority on the network? I know guests will want to keep their social media updated but, quite frankly, I don't give a damn about that. We need to make sure that the use of cellular data isn't disrupting the technology we've put in place to operate the resort."

"Of course. I'll set up system rules to prioritize traffic to those systems. The team configures immediately." Dave resumes typing on his phone, presumably keeping his team updated on their required tasks.

"Thanks, Dave." Tristan's gaze lands on mine, and his eyes hold me captive. My mind flashes to us in the pool Saturday night. His arms wrapped around my body and his erection—which was quite thick, might I add—poked my stomach. "Kennedy?"

Shaking my head once more, I snap my attention back to him and find myself wondering what it would feel like to have him poking something else. I'm met with that know-it-all smirk that tells me he knows exactly what I was thinking. "I'm sorry, the caffeine hasn't kicked in yet."

Liar.

"I was saying, I need you to email the staff, informing them that some might be experiencing limited cellular service as we work to prioritize the smart technology."

"I'll do that on my way to my next meeting," I say, jotting down the information in my physical planner quickly before rising from the chair. "Gentlemen, if that's all, I need to head into Castries."

And I need to get the hell out of Tristan's presence. He's throwing me off my game, and I cannot have that.

Not right now.

Not when I'm being entrusted to handle the chaos in St. Lucia.

Standing from my desk, I adjust the white ribbed tank top I tucked into a flowy, floral print midi skirt. The two modest slits on the slides allow the ocean breeze to flow through. My hair is piled high in a thick, messy bun, and I've curled a few face-framing tendrils. Between the high heat and humidity, my hair will be seeing lots of styles to keep the thick locks off the back of my neck.

I move through the lobby, making my way to the front desk, where a coffeepot sits. Replacing my ceramic mug with a disposable cup, I fill the dark roast to the brim. Days spent in meetings are the worst, especially Mondays, when there seems to be nothing but fires to put out. I knew this going into it, but I'm still exhausted. I'm supposed to be here for work, but it's a tropical island. Mondays in paradise should never be this chaotic.

Taking a sip, I savor the rich flavor as I watch teams of people scurry through the resort. Construction crews are busy with the final stages of the new grand entryway. Walls are being constructed as drywall seams are being mudded. The new entrance being framed, the staff huddled together training, smells from the restaurants wafting inside, and noises from machinery fill the air. A lot is happening, but in no time, we'll have a remarkable resort up and running.

"Ready to schmooze the head of planning?" Tristan startles me as he sidles up to my side. Both of our backs are leaning against the counter as we take in the scenes before us.

I refuse to turn toward him and allow my periphery to take in the man next to me. He's dressed in a tan linen suit jacket with a baby blue dress shirt tucked into navy linen dress pants, which are tapered at his ankles. I notice he's wearing brown woven penny loafers. He looks damn good, and I hate myself for noticing.

"Of course I'm ready. That's why they're sending me and not you. They know I won't be the one to screw it up since I can keep my frustration in check."

Another deep scoff sounds from him. "Whatever you say, *Firecracker*." I hate the way he emphasizes my nickname, as if I'm a device ready to explode when my fuse is lit.

Before I have a chance to come back with something witty, Jayden, our driver, walks through the construction. "Are you ready, Miss Reed?"

"Sure am." Reaching beside me, I gather my handbag, which has all the paperwork I need for the meeting, along with my takeaway coffee.

Surprised Tristan didn't have anything to say, I'm almost to the door when that surprise vanishes. "See you back in our room, Firecracker."

And this time, I let him have the final word.

• • • • • • • • • • •

Stripping out of the lightweight cardigan I put on over my tank top, I'm fuming as I storm across the grounds. Not only did I waste an entire day at the administrative building, but the guy I needed to speak with refused to see me. I mean, he flat-out *refused* to have his assistant send me back to his office.

I'm not sure what game he's playing, but consider me checked in. He's not going to get rid of me that easily.

Not only did I sit in a chair the entire afternoon, but the office space was excruciatingly hot. The air from the tiny air-conditioning unit did little to cool the space. Humidity clung to my skin like a blanket, and now the loose tendrils I curled are a frizzed-out mess and so are all the small hairs around the crown of my head. I look like Simba when he returns to Pride Rock. Only, instead of being a total badass and demanding he take his seat on the proverbial throne, I'm riding the elevator to hell, where my nemesis awaits. It won't be long until I have to face Tristian as he goads that he could have done it better. Yeah *freaking* right.

I'm hot. I'm hangry. And I'm exhausted.

I push the button on the elevator wall, tapping my foot as I wait for the car to take me four floors up. My phone died half an hour ago, so I can only imagine the emails I've missed. For the first time in forever, I don't care. Not right now. My first priority is stripping out of these sweat-soaked clothes, cooling off, and finding food.

Hell, I might even eat in the pool. *Not your worst idea today, Ken.*

The metal doors slide open, and I'm met with cool air.

At least Tristan has the air blasting through the large space. My sneakers squeak against the shiny marble floors as I make my way to my bedroom, noting that Tristan isn't in the common areas, and I don't see him outside through the windows.

As soon as I step foot inside my room, I'm digging for my charger cord, which fell behind the dresser. Note to self: have the rooms install charger clips to keep cords from falling behind dressers. Once I see my phone is plugged in, I'm stripping out of my dress clothes and not bothering to slip on a swimsuit. I'm alone in our room, after all, and nothing sounds better than sliding into that plunge pool to cool off. Besides, my strapless bra and thong are practically the same coverage as that red swimsuit.

Climbing the step, I step over the lip, but instead of sliding into the water, I lean against the ledge, allowing myself a moment to admire the view. The hot rays pour down on my exposed backside, but the cool water helps ward off some of the heat. I still can't get over the fact that the ocean is right there.

From my vantage point of the top floor, the Caribbean showcases her true allure: a blue mosaic of deep indigo toward the horizon to an almost clear turquoise once the water meets the glimmering, white sand. The gentle breeze causes palms to rustle while melodic singing from local birds fills the air in a beautiful rhythm. Nature's white noise is a beautiful gift.

"Fuuuck." The word is drawn out and deeply spoken, causing me to yelp in surprise.

I snap my head in the direction of the voice and find a half-naked Tristan standing in the doorway. His bronzed skin is on full display, showing off his physique and that damn thigh tattoo as he holds two bottles of local Piton beers with limes sticking out of the top.

His blatant perusal of my body has me wanting to squirm, but I refuse to cower. Instead, I let the heat of his gaze warm me from the inside out, wishing it was more than his eyes roaming. His hands touching, feeling, caressing my sun-kissed skin as mine do the same over his cut valley of muscles sounds much better.

What the hell is wrong with me right now?

My nipples pebble at the thought as I watch his hazel eyes turn a rich chocolate shade, much like my coffee from this morning. The large bulge in his pants starts to grow in his short swim trunks. As he reaches down with his free hand to adjust his growing erection, my eyes snap to his thigh tattoo.

"I didn't know you were home," I tell him breathily, then quickly clear my throat.

"Sorry, I was in the bedroom changing when I heard you come in. I thought you could use a beer?" He gestures to the two bottles he's holding.

Letting out a soft moan, my head falls back against the ledge, and my hand reaches forward in a 'gimme' motion. "I could definitely use a drink...or ten."

Tristan comes closer and hands me the condensation-covered bottle. With my pointer finger, I press the lime against the inside of the bottle and watch as the pulp squishes as juice runs into the golden liquid. With a long pull, the cool, fruity hoppiness slides down my throat.

"So good," I moan.

The sound of his throat clearing has my eyes snapping open. "Can you please stop moaning?"

"What's the matter, Golden Boy? Can't handle the noise?"

"As a matter of fact, I can't. And I'm wondering what else I could put in that mouth of yours to get you to moan."

My jaw drops open. It's wide enough that one of those tropical birds I was enjoying listening to could fly in. "Jesus."

"Yeah," he replies before taking a long pull of his beer. "And it's not helping when you're practically naked across from me."

Eyes widening, I remember that I'm dressed in very little clothes. "Let me go throw something on."

His hand immediately goes up to stop me. "Please don't get out of the pool. Just stay there, in your corner, underneath the water, so that I can forget what your tiny turtle tattoo looks like."

"Ahh. You spotted Donatello."

"You named your tattoo after one of the Teenage Mutant Ninja Turtles?"

"Don't sound so surprised." Wrapping my lips around the bottle, I use my tongue to lick out some of the lime pulp that stuck to the inside. The action causes another groan to escape my nemesis, and I chuckle. It was an innocent move, but apparently not to him. "You know, you're cute when you're flustered."

The hand holding his beer points to his chest as he mocks a gasp. "Did the oh-so-serious Kennedy Reed just call me cute?"

I groan. "The heat has gone to my head. I must have sweat out all my brain cells in that stupid administration building."

"Uh huh, sure, that's what it is." He winks before stretching his arms against the ledge and taps his finger against the glass. "Speaking of the administration building, how did the meeting go? I figured you'd have sent out an update by now."

Shaking my head, I feel moisture gathering in my eyes, and I will myself not to cry in front of him. I'm not typically a crier, but the stress, heat exhaustion, and lack of food have me wanting to break down right here on the balcony overlooking paradise.

"It was an absolute flop." His eyebrow quirks, as if telling me to continue. "First of all, the place is extremely hot. Their air conditioning couldn't keep up with the heat. I sat in the waiting room all afternoon because he refused to meet with me, even though we had a time scheduled and I arrived twenty minutes early. Then, about thirty minutes before they closed, my phone died. It was a complete waste of time."

"Do you need me to go back tomorrow for you?"

"No!" I practically shout. "I'm sorry, I just mean no, I can handle it. I'll go back every single day until he allows me to speak to him. Jayden had a few ideas as to how to even get him to open the door for me. So I'm going to try that tomorrow."

"All things legal, right?"

Rolling my eyes, I give him a deadpan look. "Of course, all things legal. I know this is your family's business and that this project is important, but I have no desire to whore myself out for the company, if that was what you were implying."

He choked on the sip of beer he was in the process of drinking. "Jesus, Kennedy. That's not what I meant at all. I just don't want to have to bail your ass out of jail by bribing a government official, is all I mean."

Heat creeps across my skin. "Oh."

He laughs, robust and so full of warmth. It's a sound I'm starting to crave, especially on hard days. Although I would never tell him that. He needs to know he strictly stands in the competitive pool. Speaking of warmth, my body is feeling cooled down, and as much as I'm not hating this interaction, I'm starving.

"Close your eyes, Golden Boy."

Instead of shutting them, they widen at my tone, which came out husky. "Shit, Firecracker, now I'm nervous."

"Ha. ha. I just meant I'm about to get out of this pool so close your eyes. I wouldn't want to cause any more"—I gesture to his crotch—"*reactions*."

"Funny girl," he muses. "Why are you in such a hurry to get out?"

"Not that I don't find your presence riveting, but I'm starving. I only planned on being in here long enough to cool off."

"Let's order something. We can have it sent up and put a movie on."

I pause, nibbling on my lower lip as I think it over.

"C'mon. You know you want to find out how comfortable that giant sectional is."

He's right. That oversized couch has been calling my name since we got here. "Fine."

The beaming smile that breaks free across his chiseled face is the first time since college I've seen him this excited.

And it's in this moment, as I'm entranced by his blinding smile, that I feel a tiny crack in my armored walls.

CHAPTER FOURTEEN

TRISTAN

I COUNTED EVERY SINGLE slat in the shuttered balcony doors last night. Four hundred and eighty, to be exact. But sleep never came for me. No matter how hard I tried to roll over and fall asleep, the image of Kennedy in her goddamn bra and thong flashed through my mind.

She's tantalizing.

She's infuriating.

She's *fucking* flawless.

Bronzed, glowing skin and those luscious curves leaned over the edge of the pool as she stared down below us. When I stepped onto the balcony, my tongue practically fell out of my mouth. My first thought was picking up where we left off the other night, with her body pressed up against mine. It's why I woke up hard as a rock at two in the morning. My mind kept flashing to all the scenarios I could have had her in that damn pool.

Last night felt so natural. The two of us enjoyed dinner on the couch and watched a movie. It reminded me of the night that she nearly passed out during our cycle class. How I took her home, we had dinner together, and she played a rom-com from the early 2000s. I swear she chose that movie just to torture me. The joke was on her, though. I didn't mind the *Bring It On* movies. My sister went through a cheerleading phase and would watch the entire franchise on repeat.

A restless night turned into an even more exhausting day as I was pulled into meeting after meeting. Even though my top priority is this resort remodel, I still have to oversee the projects other architects are completing. Not to mention, a weekly operations meeting, which ends up dragging.

The clock finally struck five, calling the end of my workday. If I were in the city, I'd still be working until most people's bedtimes, but I refused tonight. I hadn't seen Kennedy since she left early this morning. She was wearing a fiery red dress that flowed with every step she took. It was tantalizing to watch her move across the resort. No matter where she went, heads turned. I can't explain the jealousy that flared deep inside as the crew gazed at her, with their tongues practically hanging out and drool falling from their lips. And I know if I would've looked in a mirror, my face would've matched theirs.

Making my way across the sidewalk, I'm hit in the face with the salty ocean breeze. As I watch the turquoise water hit the white sand, I realize I still haven't had a chance to dip my toes in the ocean. I should have Sunday. I should have ignored the emails and not taken any calls from my father, but I did, as is expected of me. If I'd been in the city, I would have been attending our weekly family meal, and instead of phone calls, I'd be hearing the lectures from my father in person.

My phone ringing in my pocket pulls my attention from the sea. Again.

Speak of the devil.

"Hello, Dad."

"You've been a hard man to track down," he says by way of greeting.

Sighing, I run my hand through my hair. "I've been a little busy."

"Glad to hear you aren't just enjoying yourself."

"No, sir." Pausing, I sit down at one of the many tables sprinkled around the resort. The oversized umbrella is open, allowing a small reprieve from the bright sun.

"I heard through your brother that there are delays on the over-the-water villas. I want to know why this information didn't come from you, and why the hell this wasn't handled sooner?"

Fucking Xander.

"We filed everything when we should have. Unfortunately, there's an issue on their end. It's all bureaucratic bullshit. They don't want to approve the plans."

"You should have anticipated this, Tristan. What are you doing to get this expedited? We cannot have any more delays."

"Kennedy's on it. She's been there for the past two days working with them."

"See to it she gets it done, or we'll find someone else who can handle the job. The villas are going to be a major selling point to get guests to enjoy a secluded vacation with an exclusive atmosphere."

"I understand the urgency, Dad," I grit through my teeth. "We are on top of it and working to get the permits and plans approved."

"You better, Tristan. Don't make me regret giving you this position."

Scanning the flowerbeds lined with botanical plants, I'm about to reply but realize he's already hung up. With a frustrated sigh, I stand from the table and make my way to the penthouse.

As I wait for the doors to open on the penthouse floor, I undo the top few buttons of my dress shirt to cool down. There's nothing I need more than a drink, which is exactly what I do as soon as the car arrives. In the corner of the living room is a black bar cart lined with crystal glasses and expensive liquors. Pulling the cork on the bourbon, I pour the amber liquid into a rock glass before I carry it over to the oversized couch.

Legs spread and shirt halfway open, I rest and bring the bourbon to my lips. The urge to shoot it back is high, but good bourbon should never be shot. I know that much.

Sitting in the quiet space, I stare at the blank TV and run over not just the phone call I had with my dad but everything in my life.

The relationship between my dad and me has always been rocky. Xander was the favorite, since he was the firstborn son. He's been destined to follow in my father's footsteps since birth. Nelson Signature Hotels & Resorts is his whenever my father decides it's time for him to step down from CEO.

Xander has reveled in the firstborn duties for as long as I can remember. Throughout our years in school, he took his grades seriously. Not only was he the top student in his graduating class, but when he wasn't in school, Xander was on the green with my dad, honing his golfing skills. Dad always said that business is made on the course and not in a boardroom. He believed that it was important to harness a strong relationship on the golf course, rather than behind desks in sterile office spaces. Since Xander was next in line, the two of them would take off every Saturday morning to golf eighteen holes.

No matter how many times I asked, I was always left behind. Dad would promise we'd spend time together, but we never did. We never did a lot of things. It affected my relationship with him, but it affected my relationship with Xander even more. When I graduated from NYU, I bought a penthouse overlooking Manhattan and offered Xander one of the spare rooms. When he took it, I thought that would be the olive branch we needed to develop a brotherly relationship. The two of us have, to some degree, but it's not a relationship like most brothers.

Then there's my father's relationship with Victoria. I love my sister. Seriously, I do. We both give each other a lot of shit, but we have the closest bond. But when it comes to my father, Vi can do no wrong. As the baby of the family and the only daughter, she's been wrapped around his finger since she was born. And I know that her relationship with my father hasn't been sunshine and rainbows. He's pushed her to be the best in more ways than one, but at the end of the day, she's still his little girl.

And I'm stuck in the middle. The company will never be mine, and I'm okay with that. Honestly, I am. My dad and, some days, my brother, think I can't handle the responsibility that comes with being a Nelson. But they're wrong. Sure, I made mistakes in high school and even in college. But I'm wired differently than they are.

Making money is great, but not if that's the only thing you're known for. I wanted to experience life outside of New York and outside of the business. I wanted to do the typical backpacking in Europe to gain some true independence and have a taste of freedom. I wanted to live for a few years before I was chained to the company. It was never my dream to work for Nelson Signature, but I knew I never had a choice in the matter.

Dad had kids to run his company. To carry on the Nelson legacy, whatever that means.

Bringing the glass to my lips, I suck in a heavy sip and let the oakiness and vanilla burn my throat. I rest my neck on the back of the couch and take a deep breath. The elevator doors chime open as I'm exhaling, and in walks Kennedy. Copper frizz lines the outside of her red-tinged face. The humidity isn't helping her thick hair.

She pauses just inside the penthouse and eyes me. I feel her gaze lick heat down my face and over my exposed chest, where I couldn't be bothered to remove my shirt, opting to have it opened in a deep V. The way her eyes widen and darken to a new shade of green as she gives me a once-over. Her skin is balmy from the humidity, dark circles line her under eyes, and her shoulders are slouched. She looks nothing like her typical confident self. Instead, exhaustion and frustration radiate from her. Of course, she still looks beautiful. When doesn't she?

Shaking her head, she marches over to the front of the U-shaped couch, where she tosses her work bag onto a cushion. But she doesn't stop there. No, she marches straight over to where I'm sitting in the corner of the couch until she's standing between my spread legs. I want to reach out and pull her into my lap and kiss her perfect pouty lips. But I don't even move as I stare up at her.

Reaching forward, I think she's going to grab a hold of me, only she bypasses my arm, going straight to the crystal tumbler in my hand. Bringing my glass to her lips, she takes a sip of the amber liquid, and I watch in amusement as her throat bobs from her swallow and she sits down on the cushion next to me. Her feet fly up to the coffee table as she toes off her sandals.

"Fuck this day," she says with a drawn-out huff, and I can't help but chuckle. Kennedy's head whips in my direction, and she quirks a perfectly manicured eyebrow. "My misery brings you joy?"

"Of course not. I was just sitting here in my own misery, thinking the same damn thing."

She lifts the glass to her lips again for another sip. I've never wanted to be a glass more than I do right now.

Silence falls over the room as both of us stare into space as we work through the frustrations of our days.

"Call a truce?" I ask, shocking myself.

A truce? What am I, a child? But maybe this could be the chance to have a reprieve from the tension between us. Hell, we're stuck here in the same room. Neither one of us has our friends here to go have drinks with and bitch to.

Her head lulls in my direction as our eyes lock. "A truce?"

"Yeah. We're going to be stuck together for the foreseeable future, so might as well call a truce and vent to each other."

She shrugs. "My boss is an asshole."

My eyes widen. "What the hell did I do to you today?"

A warm smile curves at the ends of her lips. "I like how you immediately assume it's you. But no, I mean your lovely father."

"What'd he do?" I ask with more of a bite than intended, sitting up taller. I swear he better not have gotten off the phone with me and called her directly.

"He called me as I was arriving back at the resort. He informed me that I need to get the permits approved by tomorrow or I can find myself a new job."

What the fuck?

"He didn't."

"Oh, he did."

Running a hand through my hair, I push out a breath. "Shit, Ken. He shouldn't have called you. I told him we had everything handled."

"Thanks, but it's fine. I spent all day at the administrative office, only to be informed that the guy I needed to speak to took a personal day. That was after I was there for three hours."

As I open my mouth to respond, feeling panicked, she puts her hand up, shaking her head.

"It's fine. I was able to talk to someone else and explain everything. He told me he would make sure I had a meeting tomorrow. So I'll be back there at nine o'clock."

Thank fuck.

"Well, that's at least something." I stand from my seat and walk over to the bar cart to pour myself another drink. Kennedy can finish mine.

Walking back to the couch, I can't take my eyes off her. Even dripping in exhaustion from her frustrating day, she's still breathtaking.

"It is…" she starts before bringing one of her bare feet onto her lap as I settle back in my seat next to her. "Except now my feet are killing me because chairs were limited, so I had to stand most of the day. The bottoms of these sandals are hard as a rock."

Placing my hand in front of me, I gesture for her foot. "Give it."

"What?"

"You heard me, Ken. Give me your foot."

She reaches next to her for the pile of throw pillows before she arranges them in a way that has her body resting on the makeshift backrest before. Then she's bringing her foot onto my lap at a snail's pace, almost as if she's waiting for me to change my mind.

"I can't believe you're letting me do this."

A defeated shrug is all she gives me.

Adjusting her legs so that they are hanging across mine, I dig my thumbs into the arch of her foot. A soft moan comes from the woman who I can't keep out of my mind, and it's the best reward. I glance over at her and find her mouth parted, eyes hooded as they roll back into her head. And now I'm picturing her pillowy red lips wrapped around my dick as she's on her knees in front of me.

Fuck, looks like I'll be getting myself off again tonight. Only now, I know what her moans sound like...

She clears her throat. "That feels incredible."

I can think of something else that would feel incredible...

"So what's got you so frustrated?" Her breathy voice interrupts my blatant daydream.

"It's nothing."

Kennedy starts to sit up, but I hold her foot hostage. She blows out a frustrated breath as her eyes narrow.

"Uh-uh." She waves her pointer finger in my direction. "Don't do that bullshit. You wanted a truce, so spill, Nelson."

Feisty Kennedy is my favorite.

"Today, it's my dad's lack of faith in me that's got me pissed." I can feel her gaze boring into the side of my face, waiting for me to elaborate. "He's waiting for me to fail."

"Wait, what? Your dad is waiting for you to fail?"

"It's always been like this. I know you think I'm the 'golden boy' who has had everything handed to him, and in some regards, I have. But it's Xander who is the real golden boy."

For the next few minutes, I elaborate on everything that I've had to deal with by being the middle child and second boy. It's an archaic, elitist logic that only the firstborn receives the blessing of the company and everything the family name stands for. I watch as her eyes widen and her breathing increases. Anger seeps from her pores, and it's the first time I've ever seen Kennedy get defensive over me. Usually, she's finding a way to piss me off, and here she is, getting upset at the cards I was dealt.

"I had no idea." Her voice is small, and I hate that my admission is making her feel any sort of way.

"It's not your fault."

She purses her lips and stares out the window. I follow her gaze and watch the palms blow in the slight breeze.

"Do you want to be working for Nelson Signature?"

And with that question, I feel like I've been hit by a freight train. The question is jarring and has me pausing.

I shrug. "I don't know any different. Nelson Signature has always been my final destination. Growing up, the rules were simple: attend a university in New York and take my rightful place at our family's company. There was never any room to dream about anything else. My destiny was forged long before I even knew how to walk. But there was a time, back when I was in junior high, when I had different dreams."

"Tell me about it?"

Bringing my glass to my lips, I finish the amber liquid in one gulp. The welcoming burn is one I need to get through the memories flooding my mind.

"My cousin, Asher, lived in Chicago. His dad and my dad are brothers, and during the summer months, I would pack a bag and head to Chicago for a month or longer."

"Wait," she interrupts. "Your dad has a brother? Why isn't he working at Nelson Signature?"

"He's a hedge fund manager in Chicago. There was some kind of falling out with my uncle and grandfather, so he moved to another city. It sucked since Asher was our only cousin. Him and I were the closest in age and we had the closest bond."

"That's cool you could go and spend your summers there."

"Yeah…" I refuse to let my mind go to a dark place. "Asher and I had crazy dreams we knew we would never be able to do. We would talk about opening a bait and tackle shop on Lake Michigan or moving to Deer County, Wisconsin, to become hiking guides. Whatever got us outdoors and away from the suffocating city life."

Her laugh is like a melody filtering through the space as I quirk an eyebrow at her. "I'm sorry," she says in between laughs. "I just can't picture you baiting a hook."

"Believe it. Those months spent with Asher were filled with days on Lake Michigan, fishing and wakeboarding."

A wistful smile takes over her pretty face. "You were like a whole other person. So you'd leave the bright lights of the city behind to start your own outdoor adventure company?"

"I don't know what I would do now. Those were the dreams of a fourteen-year-old me who couldn't take the pressure any longer. I felt alone in the city, and the only time I didn't was when I was with Asher and his two best friends who shadowed us around everywhere."

"Trist." My name coming out of her mouth slowly, laced with caution and curiosity.

My head turns. "Yeah, Ken?"

Biting on her lower lip, her eyes search mine. "You keep talking about Asher in the past tense. Did…something happen?"

I suck in a deep breath, knowing this question was coming, but I didn't realize how unprepared I was for it. Tipping my head against the back of the couch, I take a second to calm my racing mind that's filled with images from the past. Her soft hand finds mine and she gives a gentle squeeze. It's a reassuring touch letting me know she's here for me. With a deep breath, I lean forward, my hand never leaving her grip.

"He died in a car accident with one of his best friends."

A gasp leaves her lips, and I hate that I've cast a dark cloud over this moment. She says a quiet "I'm so sorry," but I barely hear it as an onslaught of emotions I've kept buried for years hits me like a tidal wave.

For a few minutes, we sit in silence. Her hand is in mine while she rests her head on my shoulder, giving me an unspoken comfort I'm desperate for.

"I think I would've liked to see that side of you." The sincerity in her voice has me pausing. Glancing over, I expect to find pity on her face, but there's only kindness and understanding there as I search her eyes.

"I don't remember that side of me. It all turned into the pressure of getting good academics, fishing adventures turned into boardrooms, and days on the lake turned into being the director of design at my father's firm." Refusing to meet her eyes, I find that long palm branch and watch it float in the wind.

"I'm sorry for giving you so much shit."

"Don't be. Sparing with you has been the highlight of my adult life, Firecracker." I wink.

Her eyes roll, and I laugh, squeezing her calf muscle. I didn't realize I quit rubbing her feet and trailed my hand higher. I watch as her gaze lands on our connection. Kennedy's breath catches as our eyes lock, and something passes across her features. The ringing of my phone breaks our moment, and dread pools in my stomach, hoping that it's not my father calling for round two.

The number isn't one I recognize, and while I answer, Kennedy gets up from her spot and leaves the room.

I can only hope our truce will turn into more.

Chapter Fifteen

Kennedy

Lana: Just checking in! I miss your face. The house is way too quiet without you.

Me: Miss you too! Gah, how are the plant babies?

Lana: Surprisingly, I've kept them alive. How's hottie mc hottie?

Me: As annoying as ever.

Lana: You like him.

Me: Why would you think that?

Lana: You didn't correct his name *wink emoji*

THE ENTIRE DRIVE TO the administration office, all I could think about was last night. Tristan wanted a truce, and while I thought it was silly to ask, I'm glad he did.

Guilt swam in my stomach as he recounted everything he's had to endure in his life. Suddenly, the Golden Boy nickname tasted sour. Never once did I stop to assume that his life wasn't as easy as I made it out to be. I just assumed that he was the typical rich boy who flooded the streets of NYU. I never thought he might not have wanted this lifestyle.

Jayden drives us through the winding roads as I stare out the passenger window. This is now our third drive to Castries together, and I refused to sit in the back seat. He might be chauffeuring me around, but I won't treat him like the help. Besides, we've spent hours in the car getting to know each other. Jayden is nineteen, a huge American football fan, and loves cars. It's why he took the job at the resort, since we have luxury cars on standby to use for guest transportation.

Pulling into the parking lot, Jayden wishes me good luck as I step out of the pearl-white BMW. With a tight-lipped smile, I thank him before closing the door behind me. Poor guy has had to spend the last few days keeping himself busy while I wait. Fingers crossed today is the day I get my meeting.

The receptionist's eyes snap to mine as I enter, and I watch the wall go over her eyes. Clearly, she's as annoyed at seeing me as I am being here for the third time.

"Martin is ready for you." Her voice startles me.

"Good morning!" I let my cheeriness make up for her lack of welcome. She harrumphs in return.

Heat clings to my skin as I walk across the lobby and find my way into Martin's office. I rap my knuckles against the closed door, announcing my entrance, before stepping inside the quaint office. Sitting behind a desk is Martin, the man I've been desperately trying to talk to all week. His wire-framed glasses sit perched on his nose as he watches me enter his space.

"Ah, good morning, Miss…" he trails off, shuffling through papers on his desk.

"Miss Reed, but please call me Kennedy."

"Right, of course. Kennedy Reed from Nelson's Signature Hotels and Resorts," Martin replies, his voice dripping with false niceties.

As I take a seat across from him, he squirms in his chair. "You've been a hard man to track down."

"Work never ends," he pauses with a sigh. "I understand Nelson's Signatures is interested in *expanding* the resort."

"Yes, sir." Removing the file folder from my purse, I flip open the manila cover and hand him over the documents. "We've put together a detailed proposal outlining all of your concerns, as well as providing the blueprints for your inspection."

He purses his lips as he pulls the documents closer to read over. After a few seconds—but what feels like minutes of awkward silence—he shuts the folder and tosses it on his desk. "We're primarily concerned with the environmental impact and precedent this project could set."

I nod. "Of course. We completely understand your concerns, and we've addressed them in our proposal. Nelson Signature is committed to ensuring this project is environmentally sustainable and beneficial for the community."

He scoffs. "Please elaborate how on earth your resort could possibly be beneficial to us locals."

Nerves course through my veins as I stare at the man sitting across the desk. He's not going to make this easy, which means, I'm going to paste on a pretty smile and win him over with my pitch.

"We understand the locals' concerns based on the negative feedback from the previous resort owners. The resort will fund several community projects, including school improvements and support for local businesses. We'll also partner with local artisans and vendors to feature their work and products with our farmer's market initiative. Jobs are reserved for locals, and we provide detailed training to ensure no one fails at their job."

"These are promising initiatives, but we cannot guarantee anything."

"We're prepared to finalize a formal contract with the administrative offices to ensure that our promises are kept. I assure you, Martin, Nelson's Signature isn't the bad guy coming in to ruin your community."

Martin leans forward on his elbows, his fingers steepling beneath his chin. "You've certainly come prepared, Miss Reed. I'll need to review this proposal with my colleagues and discuss it internally. However, I am impressed with your pitch. You seem to have thought of everything."

"Thank you, Martin. We're committed to working closely with you to ensure this project benefits everyone involved. Please don't hesitate to reach out if you have any questions or concerns. I'll be on the island for the foreseeable future."

"We'll be in touch by the end of the week, Miss Reed."

I stand from my seat and reach across the desk to shake Martin's hand. The gesture catches him off guard. With a firm grip, I thank him again for taking the time to meet with me. Before I have a chance to walk into the hallway, I pause and turn around when he calls my name.

"For what it's worth, it says a lot about your character that you have uprooted your life to live on the island until these issues are resolved. Most companies, especially ones that we have worked with in the past, would never send someone down here. They would require only over-the-phone conversations. I appreciate your dedication to meet with me in person, and to provide many options to showcase your resort's promise to the local people."

"It's a lovely island, Martin. I'm happy to be here. And for what it's worth, I'm a small-town girl. The idea of big business is scary, and I'll do everything in my power to assure the locals we're not here to push anyone out or destroy anyone's business." With a nod and a tight-lipped smile, Martin dismisses me, and I leave his office.

"Have a lovely day," I call out to the receptionist.

One thing's for sure, I'll kill everyone with kindness because that's what closes business.

Making my way across the parking lot, I spot Jayden talking to a young group of kids. His body language is carefree, laughing at one of the boys. He spots me coming and smiles at me from across the lot.

"Oh, she's pretty," one of the girls says.

"Miss Reed," Jayden greets, standing up straighter. I send him a warm smile, one that finally meets my eyes. A weight feels like it's off my shoulders, and I can only hope that today's in-person conversation will change their minds. It seems to have affected Martin. His demeanor completely shifted as I stepped out of his office.

"Hey, Jayden," I greet before turning my attention to the group of kids. "Hi, kids."

They smile warmly. "This is my cousin, Charlie, and his group of friends. They were heading to the park to play soccer."

"How fun. I played soccer when I was younger."

Their eyes widen, making me chuckle.

"Really?" Charlie asks, and I nod. "Wanna come play with us?"

"Miss Reed has to get back to the resort for a lunch meeting," Jayden answers for me. I raise an eyebrow in his direction. I don't remember having any more meetings on my calendar today. He nods at my silent question.

"How about another time?" I ask the group of children, who look to be around the age of ten. They cheer before shouting their goodbyes as they head off to the park.

Turning toward the car, Jayden goes around to the driver's side. "I didn't know I had any more meetings."

"Mr. Nelson sent me a text message informing me to bring you back to the resort as soon as you were done."

"Oh," I answer as the two of us climb into the car. "Thank you."

As we make the thirty-minute journey back to the resort, my mind spins as I try to uncover what our meeting could be about. The IT department has managed the workaround for the internet as they continue to troubleshoot the major issues. Construction on the new entryway should be completed by the end of the week. I'm handling the approval of the new villas. Nothing comes to my mind that would be pressing.

Reaching inside my work bag, I slide out my phone. No new emails or text messages from Tristan. Then my stomach sinks at the realization. What if it's not with Tristan, but with his father? What if I'm getting fired since I don't have the approval today?

No, no, no. That can't be happening.

Arriving back at the resort takes longer than usual. It would have been fine, and a welcomed break, but my anxiety won't stop creeping in. Every minute that passes, the worse the feeling becomes.

Jayden parks under the overhang and makes his way to my side of the car while I gather my things. Stepping out, I smile at the young man. "Thanks, Jayden. Looks like you shouldn't have to drive me around for a few days."

He grins back at me. "It was no trouble at all, Kennedy. If you need anything, send me a message."

With a wave, I turn on my heels to head inside the resort. But I come up short when I find Tristan standing outside. He's dressed so casually that it has me pausing. My gaze travels down from his perfectly symmetrical face to where the button-down is left undone, exposing his tan, chiseled physique, then to his shorts that hug him deliciously, showing the black ink peeking out. But it's his shoes that have me pausing.

"Are you wearing Birkenstocks?"

He shrugs. "Thought I'd embrace the island lifestyle. How did I do?"

"I didn't take you for the hippie type, Nelson. What's next? Going to grow your hair out and sport a man bun?" With one foot in front of the other, I close the distance between us, unable to take my eyes off the man in front of me. Truth is, seeing him like this has my heart doing palpitations. If it wasn't for the fact he looks like a literal island god, I might have thought I was having a heart attack.

"Don't give me any ideas, Firecracker. Besides, you should know by now I like to keep you on your toes."

My eyes flutter with a slight eye roll as I shake my head. "Oh, you've got me on my toes alright," I snark. "But unlike you, I don't need a wardrobe change to distract my competition."

"No, you don't. It doesn't matter what you wear." His voice grows husky as he erases the remaining space between us. Reaching forward, he tucks a loose tendril of hair behind my ear. "But I like this relaxed version of you. St. Lucia looks good on you, Ken."

Heat licks across the apples of my cheeks and, luckily, it's hot out here, so here's to hoping my skin's reaction to the temperature camouflages my blush.

"Flattery won't get you anywhere, Tristan. Especially in those sandals."

The barking laugh that erupts from deep inside him has workers pausing to watch us. At this moment, I feel so content, a grin spreads across my face. Is this what true happiness feels like?

"I'm serious," he starts, trying to get control of his laughter. "It's nice to see you so relaxed. Even if you're still trying to outdo me."

"Listen, buddy"—I poke him in the chest—"just because we are in paradise, doesn't mean I'm going to take it easy on you."

"I wouldn't dream of it. I'm counting on you to keep me on my toes...even in Birkenstocks."

It's my turn to let out a cackle that has heads turning.

"You know, you just might realize you enjoy my company. Casual attire and everything." He starts moving toward the new entrance of the lobby, where I fall in line beside him.

"Keep dreaming, sandal boy. I'm here to work, not admire your mid-life crisis fashion decisions."

He pauses with a laugh as he guides me to walk through the entryway first. "Sandal boy? Mid-life crisis? You've got jokes today, Kenny. But don't be surprised if I give you a run for your money."

"Bring it on, Golden Boy."

The two of us stand alone in the lobby, smiles stretched across our faces, a lightness in the atmosphere. While my eyes are locked on his hazel ones, I can't help but look away to admire the renovations. Dust has been cleaned up from the cutting of the entryway. The scent of fresh paint mixes with the salty ocean air.

Everything's coming together. Slowly, very slowly. But together nonetheless.

"Ah, there you two are," Destiny greets us out of nowhere. Seriously, the woman just appeared. Her feet falter as she stares at us, and a slow smile spreads across her features.

"Hi, Destiny."

"Has Mr. Nelson filled you in on today's events?" Looking from Destiny to Tristan, his notorious smirk has slid into place. "Ah, I'm going to guess no based on that look."

"Your guess is correct."

She pulls open her folder and removes a piece of paper before handing it to me. I scan over the dates and items lined next to each other. Next to today's date, it says Italian, wine tasting, and helicopter tour.

"A helicopter tour?" Nerves pool in my stomach at the thought of being up in the air. The flight into St. Lucia had me ready to pass out, and now I'm going to be stuck in a tiny space hovering above a plummet to my death.

"If you want to skip the tour, I'll go, and you can stay back at the resort." Tristan offers a solution, but in my twisted brain, I take it as a challenge. An 'oh, look, I'm not afraid of heights and you are' challenge.

"No, it's fine."

"Great, Jayden is still parked outside and will take you to the airstrip." Jayden needs a raise, I decide. The poor boy has been sitting around waiting for us whenever we need a ride.

Wonderful. The last time I was in the car, I was terrified of the meeting I was stepping foot into, and now I'm worried for a whole other reason.

What could possibly go wrong?

Chapter Sixteen

Tristan

Victoria: Hey big brother! How's island life?

Me: Hot and humid.

Victoria: Still the same man of few words…have you seen much of Kennedy?

Me: Every day. We are sharing the suite.

Victoria: SHUT. THE. FRONT. DOOR!!!

Victoria: OMG! Does this mean the two of you will have an island fling?

Me: None of your business.

Victoria: OMG! That wasn't a no!

Me: *eyeroll emoji*

> **Victoria: In all seriousness…you deserve to have fun, Trist.**

> **Me: I'll keep that in mind. I've got to go. We have a reservation in an hour.**

> **Victoria: Have fun creating your own romantic comedy!! *squealing***

IT'S BEEN A WEEK since Kennedy and I went on the helicopter tour. The views were unmatched, and hearing Kennedy squeal will live rent-free in my head. With a rocky takeoff and landing, her grip left tiny half-moons on my arm. But the pure joy that radiated from her as we traveled over the Piton Mountains, red-roofed villages, the resort we're remodeling, jungles, and the ocean made every second worth it.

The truce between us remains. We've established a sense of common ground and our living arrangements have gone smoothly. Since our more meaningful conversation, I haven't divulged any more of my deep, dark thoughts. The truth is, there's still a lot I don't know about Kennedy.

I don't understand why she works so hard. Yes, I get that she's good at her job, but she goes above and beyond. She's persistent and doesn't believe in working hours. It's why when I overheard Destiny speaking to some of the resort staff, I suggested weekly trials with Kennedy and myself.

Did I have an ulterior motive of getting her alone with me in a non-work setting? Absolutely. But above all else, I wanted to see Kennedy Reed let her hair down and have some damn fun.

In college, I never heard about her attending any frat parties. She arrived early to class, sat in the front of the room, and voluntarily raised her hand to participate. Her dedication to her academics is one of the things that drew me to her. I loved her tenacity. Hell, I still do. But life is too damn short for her to spend all her time worrying about Nelson Signature. My dad's stupid comment about firing her was completely out of line, and I refuse to watch her shrink into work.

We're in paradise, while New York is sitting under a foot of snow. Fuck the conventional; we are stepping out of our normal.

And today, I'm going to push her even more.

"Ready, Kenny?" I call from where I'm standing in the dining room. I hear her sandals slapping against the marble before I even see her.

"Ready."

Fixing the collar of my shirt, I watch through the mirror as Kennedy strides past me, her nose engrossed in her phone.

Holy. Fuck.

I whirl around to take in the woman in front of me. Her hair is parted in two unique-looking braids, with a white straw fedora sits atop her head, with strands of curled hair hanging around her face. Freckles are still visible, with her light makeup, and her lashes are coated in black, making them appear longer. The coral dress with floral details she's wearing is in two pieces. The skirt hugs around her delicate curves, exposing her tight midriff, where the cropped, off-the-shoulder top sits. And I love that she picked coral. Something about her outfit screams she's up for an adventure.

"Stunning." The compliment is out of my mouth in a whisper before I can think.

Her head whips in my direction, as if she didn't realize I was standing there. Eyes wide, it's her turn to peruse. I'm dressed in the same combination, as usual. Only this time, it's a navy short-sleeved collared button-down and cream-and-navy striped chino shorts. I wait for her to get to the best part.

A brimming smile spreads across her lips that I want to kiss so badly. "Birks," she says with a laugh.

Eating up the space between us, I don't stop until we're toe-to-toe.

"Had to wear them. I know how much you love them." Clearing my throat, I watch her mouth curve up. Why is my voice so raspy?

"Come on, Golden Boy." She reaches for her handbag she left on the couch, then pushes the button to call the elevator. My heart races as my palms begin to sweat as the thrill of what's to come sinks in. With a deep inhale, I follow her footsteps. Here goes nothing—or everything.

For the past two days, Destiny and I have worked together to plan the perfect evening. Tonight is the night I make Kennedy Reed spill her truths. I need to know what I did in college to earn such an enemy status and how I can make her forgive me. She's always been more to me than competition, and it's about damn time I tell her that.

· · · · ●·●·· · ·

"Oh my gosh," Kennedy gasps as we pull into the marina.

Rows and rows of pristine white catamarans, sailboats, and yachts line the docks, with restaurants along the shoreline. Her face brightens and eyes widen while she glances from side to side, taking in the marina and tropical landscaping. A large, red-roofed building welcomes us as we arrive. The sky slowly changes as it cascades us in its golden hue.

"What are we doing here, Tristan?" she whispers in wonderment.

"Thought I'd surprise you with a sunset cruise. It's one of the resort's top excursions." Pausing to run my fingers through my hair, my nerves spike. "I thought we could be tourists for the night."

Her face softens as curiosity morphs into something I can't quite put my finger on. Jayden parks the BMW, and his eyes find mine in the rearview mirror. With a nod and a quick thanks, I step out of the car and move around the back to open Kennedy's door. When I reach inside, she takes my hand, and I ignore the electricity that sparks every time our hands brush. Only this time, I watch her features and see the moment she realizes there's a connection between us.

Hmm, she does feel this too.

Long, golden legs slip out of her slit as she exits the vehicle, and I can't keep my eyes off her. She looks stunning, but that's nothing new. Kennedy might have come from a small town in the middle of nowhere, but you would never guess that based on the way she dresses and carries herself.

Once she rights her dress, her hand slips from mine. Instantly, I find myself missing our warm connection. Sliding my hands in my pockets, I use the distraction to keep myself from reaching for her again.

We fall instep beside each other as we make our way toward the waiting catamaran. The pathway is a mixture of concrete and weathered wood. With each step, the weathered planks from years of salt and sun leave us with a symphony of creaks, telling us a tale from years of footsteps.

Briny sea air fills our noses, the perfume of the sea mingling with the mouth-watering scent of fresh grilled seafood from the local eateries. But it's the light floral fragrance that has my senses buzzing. Sweet orchid and citrus mix with the marina aromas, and it can only be coming from one person.

Sounds of seagulls and the water lapping against the hulls of boats surround us, along with chatter from radios and men on board. Through the speakers lining the pathway attached to the lampposts is a soft island melody. The atmosphere is a soothing backdrop as we continue our walk until we find the resort's catamaran.

"This marina is beautiful." Her comment pulls me from my assessment.

Finally, we find ourselves outside of our catamaran. A young woman waits for us on the cobblestones.

"Good evening and welcome aboard. We are so excited to have you joining us," she greets.

After a few minutes of pleasantries and her explaining the events for the evening, we step aboard the shiny, pristine fiberglass. The boat is in immaculate condition, not a watermark in sight. Making our way through the helm, we climb a few stairs before we're on the foredeck.

A member of the crew welcomes us with two glasses of chilled champagne.

"Thank you," Kennedy and I say in unison as we each take a glass. With a brief nod, the crew member leaves us alone. There aren't any seats on the deck, only two large netted trampolines in front of us. Kicking off her sandals, Kennedy steps down onto the trampoline and sits on the fiberglass deck.

Within minutes, we're setting sail over the glass-like blue water. "Please tell me you've been on a boat."

She scoffs. "I've been on a boat. My grandparents had a farm with a five-acre pond. We used to go out on their pontoon boat, but it was nothing like this." Pausing, she gestures around us. "It was pretty much a floating dock. I remember we all had to grab plastic chairs from the deck and bring them down if we wanted to sit. Otherwise, we sat on the floor."

"I've never heard more of a country bumpkin story in my life."

"Yeah, well, not all of us have the luxury to vacation on yachts."

With only the island melodies coming from the speakers, silence falls over us. Truth is, I would give anything to have a simpler life. I wasn't kidding when I told her that owning an outfitter was my dream job growing up.

Not wanting to waste any time, I nudge her shoulder, and she stares up at me under her long, black lashes.

"That was rude."

"It was." She chuckles.

Staring out in front of us, I watch as we slice through the water, causing splashes of waves to come up over the side of the hull.

"Why New York?"

I can tell I catch her off guard with the way her body stiffens. Turning to face me, she assesses me for a moment before releasing a sigh. "I needed to get out of the country. Don't get me wrong, I never hated living in a small town, but I always wanted more."

Hitching an eyebrow, I wait for her to elaborate. She brings the flute to her lips and takes a long pull.

"There's a certain pressure that comes from living in a small town," she says, averting her gaze. "You go to school, graduate, marry your high school sweetheart, and have babies. I'm not knocking anyone who chooses to do that, but the idea of marrying young and popping out a slew of babies never struck my fancy. Growing up and watching *Friends*, I wanted to be like Rachel Green."

"What do you mean?"

"She left the guy she was supposed to marry at the altar, moved to the city, and started her own life. She was career driven, and that inspired me." Kennedy looks down, twirling the bangles on her wrist, as if she's biding time. "My mom always told Olivia, my sister, and me how special we were. That we were courageous, strong, and smart. Of course, she told us we were beautiful, but the words she spoke to us were centered around our strengths outside of beauty. And that stuck with me."

"That's admirable, Kennedy."

She blushes. "Studying always came naturally. When most people were out partying in a cornfield, I was inside my room, reading textbooks and taking practice tests. NYU was always my dream school, so instead of nights out with friends, I chose to spend time with McGraw-Hill and Merriam-Webster."

"Who?"

Nudging into me, she fights her embarrassment. "The people who publish textbooks and the dictionary."

I can't help the chuckle that leaves my lips. "Only you, Firecracker."

She finally turns to face me and my breath catches. We stare at each other for what feels like hours, both of us trying to read the other. Her eyes bore into mine before she finally reaches for the champagne flute without another word and walks away, leaving me sitting in confusion.

When she returns, empty-handed, I watch in fascination as she climbs back down to where we're sitting. Only, instead of sitting on the fiberglass, she moves on shaky legs to the center of the trampoline, where she settles with her legs stretched in front of her and her body resting on her hands.

"Coming, Golden Boy?" Mischievous eyes stare back at me, daring me to follow. And I do just that. With her eyes on mine, full of longing and playfulness, I'd follow her to the ends of the world, it seems. Taking a seat next to her, our arms brush, and to my surprise, goosebumps trail down her bare skin at the contact. I knew she was just as affected.

The sounds of the ukulele fill the silence as we stare out at the open water and the beach houses hidden by the surrounding jungles. Many of the private estates can only be seen by water. Maybe this is what I need, a little island house to get away from the city when the overwhelming deadlines and suffocating sounds wear me down.

Would Kennedy like the escape too?

The question is on the tip of my tongue when we hit a choppier spot in the ocean from a passing ship.

A frightened gasp leaves Kennedy's lips as she snuggles closer to my side, fingertips digging into my forearm. I welcome the opportunity to wrap my arms around her shoulders. With my thumb, I rub tiny circles as I try to calm her.

"I've got you, Ken," I whisper as my lips brush her hairline. She grips me tighter, and I relish the moment, savoring every second.

The walls she's been building between us for years have slowly started to fall. As much as I want to press her for answers to why she hates me, I don't want to burst this bubble we've created.

Rounding a corner where the land juts out, the captain steers us toward a cove. Ahead of us, I spot the familiar stone buildings as our resort comes back into view. Cabanas and palm trees are dotted along the boardwalk, where the sand kisses the turquoise waters. The tower at our main pool captures your attention, as does the peer that stretches out across the sea, where flags line the wooden planks.

Everything looks so strange from our vantage point since the resort is closed. It won't be long before the white beaches are filled with honeymooners snuggled together and resort staff bustling to keep guests happy and our resort looking clean.

"You did good, Firecracker."

"The resort looks so beautiful from here. I can't wait to see what it looks like when we have guests."

I hum against her warm skin. "I was just thinking the same thing."

"Excuse me, Mr. Nelson," a crew member interrupts. "Would you and Miss Reed like another glass of champagne as we prepare to watch the sunset in the next few minutes?"

"That'd be great, thank you." He steps down onto the trampoline, handing Kennedy and I each our own flute before he pours the bubbly into our glasses.

Within minutes, the golden hue melts away and transforms into shades of purple, orange, and pink across the horizon. We sit there in awe at nature's painting. The engine cuts off, blanketing us in a peaceful quiet as soothing sounds from the waves lap at the boat as we float.

Kennedy rests her head against my shoulder as her soft voice breaks the silence. "This is breathtaking. Thank you for doing this."

Turning her attention upward, our faces are only inches apart. Our gazes lock, and I watch as she scans my face, her eyes landing on my lips. Her tongue peeks out and licks at her lower lip, and my body urges me to make a move.

Does she want me to kiss her? Because I want to. I've been desperate to know what those plump lips feel like. It's all I've been able to think about. Every night before I fall asleep, I'm tormented by images of her. Seeing her outside of the office, and in a setting where she's let her guard down, has me wanting to explore this newfound comfort between us.

Leaning forward, I slowly, painstakingly, erase the space between us. So many thoughts flash across her eyes, but she never moves away. In fact, I think she leans closer, which has my heart racing.

Without any more hesitation, my mouth finds hers. Fireworks flash through my mind at the contact, at how soft her lips are, how she kisses me back so effortlessly. Before I have a chance to deepen our connection, the captain's voice sounds from around the corner. Kennedy springs away from me with wide eyes, her fingers grazing her lips as she puts space between us.

"Thank you so much for joining us tonight," the captain says, before explaining what the next steps of the night include for guests. He tells us how the staff will transition the salon into a nightclub atmosphere where a DJ performs with LED lights to set the mood while unlimited rum punch is served.

"Oh wow, that sounds like so much fun," Kennedy says from her new position, where she stays at a distance.

"The guests seem to think so. Would you like me to have them set it up for you two to enjoy?"

With a warm smile, she shakes her head. "No, thank you. As much fun as it sounds, we'll just sit out here and enjoy the ride back."

"Of course." He nods. "Is there anything else I can do for you two?"

We shake our heads. "No, I think we are good. Thank you, though. This has been a lovely evening."

"We're glad to have you on board." And with that, he leaves, and an awkwardness settles over us.

Within minutes, the captain has the engine started, and we're returning to the harbor. My mind spirals with ways I can salvage this evening. I want more of what we started. More touching. More kissing. More relaxed Kennedy. Wordlessly, she moves up from the trampoline to sit on the fiberglass deck, her feet dangling over the netting. The soft chords of a ukulele still play, and I recognize the melody this time.

Standing to my feet, I move on wobbly legs until I'm in front of her. "Dance with me?"

"Wh-what?" she asks, a pinch to her brow.

"Dance with me, Kennedy."

For a moment, she only stares at me. I can see the gears turning in her mind, debating if she should embrace this moment. Selfishly, I hope she does.

When I think she's going to ignore my hand, she accepts.

With a nod, she takes my outstretched hand as I pull her up so both of us are on the flat deck. Wrapping my arms around her waist, I pull her in close to me as her arms circle my neck. The lyrics to "Somewhere

Over the Rainbow" begin as our bodies sway together. Daringly, I pull her closer until our bodies are flush.

"Tristan..." Her breathy voice is laced with confusion and desperation.

"One song, Ken. That's all I'm asking for."

Soft curls tickle my chin when she rests her head against my chest as my thumb grazes against the exposed flesh above her skirt. A shiver runs down her spine, and I long to see how else she'd react to my touch.

"Cold?"

"No," she whispers against my chest as the two of us continue to sway.

"My mom used to sing this song to me. She loved *The Wizard of Oz*, so whenever she would rock us to sleep, or whenever we needed comfort at night, she would sing this song."

She doesn't lift her head from my chest and doesn't respond. Her silence is deafening and has me paranoid I shared too much. Just when I'm about to open my mouth to say something else to ease the tension I feel, she lets out a soft exhale, relaxing deeper into our connection.

"I can see why she did that."

I swallow, unable to find a response as I trace shapes against her skin.

I savor this moment for as long as I can, before the bubble we've found ourselves in is inevitably broken. But she surprises me by pulling me close to her as the song ends. The two of us stand against the railing and watch darkness settle around us. It didn't happen overnight, but somewhere along the way, our time together on the island has shifted everything between us. The quiet nights spent together relaxing after work. The way we no longer struggle for conversation, but speak freely. Her smile is no longer forced and fake, but has brightened in a way that takes over her features. I no longer feel the need to prove myself to her. There's no edge, no rivalry. Just us.

CHAPTER SEVENTEEN

KENNEDY

"Welcome back." Destiny greets Tristan and me as we step into the lobby. Our voices echo around the space. "How was your evening?"

"It was perfect," I reply, flashing Destiny a warm smile. My heart stutters as I replay the night, especially the brief kiss I'm still reeling from. I cannot believe Tristan planned all of this. Like, who is he and where has my rival gone?

Destiny's eyes peer over my shoulder and the subtlest smile graces her face as she looks at Tristan. Something tells me the two of them worked together to plan this evening.

"If you two are ready, I'd love to escort you to dinner."

My head whips around to Tristan as shock covers my features. "There's more?"

"Of course we've gotta eat." He flashes me that devilish smirk, causing a tingling sensation to erupt between my thighs.

Seriously, what's happening here?

Tristan's hand interrupts my thoughts as he waves it, encouraging me to follow Destiny through the vacant lobby.

Long gone is the beautiful sunset. But in her place is a mixture of dark blues as the sky has fallen into complete darkness. The warm orange glow from lampposts illuminates the sidewalks as we make our way to the end of the resort. Cicadas are the only soundtrack we need as both of us seem to be lost in our thoughts.

My mind is swirling, in a battle with itself as I fight the urge to grab hold of Tristan and feel his body against mine. But at the same time, he's still Tristan Nelson, the man I swore was my enemy. I'm stuck rethinking everything. Was the competition one-sided? Have I made a bigger deal out of our history?

It wouldn't surprise me. I'm a constant over-thinker, and I have a bad habit of jumping to conclusions. It's something I've always struggled with, almost an inner paranoia I haven't been able to work past. Maybe it's from years of wanting to stand out in a town that constantly looked past me. Or the competitive nature I adapted from years of fighting for my place in school to be the best and win scholarships that would lead me to my dream college.

Warm sand covers the weathered boardwalk, still warm from the hours in the sun. The gritty feeling slides between my toes, making my steps slow as my foot slides against the footbed of my sandal. Reaching beside me, I grab Tristan's forearm and feel the muscles flex underneath my touch.

"You okay?" he asks, pausing next to me as his other hand grips my wrist that's clutching him.

"Yeah," I say, bending down to unclasp my sandals and carry them instead. "I keep getting sand in my shoes."

"Well, we are at a beach," he snarks. But the comment doesn't grate on my nerves like it normally would. No, it's playful, and I kind of like it.

Have I been reading into his smart-ass comments all wrong? Has he been playing with me, and I've twisted everything into a darker meaning?

I don't have a chance to ponder as we climb the few stairs to one of the piers. Pausing again, I slip my sandals back on, not wanting to risk a splinter. Chatter at the end of the pier draws my attention as I notice a group of resort staff inside the black structure. Light pours from the windows as music plays. Walking down the planks, the wood creaks beneath our steps. We pass a small sitting area with cushioned chairs and a large stone fire pit. Heat licks across my skin from the roaring flames as we pass by.

"Tonight, the kitchen is providing a tasting menu. They've been busy working on new recipes, and as a trial run, they'll be serving the staff and, of course, you too," Destiny informs us as we stop outside the restaurant.

Lullaby Lagoon sits over the water at the end of the pier. What I thought was black is a dark brown stain covering the exterior, with medium-brown stained shutters over the windows. What's unique about this restaurant is that there aren't walls separating the inside from the outside. Instead, it's an open space that provides unobstructed views of the ocean on three sides.

A waist-high picket fence separates the space as the property encourages indoor and outdoor dining options. Black wicker chairs and gray metal tables line the outdoors, while white chairs and silver tables brighten the interior. Candles are lit on every table and tan woven chandeliers glow from above. It's a very intimate setting.

Staff quiets as we walk past, and I hate that they feel the need to do so. With a smile, I wave as we enter, hoping to reassure the group that they do not need to act differently on our behalf.

Destiny escorts us past an outdoor sectional that hangs off the side of the pier on its platform to a secluded table on the patio. Like the other tables we passed, this one has a few more candles and glasses waiting for us.

Tristan slides my chair out for me as I sit, and my belly swarms with butterflies. "Tristan, what is all of this?"

"Dinner," he says with a grin, before taking the seat across from me. I'm stuck in a trance when our eyes meet. For some reason, this feels a lot more like a date than a dinner to sample the menu. Maybe I really am hungry and the champagne on an empty stomach has gone straight to my head.

"But why are we not eating inside with the rest of the staff?"

He shrugs. That stupid shrug of his gives nothing away. Since I won't be getting any more answers from him, I grab the menu, which is sitting on top of the place setting.

A waiter approaches and pours us each a glass of water. "Hello, I'm Zeb. Can I interest either of you in a glass of wine?"

"Top-shelf bourbon, neat, please," Tristan orders while I scan over the menu, trying to decide what entree I'll go with so I pick the correct wine.

"And for you, miss?"

"The house red, please."

"Certainly," our waiter says, scribbling down our order. "I'll bring out a few appetizers the chef has prepared as well."

Once our waiter leaves, I scan the property in front of me. I've never been one to dream about my wedding, or even a honeymoon, but sitting here under the stars, with the mountains and jungle surrounding us, as the waves lap against the wooden beams of the pier, I understand the fascination. For maybe the first time, I can picture being on vacation in paradise with someone you love.

It's not long before our waiter returns with our drinks. He places the glasses in front of us before reaching onto his tray to set down our appetizers. The tasting tonight is nice since we have an opportunity to try a variety of menu options.

"Here you have our pan-fried scallops, with a cornbread breading and anchovy mayonnaise, our panko-crusted crab cakes served with mango, chili, and scallion salsa, and lastly, our curried butternut squash soup garnished with herbed croutons, roasted cashews, coconut cream, and chive oil. Enjoy."

My mouth waters at the food in front of me, and maybe at the man across from me too. From my vantage point, I have the perfect opportunity to take him in and all his handsome qualities. Not much about Tristan has changed. A smattering of dark brown hair still covers his face, only his beard has been cut shorter, taking on a permanent five o'clock shadow, while his golden skin is even darker, thanks to his evenings spent in the plunge pool.

I watch in fascination as his forearms flex when he cuts into a scallop. And seriously, what is it with his forearms? Thick veins journey up his arms, and it's seriously like forearm porn. My body begs me to find a way to be wrapped up in his arms again. Sitting on the trampoline in his embrace felt natural, like it was something we'd been doing for years.

"Not hungry?" he interrupts my thoughts.

Startling, I reach for my spoon and scoop up the burnt-orange-colored soup. The flavors explode on my tongue, and I let out a very unladylike moan. "Oh my gosh, this is the best thing I've ever put in my mouth."

His fork pauses in the air as his jaw hangs open. The realization of what I just said hits me, and my cheeks heat. "If that's the best thing that's been in your mouth, clearly, you've been doing things wrong."

"Tristan!" I mockingly scold, holding in a laugh as he tips his shoulder up in a shrug.

A comfortable silence falls over our table as we enjoy the food. Halfway through the appetizers, our waiter comes back to take our entree orders while we finish the food in front of us. One thing is for certain, if I keep eating like this, I'll be finding myself in the gym at the start of every day. Cycling in New York was a part of my weekly routine, but since being here, I haven't felt the need to hit the gym. Maybe it's because I'm forced to be outside and not confined to a stale office. Whereas in New York, I needed that sense of adventure, of movement. Here, I get that every day when I walk across the property.

Our food arrives, and I admire the creative plating. Asparagus fricassee sits in the middle of my plate, with three grilled lamb chops placed over top and a red wine reduction drizzled around the outside. Tristan's plate is similar. Only he has whipped potatoes in the center of his and his beef tenderloin on top. Next to the beef is a skewer of perfectly grilled shrimp and a port wine reduction is drizzled across the plate. My mouth waters.

Slicing into the lamb, I blurt out the first thing that pops into my head. "I used to show sheep at the county fair."

Tristan chokes on his mouthful of water. "What?"

"Yeah, we would get lambs and walk them around the property."

"Then what did you do with them?"

"At the end of the fair, there would be a livestock sale, where people and local businesses bid on the animals."

"What happens when they buy them? Do they have sheep running around the car dealerships?"

I chuckle, shaking my head. "No, silly. They take them to market, where they become…" I gesture to my plate with my fork.

"Jesus. That's morbid," he laughs out as he cuts into his tenderloin.

"Facts of life." Taking a bite of my lamb, I moan again at the rich, juicy flavors. "This is delicious."

"Would you stop moaning," he mumbles.

Daringly, I take my foot and run my toes up his bare leg, slowly and seductively, to tease him. "What's the matter, Golden Boy? Turning you on?"

He reaches under the table and grabs my ankle. I try to jerk it away, but his grip tightens. "Yes."

Chills skate across my skin, even with the humidity. My eyes snap to his and find him already watching me. Warmth radiates from his gaze as if I'm genuinely affecting him. What's happening between us?

The sound of steps on the wooden floor pulls our attention, snapping the trance we've found ourselves in. Our waiter returns to top off our water glasses. The magnetic pull swirls in the air, growing thicker than the humidity, and I try to take my foot back again. Only this time, Tristan's fingers trail up my skin, leaving goosebumps in his wake. I'm fighting to squeeze my legs together to relieve some of the pressure and lessen the tingling ache that's settled between my thighs. Once our glasses are filled, I thank the gentleman as he scurries away, no doubt feeling the tension around our table.

Dinner feels like it drags on for hours as we envelop ourselves in our tiny bubble of foreplay. With each bite I take, my lips wrap around my fork in a slow manner, which has me closing my eyes and releasing soft hums. Tristan's touch rarely leaves my ankle as he continues to tease me with soft caresses whenever I find myself enjoying my meal a little too much. Reaching for my wine, I let the medium-bodied red liquid glide into my mouth. The wine is the perfect mix of acidity and boldness to complement my dinner. Flicking my tongue against my lips, I lap up the tiny droplet that escaped. This time, it's Tristan's turn to groan.

I can't explain what's gotten into me. It's been so long since I've been entertained by a man, even if this isn't a date and it's *Tristan*. The idea of being wined and dined isn't lost on me. Is this what it's like to date? Or is it what it feels like to date *him*? Maybe when I get back to New York, I'll make it a point to go out on more dates. That's if Tristan doesn't ruin me for all other men in the meantime.

Who am I kidding? Once I step foot back into New York, I'll be more invested in the office. But maybe I'll try.

After our plates are cleared, Tristan and I make our way over to the seating area, where the fire pit is, for our dessert. He takes the seat next to me, and I enjoy the feeling of his skin brushing against mine. I'm grateful for the heat from the flames, as the air has started to cool.

"So this is what it would be like to date Tristan Nelson?" I blurt, taking a bite of the mango chocolate cheesecake.

A quizzical expression morphs his features. "What?"

"This…" I gesture around us. "The sunset cruise, the candlelit dinner, the caresses, and now dessert by the fire."

"This was all for you."

My body alights at his husky tone, stomach flip-flopping as I meet his gaze.

"Wh-what do you mean?" I fumble over my words.

He leans in closer, and the urge to feel his lips against mine is strong. "I did all of this for you, Firecracker."

My eyes bounce back and forth as I seek out any detection that he's lying. "Why?"

"Because contrary to what you believe, I'm not the enemy, Kennedy." His fingers graze my cheek as he curls a loose piece of hair behind my ears. The gesture has me melting into his touch as our bodies press together as if they're magnified. My lips find his first, and my body relaxes instantly, like it was waiting to feel him again. When his tongue flicks the seam of my mouth, begging for me to open, I grant him entry.

The kiss quickly turns heated as the overwhelming urge to climb into his lap hits me like a wave crashing over my senses. I reach for his head and tug his mouth closer to mine, wanting, *needing,* to erase the remaining space between us. The sound of a fork hitting a plate has me springing apart from him, taken aback by how entranced I was by that kiss. Chest heaving, I glance behind me to see if anyone noticed the makeout session we were having like two horny teenagers.

"Shit, Firecracker." He trails his hand down his front as he adjusts the bulge I can barely see from the minimal light around us.

"Let's go home."

Chapter Eighteen

Tristan

"Let's go home."

Three words have never sounded so sexy. One minute, the two of us are enjoying dessert in silence, and the next, Kennedy's lips are smashed against mine. The urge to pull her into my lap was overwhelming.

But when she uttered those words, I don't think I've ever moved faster than I did right then. Setting our plates on the table, I pull her to her feet and basically drag her off the pier. I'll thank Destiny and the chef tomorrow for the wonderful evening. And as much as I was enjoying dessert, I could think of something else I'd rather taste than carrot cake.

With her hand grasped firmly in mine, we make record time getting across the courtyard and to our building. As we wait for the elevator, I take the opportunity to push Kennedy against the wall. Trapping her arms above her head, I lift off the fedora that has been obstructing my angle all night. Our lips meet in a searing kiss as she moans into my mouth. We duel in a heated kiss, our tongues meeting as her body melts against mine. My erection presses into her middle, leaving no doubt she has me so turned on. The bell dings, and we tumble into the waiting car as it carries us to our shared space. She falls against me, and I land with my back to the wall. My hand holding her hat battles to grip her lower back while the other plunges through her hair, holding her mouth to mine.

I've never been so grateful to be sharing a room.

Her hands battle the buttons of my shirt as she tries to unclasp them, our mouths never disconnecting. Finally, the buttons free, and her cool hands graze my chest, pulling a hiss from the contact, and her mouth curves in a smile. With my hand still on her back, I trail it down, gripping her ass as she grinds into me, dropping her hat in the process. When she rewards me with another breathy moan, I slip it lower, pulling at the satin material of her skirt until my hand smooths beneath the slit to her thigh.

My fingers graze up her silky skin until I reach her apex. Heat radiates from her as my knuckle rubs across her wet panties.

"Fuuuuuuck," I groan. "You're dripping for me."

Her body shudders. I pull the material to the side with a finger, allowing my thumb to brush against her swollen clit. Satisfaction fills me as her hips buck at the contact and she deepens the kiss. I'm about to sink two fingers inside her when the doors chime open. The ding has Kennedy forcing her back ramrod straight, and whatever spell we've been under this evening is immediately busted.

She pushes off my chest and storms out of the elevator without a word.

What the fuck just happened?

The doors start to close as I'm standing there watching her retreat across the suite. Reaching out, I keep the car from closing while grabbing her stupid hat. Frustration fuels my movements as I move through the room, trailing after her. My insecurities crash down around me and tendrils of anger flicker to life.

Did I do something to her? Was she not feeling things the way I was?

The date was perfect, couldn't have asked better, really, and she definitely seemed all in when we ran out on dessert. She's the one who wanted to leave. We practically inhaled each other in the elevator. It had felt like a connection, something deeper than co-workers forced to share space.

Her door is wide open, and her back is to me as she reaches for the zipper on the side of her skirt.

"What did I do?" My words come out harsh and startle her. She jumps, her hands going to her chest.

She scoffs and turns her attention away from me. "What don't you do?"

"Elaborate." I don't ask, but demand while flinging her fedora like a frisbee toward her bed, because fuck this. I'm done with this back-and-forth, hot-and-cold bullshit. She's had a problem with me since college, and it's about time we settle the dispute now. I've gone and fallen for a woman who wants me one second and hates me the next.

I watch as she inhales and exhales, not looking at me. Her back moves with each breath, and I want to spin her around until she spills all her truths. She spins on her toes and marches toward me.

Fiery Kennedy might be my favorite Kennedy, but right now that glare of hers has my balls wanting to shrivel. She jabs her finger into my chest, which was still exposed from moments ago when she was practically ripping my shirt off my body.

"You get *everything* I want."

"What are you talking about?" I ask, exasperated.

Her chest heaves and her face falls. I want to erase the pain and go back in time when we were sailing across the ocean in our little bubble. Gone were the worries of tomorrow and the pain from yesterday. We were living in the moment and soaking up each other's company for the first time in our entire relationship.

"Kennedy," I press, searching her face for any clues as to what's racing through her mind. "Talk to me. I can't fix things if you won't tell me what I did to royal fuck up when it comes to you."

She shakes her head. The beautiful head with the delicate features and the swollen lips from our kisses. "In college, I would work my ass off. I didn't party. I didn't make friends. I didn't do anything but study, and there you were, constantly swooping in with your arrogant ways to gain the attention of every professor in our major."

"That's why you're so pissed off with me? Because I received more acknowledgments than you?"

"Well, it sounds really fucking stupid when you put it like that."

"It kind of is."

"No, don't do that." Her voice rises before pausing. She shakes her head in disbelief. "Don't make my feelings invalid. They were real for me."

"Of course, your feelings are valid, Kennedy. I guess I just don't understand."

"You don't have to understand." Her face is filled with anguish, and I hate that I'm the reason for it. I can feel her walls rebuilding. I can't watch it happen, not again. We've come too far to go back to the beginning.

"You're right, but I want to. Can you try to explain it to me?" Shoulders relaxing, I take a tentative step toward her as I lift my hand to brush a strand of hair out of her face, but I don't get the chance.

She shakes her head, turning and walking away, putting distance between us. I think she's going to ignore the question, but she turns around and flails her arms out, her soft voice filling the room. "Getting to NYU was my only dream. I have given up a lot of my life to achieve my dreams, and that was fine; it was a sacrifice I wanted to make. But I thought when I got to NYU, it would be easier. I'd work hard, study, and finally get the praise I guess I was desperate for. No one back home, not even my parents, gave me the credit that I deserved for getting a 35 on my ACT and a 1540 SAT score. Not to mention, graduating with a 4.0. It hurt that no one gave me the credit I deserved. But I thought when I got to college, people would recognize how much grit and determination was needed to get to where we were.

"So I'd sit in the front row, participate in class, and focus on everything the professors had to say. But then you would show up late, sit in the back, and constantly get called in when I was the one showing up early, taking notes, and voluntarily raising my hand to answer questions."

Thinking back on my time in NYU, I can see where she developed a negative impression of me. The Nelson name carried a lot of weight on campus. While I wasn't in a fraternity, like my father, the attention was still drawn to me. I was treated like a celebrity, and the professors noticed my name on their rosters. They gave me extra attention in hopes that their goodwill would make it back to my father. I couldn't have cared less about their attention. I was there because I had to be there.

"I didn't realize how much you wanted it."

She huffs, but then whispers, "No one knew how much I wanted it."

"Things were rough for me, and I used my name to get by with a lot of things. I'm not proud of it, and I know it was a shitty thing to do, but I felt like my life was imploding. So even though I've never been one to want the fame that came with my name, there were times when I milked the system," I admit, not proud of the fact that, in my time of need, I was using everything I could to keep my head above water.

"I'm sorry you were going through a tough time."

Our eyes lock, emotion coursing through hers as we stare at each other. "It's not your fault, Ken."

And it's not. That time of my life has been put in a locked box. I refuse to fetch the key and open old wounds. I spent a lot of time in therapy working through things, and after graduating college, I finally felt like I was becoming a new, better version of myself. Only to find myself working for my father.

"I hated you for a long time. I hated that your papers were always used as examples, that you had an article posted in *Architectural Digest* about the next up-and-coming in the industry, and I hated how you won that damn senior project. You didn't need that prize money. That two-grand would have helped me feel a sense of security as I was struggling to make ends meet. The billionaire's son didn't need it."

"For what it's worth, I donated the money." Her eyes widen.

Running my hands through my hair, I stare out the window at the dark waters. The black night seems fitting for the ominous mood that has settled over us. "I hate this, Kennedy."

She ignores me as she stands across the room, her shoulder leaning against the glass panes of her sliding patio door, her gaze is locked on the world around us.

"How can I fix this?" I plead, knowing how desperate I sound. "Tell me how I fix this, Kennedy."

Turning her attention toward me, I watch that confidence slide into its rightful place across her beautiful face as she steels her shoulders.

What she says next has me sucking in a breath of pure and utter shock. Three words I would have never imagined come flying out of her mouth with such conviction, it sends a shiver of pure anticipation down my spine.

"Crawl to me."

CHAPTER NINETEEN

KENNEDY

"Crawl to me."

The words are out of my mouth before I can process the weight they carry.

What did I say?

Am I having an out-of-body experience?

Who is this person who uttered such powerful words?

Refusing to back down and hide from what just escaped my mouth, I keep my shoulders squared as I stare at the man before me. Something about being in Tristan Nelson's presence emblazons me with a boldness I've never felt before.

The air around us swirls and thickens, more palpable than the St. Lucia humidity. The tension we've both been fighting for so long has built to the point it can no longer be ignored. Standing across from him, my heart pounds the soundtrack of every emotion coursing through my body, getting louder and louder, and I'm sure he can hear it too. A tremble ripples through my limbs, and I clench my fist, hoping he can't witness the nervous energy I'm expelling.

With wide eyes, I watch his conflicted expression. He looks as caught off guard as I'm feeling. Right here, right now, we're throwing caution to the wind. This moment will alter us for the foreseeable future. "Wh-what did you just say?"

"Crawl to me." My voice shakes subtly, with a mixture of defiance and desperation, but the words have never been clearer. "You want to know how you can fix it? Then show me."

Those hazel eyes I've found myself staring into far too many times darken to a rich mocha. Stunned, his chest rises and falls in rapid succession as silence falls over the room. Neither of us moves as our eyes stay locked. The command hangs in the room, a challenge, a plea waiting to be answered.

In a flash, long gone is his moment of hesitancy, and my heart skips a beat. In its wake is something deeper, something raw, something unguarded.

With a slow step, he starts his approach. One foot and then the other. His movements are deliberate as he eats up the space between us. My pulse races as my nerves quickly melt into something else. Desire courses through my veins as flutters take flight in my stomach. My core aches at what's to come, wetness ruining the lace panties I wore tonight.

Just when I think Tristan's not going to listen, he falls to his knees. My breath catches in my throat as I struggle to breathe. The urge to rub my legs together to satisfy the ache as I watch my enemy submit to my words has my pussy clenching.

He's doing it.

Tristan Nelson is *crawling* to *me*.

Jaw clenched, his darkened gaze never leaves mine, my own desperation reflected back at me. Each inch he closes feels like an eternity, and it won't be long before I'm a mess before him. I'm beyond desperate to feel his touch.

The air crackles, sending out electric shocks. Rivalry and resentment give way to raw desire. This was a surrender, a breaking of barriers that had kept us apart. Years of our competition, torment, childish digs, and professional facade all fade into a problem to be dealt with another day.

Witnessing this man, who oozes confidence and charm, drop to his knees to prove I can trust him is liberating. Seductive and erotic. It's opening doors I never knew were kept closed inside my brain.

When there's no more space to erase, he leans back to rest on the backs of his legs as his fists twitch at his sides. It's nice to see that he's having a hard time fighting this pull as much as I am. My heart hammers harder as his perusal trails up from my feet to where our eyes meet once more.

His hands hesitate briefly before I feel his warm touch against my ankles, making my breaths shallow. Shivers race down my spine as goosebumps erupt over my skin, and he slowly glides up my legs. His touch is light, almost non-existent, as if he was afraid I might pull away.

Only, I won't. I'm fully immersed in this force field. My feet are rooted to the ground as if they were mixed with cement. As terrifying as this feels, a thrill rushes through me, the anticipation seeping into every fiber of being.

He parts the slit of my skirt, exposing my golden skin as his lips meet the sensitive flesh outside of my knee. My breathing becomes ragged as my skin tingles everywhere he touches.

The languid ascent continues as his fingers trace the curve of my thighs while his mouth trails over everywhere his hands reach first. As close as he is to the apex of my thighs, Tristan never allows his fingers the chance to graze my pulsing center, where he would no doubt find me embarrassingly soaked.

Those darkened eyes are laced with so many emotions swirling around the amber, green, and brown specs as he stares up into my soul. Lust mixes with a promise of trust, but underneath it all is submission.

Is Tristan giving himself to me? Has this been something he's been desperately craving?

"I've wanted this for so long." His whispered admission is rough with emotion, spoken against my hipbone as he leaves a featherlight kiss. "I've wanted *you*, Firecracker."

Flames lick across my body as his words ignite a fire deep inside my soul. The walls I've built around my heart start to crumble. Reaching down, I trail my fingers over the neatly faded sides of his dark brown skin. It's his turn to shiver at my caress before my fingers thread through the longer hair on the top of his head. I can't resist the urge to tug at his soft, messy locks. A soft groan escapes his perfectly parted lips as I continue my perusal. Our eyes never break contact as I cup the side of his angled jaw, feeling the stubble against my palm. I'm eager to feel it graze against my inner thighs.

"Then show me, Tristan," I say, the words tumbling out as a low tremble mixing with my breathy tone. "Show me how much you want me."

Before I even blink, he's rising from his kneeling position, his hands never leaving my body as they roam over my hips. His exploration continues over the sliver of exposed skin, over my ribs, before cupping my breasts and rubbing his thumb over my hardened nipples. Each touch is like a jolt of electricity slicing through my body and straight to my throbbing pussy.

Tristan's six-foot-three frame hovers over me as he leans in. His eyes dart from each of mine, as if he's reading my soul, waiting for me to shatter this moment. There must be something in my gaze he approves of because, within seconds, he's leaning into me. My pulse stutters as he captures my mouth with his.

The kiss has fireworks exploding behind my closed eyes. Colors burst in this fierce, all-consuming kiss. Years of pent-up energy and longing are erased in seconds. His hands dart to my hair, where he tangles his fingers in my loose curls before he's gripping the back of my neck.

Gone is the swishing of the overhead fan blades and the whirring of the air conditioning unit. No noise is left except for the whooshing of our hearts beating at a rapid pace.

His hold tightens, squeezing the delicate flesh near my thundering pulse. When I gasp at the feeling, Tristan takes full advantage of my lips parting as he plunges his tongue into my waiting mouth. The movement has me melting into his broad chest.

As our tongues tangle and lips devour, we exchange moans filled with hunger. Everything in this moment is heated with raw desire. This is when everything changes. Our working relationship will never be the same again. All the years of dueling are being erased with every kiss and sensual touch.

Tristan is the first to break the kiss as his eyes land on mine. Our chests heave, my panties are completely soaked, and I can tell he's just as aroused as I am based on the erection digging into my stomach.

As we watch each other, our gazes reflect the same thing. This was just the beginning. It's been a long time coming and both of us are ready to embrace whatever this spark between us is.

"Dammit, Firecracker," he rasps. "I knew kissing you would blow my mind, but I never realized how much you would ruin me."

"Then why did you stop?" I ask, holding back a whimper. He has me feeling needier than I ever have and we've barely done anything.

He flashes me his signature smirk. "Oh, we're just getting started."

Tristan drops to his knees in front of me again. Never in my wildest dreams would I imagine this scene. Fingers trail up my legs as he finds the hidden zipper on the side of my skirt and pulls it down the rest of the way from where I started it before he came marching into my room. Fabric pools at my feet and I watch his eyes widen. I'm standing before him in sandals and a sage-colored lacy thong, my upper half still covered by the off-the-shoulder cropped top.

"So fucking perfect." His voice is deep and raspy as his fingers smooth back up my legs before slipping underneath the tiny strap holding the scraps of fabric together. Trailing the lace down my legs, he tosses it behind him before finding me watching him again.

"Such a pretty pussy." His eyebrow quirks, as if he's asking for permission, and with a terse nod, I grant him what he's desperate for. His nose slides across my bare pussy, a groan rumbling past his lips before he's covering my mound with his mouth.

His words make me tremble. I've never had a man speak to me in such a filthy manner. The words only turn me on more, causing me to spread my legs wider to make room for his strong shoulders. I've become so desperate for this man's touch, and we've barely begun.

Tristan licks me from slit to opening, before flicking my clit with his tongue. My head snaps out as I release a guttural moan, one I don't even recognize the sound of. It's been so long since I've been touched by a man. So long since someone has tasted me. Not that I have much experience in that department, which is why his sudden action surprises me most. Reaching one hand behind my thigh, he widens my legs before propping my leg on his shoulder. "Keep this here, baby."

He sucks my folds into his mouth as he places a finger at my entrance. I'm wet and needy and desperate for more, more, more. Looking up at me, he chuckles against my skin. Apparently, I mumbled "more" because that's what Tristan gives me.

"Oh god," I moan.

He plunges a second finger into my pussy as he begins working me from the inside while he sucks my sensitive clit into his mouth and nibbles. A tightness coils inside my belly as I ride his face and fingers.

"Yes, Tristan. Oh my god, right there," I chant, reveling in the way he's playing my body as if it's his favorite instrument.

Breaking away, his tongue laps at my entrance as he eats me like a starved man while he finger-fucks me with fervor. It doesn't take long before I feel the build-up pushing me right over the edge of ecstasy.

"Tristan!"

His mouth pops free, but his fingers continue pumping in and out of my pussy. I can hear how aroused I am by the sounds of my wetness against his hand. He stares up at me from his vantage point on the ground as he watches me fall apart.

"That's it, Firecracker," he grunts as he pushes a third finger inside of me. "Fuuuuck. You look so perfect coming on my fingers. I can't wait to watch you come on my cock."

His filthy words are the final push I need before I'm coming with a cry as my body trembles. Chest heaving, Tristan continues to rub circles against my swollen clit as he milks the rest of my orgasm, which feels like it's never going to end. My knees weaken, and before I have a chance to sag onto the carpet, a strong arm wraps around my waist.

Looking up in a pleasured daze, I find my Tristan's lust-filled eyes. He brings his fingers to his mouth, the ones that were just inside of me, and sucks them clean. I swear I could come again just from the sight. A drunken smile spreads across my face, and I reach my hand around the back of his neck. Pulling his face to mine, I kiss him deeply. The saltiness of my essence hits my tongue as I let out another moan.

But before I have a chance to climb back onto my bed and pull Tristan on top of me, he's planting tiny kisses on my forehead before trailing them down my cheek and across my jaw.

"So fucking perfect when you come, Kennedy," he whispers in my ear. Grazing my hand down his still-clothed body, my fingers find his hard cock and, suddenly, I feel the moisture beginning to drip down my legs. He's huge, and my pussy throbs at what it would feel like to have him sink inside me.

A soft chuckle leaves his lips, always reading my mind. "Not tonight, Ken."

I can't help the pouty lips I give him, which has him even more amused. "Tonight was about you, but don't worry, Firecracker. I cannot wait to sink my cock inside your tight pussy."

"Who knew you had such a filthy mouth?" I question on a sigh. "And who knew I would be into it?"

"Only with you," he whispers against my lips before he kisses me. It seems he can't keep his hands off my body now that we've opened the door. And I can't say I hate it.

With a smack to my ass, he reaches for my hand and ushers me to my bed. "Now sleep, pretty girl."

Nibbling on my bottom lip, I start to crawl into my bed. As I stand on my knees, facing him, a brazen feeling rushes over me, and I reach behind me and pull down the zipper holding my top in place. The material skims down my arms as my breasts bounce free. Tristan's eyes widen and flare with desire.

"Stay with me tonight?" My question sounds meek, nowhere near the confident woman I was when I forced the man to crawl on his knees to me.

He nods, running a hand through his mussed hair. "I'll stay with you, but we're sleeping tonight, Ken. I've waited way too fucking long to have this, and I'm not fucking rushing it."

His admission has my heart sputtering against my ribcage. How long has he been wanting this? Us?

Lying back on my bed, I pat the space next to me, a silent agreement that nothing more will happen. But after everything he's arranged tonight, I need him next to me.

After stripping down to his boxers, Tristan slides under the covers and wraps his arm around my naked waist as he pulls me to him. Our heated skin meets, and we both let out matching sighs of contentment.

Tonight, I'm falling asleep wrapped in the arms of Prince Nelson, my enemy turned rival turned something much, *much* more.

Chapter Twenty

Tristan

The golden glow of a new day spills in from the open shutters that line Kennedy's windows. Her gorgeous, naked body is tangled up in my legs as her head rests against my bare chest. For the past few minutes, I've been lying here like a creep as I watch the rise and fall of her chest as her soft snores fill the room. She's breathtaking, which isn't anything new for me to discover, but there's something different about seeing her sleeping. Kennedy's features are softened, and the worry lines have smoothed away, as she's completely unguarded.

I knew her body was perfect. It's evident in her outfits how hard she works to keep her physique, like everything else in her life, but seeing her naked...it was even better than I had imagined. Over the years, I've thought about Kennedy beneath me as I worshiped her body, and I've had my fair share of cold showers. Her passion in the office is sexy as fuck and turns me on in a way I never could have imagined. But getting a real glimpse of her, all of her, was better than any fantasy. The smattering of freckles across her creamy skin is perfect. Hell, even the tiny scar on the inside of her knee adds to her charm.

For so long, I've wanted to push her into telling me what I've done in my past to cause such pain in her eyes. I never could have imagined the truths she spilled last night. My privilege is clearly showing, because it never dawned on me how desperate she was to fit in. To find her place in a completely different world than what she grew up in. I've always had most of everything handed to me. I've never had to walk into a room where people didn't know who I was. I've had the privilege of being a Nelson and, selfishly, I never realized the full extent of the meaning behind my name.

Then, there I was, constantly shitting on everything Kennedy worked so damn hard for. I would've hated me too—the pretentious golden boy who won everything and everyone.

Last night, I would've gladly gotten on my knees and begged for her forgiveness, but then sweet Kennedy uttered those three words.

Crawl to me.

And holy fuck. That was the hottest thing anyone has ever demanded from me. It wasn't just the weight of those words; it was who said them. Her sexuality oozed from her, and I would have crawled the island just to see her eyes heat with the same desire that coursed through my body. Her innocence caught my attention, but it was her confidence that drew me to her.

Kennedy Reed is an anomaly. She never backs down from a challenge. Instead, she stands toe-to-toe with whomever is making her feel small. Her shoulders square up as if she's preparing for battle. Her looks are definitely captivating, all that thick copper hair, but it's her mind that makes her shine brighter than anyone else.

My cell phone ringing breaks the stillness in the quiet room, causing Kennedy to wake. She moves her head until her sleepy, green eyes snap to my face. I'm waiting for the moment when she freaks out about the two of us lying in bed together. But it never comes. Instead, a sheepish smile spreads across her face as a slight blush creeps over her freckled cheeks.

"Morning, Firecracker."

She snuggles in closer and turns her head away from me before mumbling against my chest. "Morning, Golden Boy."

Ignoring my phone, I take time to properly wish her good morning. Slipping two fingers underneath her chin, I tilt her face up to mine. Her head shakes as she hastily covers her mouth with the hand that was resting on my thigh.

"Uh-uh," she mumbles. "Morning breath."

"Jesus, Kennedy." I roll my eyes. "I was eating your pussy like a goddamn delicacy last night. Do you think I give a fuck about your morning breath?"

Her eyes widen with a flash of desire at the reminder. Taking advantage of her state of shock, I remove her hand and lean forward until my lips touch hers. Thick, swollen, and bruised from the night before. Heat swirls through my veins at our connection.

I hope Kennedy doesn't plan on letting me go, because there's no way in hell I'm letting her slip past me again.

She melts into my side as she deepens our kiss, fully embracing the connection. Trailing my fingers up her bare back, goosebumps erupt in my perusal, waking something else up beneath the sheets.

The blaring sound of my phone ringing again startles us. Kennedy jumps apart as if we are two teenagers being caught by their parents. Internally groaning, I reach over blindly and feel around until my fingers hit the cool surface of my phone. Bringing it to my face, 'Dad' flashes across the sheet.

It's like a bucket of cold water splashes over us as Kennedy rolls out of my hold.

"Take it," she says. Her legs escape the sheets as she slips from the bed. "I've got to get ready for work anyway."

I know she's right and we both need to get ready for work, but after last night, I wanted to steal a few more moments before she freaks out. There's no doubt in my mind that Kennedy is going to have a mental spiral where she completely panics over her sleeping with her "enemy."

Dragging my thumb across the answer button, I bring the phone to my ear as I scoot higher up the bed, the white sheet pooling around my waist. "Yeah?"

"About time you answered," Dad barks on the other end, stern and impatient, like he always is with me. Now I'm really glad I ignored his call earlier. "Are you sleeping through my calls? Just because you're at a tropical resort doesn't mean you're on vacation."

I adjust my position on the bed, the slightest bit self-conscious about being naked while speaking to my father. The sheets rustle against my legs, the cool fabric contrasting the warmth of my skin—which is heating by the second. The urge to snap back with a sarcastic comment has me biting my tongue.

"Of course, sir." Scrubbing a hand down my face, the rough texture of my trimmed beard meets my palm. My dad has a knack for making me feel like a kid again every time we talk.

His voice drones in my ear, going on about my responsibilities in the company, how deadlines are suggested, and that he's extremely frustrated the building plans haven't been approved yet. Once again, he's threatening to fire Kennedy and, once again, I'm reassuring him that they will be approved by the end of the week. Kennedy is doing the best she can, given the circumstances, and there's no way in hell I'm letting him fire her over something out of her control. Not when I've had a front-row seat to witness how hard she's fighting for our company.

I should be taking this call seriously—it's one of Dad's biggest complaints, my lack of dedication, but my mind is elsewhere. Through the open bathroom doorway, I catch a glimpse of Kennedy's bare back as the sound of the shower echoes softly in the background. She moves with a casual grace as steam billows around her. The sight of her flawless skin brings me back to last night—the arousal in her emerald eyes, the daring light in them when she told me to submit to her, and the way her moans filled my ears. Everything about Kennedy Reed is sexy. She exudes confidence that would make lesser men crumble at her feet.

The memory of her breathless laugh, her satiated smile, and the way her eyes danced in the dimly lit room makes my pulse quicken.

Fuck, this woman.

Waking up with her snuggled into my chest, her red hair cascading over the white sheets, and our legs tangled together felt like an alternate reality. One I never wanted to wake from.

Too bad life doesn't work that way.

Squealing from the bathroom interrupts my daydream. I jolt upright, ready to burst into the bathroom, when she comes sprinting into the bedroom, completely naked, her phone clutched to her chest. A brimming smile spreads across her face, causing her freckles to dance.

"Babe! The plans got approved!" she shouts, eyes wide with excitement, but it's the term of endearment that has *my* eyes widening.

I almost missed it. Almost. One word caused my brain to short circuit, but as soon as it caught up, the weight of it hit me. Did she mean to say it? The way the word rolled off her tongue, all casual and sure, she might as well have called me "hers." And I know to most, it's not a big deal, but to me, it felt like everything.

Realization of what she just called me flashes across her face as she bites down on her lip, uneasiness marring her features. It's as if she didn't mean for the word to slip. But her features quickly change. With a quirk of an eyebrow, a sly grin tips the corner of her lips, Kennedy gives me a small shrug as if to say 'yeah, I just called you babe. What are you going to do about it?'

I can't help but grin, her energy infectious. My dad's irritated voice in my ear breaks the silence. "What the hell was that?"

I quickly cover the phone with my hand, muffling our sounds as she dances around, still buzzing from the news. "Uh—nothing, just...the plans. She just got the email. They're approved," I explain, trying to keep my voice steady as she bounces around, completely carefree and very much unclothed.

I never want to go a day without seeing her like this.

If only there was a way to freeze time.

Informing my dad that I will call him back later, I end our call and toss the phone haphazardly on the bed as I continue to watch her.

I'm paralyzed in this spot—unable to take my eyes off her. Barefoot, red hair messy from yesterday's curls, naked as the day she was born, she's twirling, dancing, laughing—so full of happiness it's impossible not to smile.

I lean against the headboard, arms crossed over my chest, watching her with this stupid grin on my face.

God, she's beautiful.

I've never seen her like this, and it does something to me, makes that slow-burning attraction flare into a full-blown inferno. Every step, every spin, it's like she's putting on a show for me.

Only, I know she isn't. It's almost as if she's forgotten I'm here and this is the real Kennedy. No walls, no guards, just her.

Her hips sway and I'm gone. It's all I can do not to reach out, grab her, and worship every inch of her flawless body, but I'm perfectly content to just watch. I know how happy she was to land the lead on this project and how worried she was about losing it, especially with my dad threatening her.

Then it happens. Her foot catches on a shoe, and in slow motion, she's flailing, arms windmilling as she goes down. I'm already moving, heart in my throat, ready to catch her, help her, do something—but before I can even get to her, I hear it.

Laughter. Her laughter is bright and loud as she sprawls on the floor, totally unbothered by the fall.

I pause, torn between concern and amusement, until her eyes find mine, twinkling with mischief. "I'm fine," she says, still laughing, and I can't help but laugh too, shaking my head. Of course she is. That's her, always full of surprises. The chemistry between us is electric—I can feel it buzzing in the air—and now I'm standing over her, rock hard at the sight of her naked below me, holding out my hand to help her up. There's no use in playing it coy by trying to hide how badly I want her, not with my dick standing at full attention.

"You sure you're okay?" I ask, my voice a little rough, the words coming out huskier than I intended. Her hand slides into mine, warm and soft, and when she's back on her feet, we're standing too close. Too close not to kiss, but just far enough to keep the tension simmering between us.

"Never better," she says with a wicked smile, her gaze lingering on mine. And damn, I want her.

Chapter Twenty-One

Kennedy

Whirlwind.

That's the only word I can use to describe the last forty-eight hours. I can barely wrap my head around everything that's happened. It's like I blinked, and I've gone from being buried under the stress of trying to get the building permit approved to standing on-site, watching crews prepare for the construction of the overwater villas. My mind is still reeling from it all—racing through the frantic phone calls, the long meetings, and the nagging pressure that we were behind schedule and the threat of losing my job. It wasn't until the plans were finally approved that I even allowed myself to breathe again.

Then, of course, there was *him*.

As I'm standing here on the resort property, watching the construction crews move like ants as they start work on the villas, I feel like I've been spun in a thousand directions at once. My mind is a mess, constantly shifting between excitement and anxiety, between thinking about the project and *him*. It's like I can't separate the two—this mix of professional and personal chaos—and I don't know which is making my heart race faster.

This villa project is going to be a massive success, but I can't help thinking about how last night seemed like the start of something just as big. Something I'm not sure I'm ready for.

My phone ringing in my pocket has me startling out of my daydream. The tropical heat and humidity are fogging my brain. Glancing at the screen, I see Lana's name and smile. It feels like forever since I've talked to my bestie. Knowing that it's too loud to answer, I decline her call and type out a text, letting her know I'll call her back shortly.

With one last glance, I find the foreman and make my way toward him.

"Miss Reed," he greets.

I smile warmly as I glance around. Lumber lines the beaches, the sounds of heavy machinery humming and roaring as workers drill deep into the sandy soil, installing pilings that will support the villas. Metal clanking against metal echoes across the shoreline as cranes move in, lifting beams and foundation supports into place. Teams of workers in neon vests and hard hats move with precision, shouting instructions and coordinating tasks as they lay the groundwork for the structures. The air smells of saltwater and fresh lumber, the faint scent of sawdust mixing with the tropical breeze.

"Everything is moving quickly. Thank you for being prepared as soon as we got the go-ahead," I say to the foreman.

"Of course, Miss Reed. We should have the site work and framework finished by the end of next week. We have teams in place to have around-the-clock crews working to ensure we hit the new deadline."

I nod, jotting down his update in my notebook. "That sounds great. I wanted to let you know I'm taking off for the evening, but if you need anything at all, please don't hesitate to call me."

We shake hands on that promise, and I move through the silky sand as the early evening sun beats down on me. A glass of wine and my bikini are calling my name. It's been an exhausting work week, so I'm ready to be out of work mode.

I'm met with the rush of air-conditioned air as I step out of the elevator, a welcome contrast to the heat that's been clinging to my skin all afternoon. Hours under the beaming sun with the construction crew, overseeing every detail, left my skin warm and tinged pink. I'm sure I was a pest to them, but there was no way I wasn't going to verify they were in line with the blueprints and the very specific building permits. I wasn't risking any more delays on this project.

I roll my neck and feel the twinge of my muscles as I let my bag slip down my arm and land on the couch with a soft thud. Slipping out of my sandals, I head straight to the galley kitchen. The penthouse is quiet except for the soft whir of the A/C unit, which is a stark contrast to the bustling resort. Normally, I'd be welcomed with Tristan's deep timber, but right now, it's just me. It's well after five on a Friday, and he's been a firm believer of business hour boundaries since we arrived on the island, which means he must've gotten caught up with something important.

My fingers instinctively swipe across my phone, pulling up my best friend's name. A quick tap and the FaceTime call rings out as I prop the phone against a decorative bowl on the counter. The fridge door effortlessly pops open, and I smile at the sight of the chilled bottle of rosé, which has been calling my name for the past hour.

I reach for the bottle and bring it to the counter as I pull a crystal glass from the cabinet and wait for Lana to answer. Pulling the cork out, the pop sounds as my nose is met with the sweet, fruity scent of the wine. The call connects as I pour the blush-colored wine into a glass, the soft glug filling the silence.

"She's aliiiiive," my best friend answers in dramatic fashion as her face fills the screen.

"Lana, Lana, bo-fana," I say by way of greeting.

We share a chuckle as I bring the glass to my lips and savor the light, refreshing taste of the fruity wine. Grabbing my phone, I hold it in the air until I have the perfect angle as I wander toward my room—phone in one hand and wine in the other.

"How's my badass designer queen doing?" my bestie asks, her voice crackling. I walk through the doorway of my room and feel my shoulders relax.

My eyes land on my bed as images of Tristan and me tangled in my sheets flash through my mind. Last night, we each slept in our own rooms, and I'm not even going to lie, I missed being in his arms. I can't explain the cosmic shift between us. How I went from hating him to drooling over his delicious body. All I know is that one night with Tristan will never be enough. Well, until reality slaps us in the face and we go back to New York.

"Earth to Kenny..."

Shaking my head, I fix my eyes back on my screen. "Sorry, girl, it's been a crazy couple of days."

I toss the phone onto the bed, flipping it so she can still see me, then set the glass of wine on the dresser. The air is lighter now, my shoulders no longer weighed down by the stress of the day. I open the closet and thumb through bikinis, finally settling on one with tropical colors.

"Spill. The. Tea. I know that look on your face. It's the look of you hiding something from me."

I snort, grabbing my bikini from the drawer. "You have *no* idea."

"Oh, I think I have some idea," she teases and leans in closer to her screen. "That grin is telling me everything. Something definitely happened. Did you finally—"

"Make out with Tristan? Oh yeah," I blurt out, heat rising to my cheeks. "A few times. It wasn't planned. I mean, one minute, he's surprising me with a sunset cruise and dinner at the resort. Then, the next thing I know, I'm basically mounting him in the middle of the restaurant."

I can't help the smile that spreads across my face as I tie the bikini strings behind my neck. The memory of his lips on mine, the way his hands held me so close... My stomach does a little flip just thinking about it.

Her jaw drops, eyes wide as saucers. "Wait. Hold up. You kissed *Tristan*? You kissed him after months of all that tension and denial? Oh my god. Tell me everything!"

With my bikini on, I turn back to the phone, pausing long enough to grab my glass of rosé off the dresser. "It wasn't just a kiss. I mean, yes, we kissed, but it was more than that. It was..." I hesitate, unsure how to explain the intensity of the moment. "It was like everything that's been building between us finally snapped into place."

As I head toward the balcony, her squeal of excitement rings through the penthouse. "Oh my god, this is like a *movie!*"

Laughing, I step outside, where the warm breeze greets me. The sun is just beginning to set, casting a golden glow over the ocean. I settle onto a lounger, stretching out as I sip my wine. "I know, right? It felt surreal. But now I don't know what happens next. He's still technically my boss and *Tristan*, and that complicates everything."

She rolls her eyes dramatically. "Girl, you kissed him! That's huge! Was it everything you imagined?"

I pause, closing my eyes for a moment as I replay the memory of his lips and the feel of his hand on the small of my back. "I never imagined kissing Tristan Nelson. You and Zoe have always thought this would happen, not me. But if I'm being honest, the man can kiss."

She claps her hands in delight. "I knew it! The tension has been driving me crazy through the phone, so I can't imagine what it's been like for you. I've got to know all the details. What the hell happened to change things?"

"Two nights ago, I came home from work with a surprise sunset cruise planned," I start, settling deeper into the lounger as the breeze teases loose strands of my hair, carrying the faint scent of salt and hibiscus. "Never in a million years would I have imagined that Tristan Nelson would plan a sunset cruise and dinner for us."

"Wait, what?" Lana's surprised expression reminds me of exactly how I felt that day.

Lifting my glass, I take a sip of wine before continuing. "Yeah, imagine my surprise..." I pause, a soft smile tugging at my lips. "Lan, the way he looked at me as the sun faded, it was like he could see right through my walls. It was everything I didn't know I needed from him. Like he could finally see *me*."

"Aww," she coos, her eyes softening.

"For so long, we've been at war with each other." I look away sheepishly. "A battle I started, only for him to prove me wrong in the most epic of ways."

"What do you mean?"

Resting my wineglass on my stomach, I stretch my legs and let the warmth from the setting sun sear my bikini-clad body. "He confessed that he's never viewed me as the competition or his rival. Which means I created this entire narrative in my head and was so hellbent on proving I was right, only to be completely wrong."

"I told you that you were making a bigger deal out of things," she says with a shrug, and I glare at her.

"Not the time."

She chuckles, and I stare out over the phone at the birds floating in the ocean breeze as images of that night flash in my head. I nibble on my lower lip as a blush creeps across my cheeks. "I didn't expect the night to end the way it did."

"What happened?" Lana gasps, bring the phone closer to her face. "I swear, Kenny, I'm going to hang up the phone if you don't get on with it."

"Okay, okay." I huff a laugh. Leaning closer to the screen, I lower my voice, even though no one else is around to hear. "You're not going to believe what I said to him."

Her eyebrows shoot up, intrigued. "Oh, this is going to be good."

"I told him to crawl to me," I whisper, my lips curving into a shocked grin. "Like, literally crawl to me. I have no idea where that came from. He asked what he could do to fix things between us, and that's just...what popped out."

Her mouth falls open, and I can practically feel her jaw hitting the floor through the screen. My expression mirrors hers—eyes wide, cheeks flushed, my fingers still clutching the side of my face as if that might stop the heat from spreading.

"Oh my god, Kenny, you did not?"

I nod.

"What did Prince Nelson do?"

"He did it." I shake my head, almost like I'm trying to wake up from some crazy dream. But the smirk tugging at my lips gives me away.

Giddiness radiates from Lana as she squeals with excitement. "I am so here for this new Kenny."

With a smile, I take another lazy sip of rosé, letting the chilled wine roll across my tongue before I glance back at the screen. "Oh, there's more."

"Spill!" Lana demands.

I roll my eyes and adjust the screen. "The next morning, I woke up with him still in my bed."

Lana's eyebrows exaggeratively wiggle in a suggestive way, causing me to giggle.

"Anyway, I went to take a shower, and that's when I got the email that the plans had been approved. Without a thought, I took off back into the bedroom, completely naked, might I add, and started moving in this ridiculous celebratory dance."

"Oh my god." She cackles, throwing her head back as the phone shakes in her head.

Nodding in disbelief, I add, "Not only did I dance for him, naked, but he was on the phone with his dad. And then I tripped over my shoe and fell flat on my face."

"Kenny, that's classic. I wish there was video evidence."

My face scrunches. "Ew, I was naked."

"Semantics." She waves me off. "Happiness looks good on you, babe."

I try to keep the smile on my face, but I feel the corners sagging as doubts cripple my mind. Adjusting the strap of my top, I battle my inner overthinker.

Lana notices the shift in my mood. "This is your moment, why are you hesitating?"

I shift on the lounger, staring out at the waves. "It's just... I went from hating him to wanting him in the span of, like, forty-eight hours. One minute, he's infuriating, and the next, we're making out, sitting around a fire pit like it's the most natural thing in the world. What if it's just a phase?"

Her expression softens as she tilts her head. "Look, it's clear you're not just physically attracted to him. You've been stewing on this for a while. Maybe now that things are happening, it feels like too much, too fast, but that doesn't mean it's not real."

"I don't know. We kissed, and I can't stop thinking about him, but he's still my boss, and that power dynamic...it's weird."

She shakes her head, taking a long sip of her drink. "Okay, but think about it this way—if the roles were reversed, and you weren't working together, would you still feel this way about him?"

I bite my lip as I consider it. "Yeah. Yeah, I think I would."

"Then that's all you need to know," she says with a grin. "Boss or not, you're into him and, clearly, he's into you. This isn't some office fling—it's been brewing, especially on his side. You don't need to know all the answers right now."

I take a slow sip of wine as I let her words sink in. "I just...don't want to screw it up. We're in such a weird spot. What if this ruins everything?"

Her voice drops to a more serious tone. "Babe, if you're worried about screwing it up, that means you care. But you can't let that fear stop you from exploring something that could be great. You've already got chemistry—don't let logistics ruin that."

I laugh softly, feeling some of the tension ease. "You always know what to say. And yeah, I guess you're right. It's just...a lot."

She raises her glass. "To 'a lot,' because that's where the good stuff happens. And to you finally making out with Tristan!"

For the next fifteen minutes, the two of us continue catching up before she has to hop off for dinner reservations.

The sun slowly dips lower, and as I lie back on the lounger, the uneasiness remains in the back of my mind, but it's lighter now. Maybe she's right. Maybe I just need to lean into whatever this is and see where it takes me—after all, the chemistry is undeniable.

Chapter Twenty-Two

Tristan

I hate working late on Fridays.

By the end of the week, I'm tired of being in a suit and tie, of sitting through meetings and being under my father's microscope. It didn't bother me as much when we were in the city, but now that paradise is out my window, I'm ready to call it a day.

I'm ready to spend time with *her*.

Especially now that I've had a taste. My fingers twitch in my lap as I listen to Xander drone on about something. I quit listening as soon as the clock struck five and I saw a flash of copper through the window.

"Tristan, are you still with us?" My eyes snap to the video meeting, where my brother's face fills the screen.

Nodding, I glare at him, which causes him to smirk. The asshole.

"Great." Xander claps his hands together. "If no one has anything else, we can call this meeting. Have a great weekend, everyone." No one says anything and I quickly end the meeting. An ice-cold island beer and an evening with Kennedy are calling my name.

I unplug my laptop and gently slide it into my bag before wrapping the charging cord and placing it next to my computer. Flipping my notebook shut with a soft *thud*, it's the only sound in the room except for my rapidly beating heart. My body moves with purpose, as if it's on autopilot, thankfully, since my mind is elsewhere.

My thoughts drift to the penthouse—*our penthouse*—and I wonder what she's doing. Is she relaxing with a glass of wine on the oversized couch, catching up on a reality show? Or is she slipping out of her work clothes and dipping into the cool plunge pool, wearing nothing at all? She has no idea how badly I want to demand—no, beg—her to never wear clothes in that pool.

Standing from the chair, I sling the strap of my bag over my shoulder. My fingers drum against my slack-covered thigh as nervous energy bubbles beneath the surface. She's always pushed my buttons and challenged everything I do to keep me on my toes, but this tension is unlike anything else.

I flick off the light, then move through the quiet hallway as I make my way to the exit. Pushing open the glass door, I'm hit with one last burst of cold air, contrasting sharply with the hot, humid tropical air that greets me. The resort's white stucco walls glimmer in the sunlight and the palms sway lazily in the breeze. As I walk along the sidewalk, the sound of distant ocean waves mixes with the whir of heavy machinery as crews continue their construction on the villas.

The walk is short, but it doesn't keep my mind from spinning. In the office, we clash over everything—design elements, timelines, and budgets. Hell, even here on the island, she finds new things to fight me on. We butt heads like it's part of our job requirement.

But in the penthouse... God, the tension between us is a whole different beast. Or maybe we're finally accepting the pull that everyone in my life seems to sense. The silent moments hang thick in the air with something unspoken. Every glance feels charged. Each moment we share a game we're both playing, but no one gave us the rule book.

Despite how fast everything seems to be moving, I miss having her near. Last night, we both slept in our own beds, but it felt wrong. After one night of having her in my arms, it was like she was always meant to be there.

I know it's crazy how quickly things are shifting, but it feels real—like I've been waiting for her all along. There's the other side to it, though, the part that keeps me up at night. I'm her boss. This isn't just some fling. Is it even acceptable in the company? I know what people will think, what they'll say about her. She's too good at her job to be reduced to some baseless rumor that she's sleeping her way to the top. I want to protect her, shield her from the gossip mill that will undoubtedly churn the second we arrive back in New York.

I know she needs time to catch up to these new feelings, time to make sense of all this. And I'll be patient. I will because she's worth waiting for. But God, I hope she realizes soon. I don't want to waste any more time not exploring this. It's like the universe finally aligned to bring us to this point, and I can't let that slip through my fingers.

As I'm reaching out to press the button to call the elevator, my phone rings from my pocket, causing my thoughts to evaporate. A deep sigh leaves my lungs as I glance down at the screen.

"Great," I mutter under my breath as I see Xander's name flash across the screen. What else could he have to talk about? I've just listened to his voice for the last two hours in back-to-back meetings.

Swiping the phone, I move away from the elevator toward a bench as I bring the phone to my ear. "It's after five on a Friday. I'm off the clock."

Xander chuckles, and I roll my eyes. "Aw, little brother, you're a Nelson. There's no clocking out."

"Yeah, well, I'm turning over a new leaf and embracing island time."

"Speaking of island time, how're things with your fiery roommate?"

"Things are fine," I say, hoping my tone doesn't give anything away. Xander has a gift for reading between the lines.

When he hums, the hair on my neck rises. Has someone from the resort reported to him that Kennedy and I have been going on dates? I mean, yeah, I'm using them as dates, but they are test runs for the resort.

"Interesting." He pauses as another voice can be heard on the other end of the line. Xander muffles the receiver. Taking the opportunity, I stand from the bench and make my way back over to the elevator. I press the call button while he has a side conversation, and I hope the metal elevator causes the signal to drop.

"*Fine* is an interesting word," he says as I step into the elevator. "You've always said how challenging she can be."

"She is, but we have to spend a lot of time together, so we're making the best of it."

"Yeah, I bet you are."

A surge of warmth rises to my face. Xander always has a way of getting under my skin, but this time, he's right on the money, and if I'm not careful, he'll figure it out completely. Then who knows what he would do with that information? He'd no doubt tell my sister, and Victoria would have no problem blabbing, especially to my mother. Mom is ready for grandkids, which are not on my radar.

The elevator dings, and the doors slide open, revealing the penthouse floor. Stepping out, adjusting the strap of my bag, I let my gaze roam over the space that is free of Kennedy. Disappointment flashes through me as I stride to the end of the hall, where our rooms are.

"I'll catch up with you later, alright? I've got to check on some things here."

Xander chuckles on the line again, and it grates my nerves. "Yeah, yeah. Don't let her run you ragged. Or, you know, maybe do. You need to get laid, little brother. You're too uptight."

I shake my head, my lips twitching into a grin. I'm the least uptight out of all of my siblings. It's the reason why I'm always on my father's shit list. "Later, Xander."

Ending the call, I tuck my phone back into my pocket. My heart beats a little faster as I approach the doors to our bedroom. The memory of our last conversation replays in my mind. That stubborn fire in her eyes when we disagreed. The way she leaned over the counter late at night, casually eating takeout like we weren't at each other's throats just hours before.

Kennedy's voice filters through her open patio doors. She's on the phone, and I don't want to interrupt her. The sound of her laughter causes a smile to spread across my face. I love hearing her laugh. So carefree and happy.

Turning toward my room, I loosen the tie on my neck, which feels like a noose. With it removed, I let out a relieved sigh as the tension from the day melts away. The dress shirt comes next, buttons undone one by one until I shrug it off and toss it onto the bed. I kick off my shoes, then step out of my dress pants, leaving them in a heap with the rest of my workday. My hands automatically reach for the cargo shorts I threw in the closet, paired with a casual tee.

But I can't forget the finishing touch—my Birkenstocks. She teases me relentlessly about them, but the way she laughs when she sees me in them? It's worth it every time. It's this little inside joke between us, one that seems to soften whatever tension lingers in the air.

As I pull on the shorts and slip into my sandals, I decide tonight's the night. We've both had a whirlwind of a week, from the building plans finally being approved to everything that's been brewing. We need to celebrate. Not just the end of a crazy week, but...whatever this is between us. Maybe tonight we'll figure out where it's going.

"Hey, you're home." Kennedy's voice is sweet from behind me.

After I changed, I decided to give her more time to herself. So instead of joining her on the balcony, I cracked open a bottle of beer and enjoyed the silence on the couch. Turning my head, I watch her strut her bikini-clad body closer to me, and I fight the reaction in my shorts. Her smile is bright, her cheeks flushed, and my heart races at the sight.

"Want to go out tonight, Firecracker?" My voice is husky, and I clear my throat, shaking off the stupor I find myself in whenever she's near.

She makes her way around the coffee table until she's between my spread legs. Her gaze trails over my body, leaving a heated path as they roam. Reaching forward, she plucks the beer bottle from my hand before taking a sip. I shake my head as a grin spreads behind the bottle.

"I'll never say no to a night out with you."

Chapter Twenty-Three

Kennedy

Thick and warm air wraps around me like a blanket as we step out of the penthouse elevator. The island feels so still, almost eerie, without the usual sounds of tourists. I still can't get used to a vacant resort. The clanking sounds of construction that fill the day can be heard in the distance as crews work around the clock. But right here, it's just us, the quiet hum of nature, and the soft rustle of palm leaves in the breeze. I breathe in the salty air, the scent of the ocean filling my lungs and the slight masculine smell from Tristan's cologne floods my senses as I try to ignore the nerves twisting in my stomach.

The path beneath my sandals is hard against my feet as we walk, the faint sound of our footsteps the only noise breaking the silence. His hand brushes mine, just barely, but it's enough to send a spark along my skin. Every time he touches me, it's like a fire ignites in my chest, and I'm not sure if it's the island heat or just him.

Probably him.

I glance over, his laid-back island vibe evident in the way he's dressed—khaki shorts, a loose button-up shirt left half undone, and those damn Birkenstocks. It's casual, but it looks so good on him. *Too good.* He walks with an easy swagger, the same that's always had me on edge since we started working together. The tension between us is undeniable, simmering just beneath the surface, and tonight...I don't know if I'll be able to keep myself from falling into it completely.

"*Don't overthink it,*" Lana told me on the phone a few hours ago. "*Just go with it. Get out of your head.*"

It's not that simple, though, is it? How do I just let go of all the worries, the doubts, the fear that maybe I shouldn't want this as much as I do? But then I feel his arm brush against mine again, and I think maybe she's right. Maybe I do need to let go.

Glancing up once more, I find his gaze locked on mine, as if he were waiting for me to look at him again. There's a softness around the edges of his eyes—a sexy smirk toys on his face. This version of Tristan is my favorite Tristan. The island life looks good on him.

Smiling, I bite the corner of my lip, and I swear I hear the man growl.

I'm wearing a dress that's a little more daring than I'd usually choose—something tropical, sexy, and fitted just enough to make me feel bold. The dark green fabric clings to my body in all the right places, and I feel his eyes on me as we walk, his gaze lingering on the hem as it sways with each step. It makes my skin tingle, and I bite back a smile, trying to play it cool, even though my heart is racing.

"You're killing me, Firecracker." His words are deep and send a vibration through me. I feel him rake over my body as he inhales deeply before casting his gaze forward.

We reach the edge of the property, and the bar comes into view, its neon sign flickering in the dim light. It's small, the kind of place locals hang out at, and even from here, I can hear the raucous strains of music drifting through the open walls. The lights inside are soft and warm, and there's a buzz of energy that makes my stomach flutter with excitement. Or maybe it's the nerves again.

As we step across the empty parking lot, I glance at him from the corner of my eye, catching a lazy smile on his face. He's in his element, comfortable and confident, and I envy how easy it seems for him. Meanwhile, my mind races, and my thoughts are a jumble. What am I doing? I'm supposed to be working, supposed to be keeping things professional, but all I want to do is give in to the pull between us. My friend's voice echoes in my head again: *Get out of your head.*

Tristan reaches down, and my fingers automatically intertwine with his as we move closer to the lively bar. With a gentle tug, he pulls me to his front as he steps behind me, and we enter the bar. Inside the bar is exactly what I expected—a local dive, half walls separating the inside from the outside, tables scattered around with just a handful of people sitting at them. The stage in the corner has a microphone, and I realize, with a thrill, that it's karaoke night.

"Karaoke," I say with a growing grin. I can't help it—this is exactly the kind of distraction I need.

He chuckles and shakes his head. His lips find the shell of my ear as goosebumps erupt at his nearness. "Don't even think about it."

The crowd cheers for the current singer, who's belting out a song that's way out of their range, but the energy in the room is contagious. For a moment, I forget about the tension, about everything that's been weighing on me.

"I'll get the drinks. You grab us a table," he says, giving me a playful nudge toward the seating area.

I nod, smiling as I slip through the tables, finding one near the back, but still close enough to the stage. Sitting down, I smooth my dress over my legs and let out a breath I didn't realize I'd been holding. The cool plastic of the chair feels good against my skin, grounding me as I try to gather myself.

When he returns with two beers, I take one, our fingers brushing in that electric way, and I can't help but look at him as I sip from the bottle. His hand lingers just a little too long, and my heart skips a beat. Every touch between us is charged with something I'm not sure I can ignore much longer. Maybe I don't want to.

We drink, listening to the locals take the stage one by one. Some of them are surprisingly good, others...not so much, but everyone's having a good time, clapping and cheering, regardless of talent. I laugh more than I have in days, my stress melting away with each swig of beer.

Tonight is everything I didn't know I needed. At some point, Tristan moved his chair closer, erasing the space between us. His tan arm wraps around my shoulder and rests on the back of my chair. The weight of his arm is strong and warm, settling as if it belongs there. The rough pad of his thumb traces slow, absent circles on my bare skin, each motion sending shivers along my spine.

I glance up at him, expecting to catch his eyes, but he's focused, watching the singer with that casual ease I envy. The bright lights of the stage glimmer across his face, casting shadows along his sharp jaw. I want to pepper that jaw with kisses and feel the stubble against my delicate skin.

He's leaning back in his seat, legs spread wide in that infuriatingly attractive way men seem to own without even trying, everything about him content. He's completely at ease, like this—like us—is the most natural thing in the world. But every brush of his thumb tells a different story, one that makes it harder to breathe.

"This place is really cool." My eyes scan around the bar and land on a group of locals throwing darts.

"You ever play?"

Turning my head, I find Tristan watching the same group. "Darts were never my thing. Pool, I can play, but not darts."

He hums as he brings his bottle to his lips, his Adam's apple bobbing as he swallows. His tongue peeks out as he licks the drop that escapes. My thighs clench at the idea of his tongue on me again.

"I never would have pegged you for a pool shark."

"I'm full of surprises, baby," I say playfully, flashing him a wink. His chuckle rolls warmly over me like the waves crashing on a nearby shore—powerful and soothing.

"Yes, you are, Firecracker. So many surprises." Tristan's husky voice is like velvet as his smooth lips land on my skin. He trails soft kisses around my collarbone and higher up my neck before he's sucking my flesh between his teeth. With a gentle bite, he laps at the mark before he's pulling away, and I'm fighting the moan desperate to break free. Then he moves fluidly and positions himself in the same casual manspread, as if nothing just happened.

Meanwhile, I'm a soaked, achy mess, waiting to be devoured. His arm finds the back of my chair as his thumb resumes rubbing against my skin.

"Is this everything you ever wanted?" His question causes me to pause as I look over at him.

My face scrunches with confusion. "What do you mean?"

"Your dream of being an architect. Is this everything you imagined it would be?"

I stare out in front of me as I watch the guy sing a terrible rendition of "Dancing Queen." "Did I imagine that the company I thought I was going to make me senior architect, with the promise to be chief architect in the next two years, would be swallowed up by my college rival family business? No, this isn't everything I imagined it would be."

Tristan's shoulders slump in the seat next to me.

"But I can't imagine it any other way. Turns out, I missed fighting with you."

I feel his deep chuckle reverberate through my body. "Is that so?"

A smile spreads across my face as I nod. I really did miss this. Not only does competing with Tristan fuel my desire to win and be the best, but it gives me a spark of joy.

By the time we're on our fourth round, I'm feeling the alcohol buzz through my system, my body relaxed in a way that makes everything feel a little lighter as every one of our touches lingers longer than the last.

Then, without warning, the DJ's voice booms over the speakers. "Next up, Tristan!"

He freezes, his eyes darting to me, and I can't help my mischievous grin.

"You didn't..." he starts, but I just shrug, trying to look innocent.

"I might've signed you up while I was 'using the bathroom,'" I say, laughing as he groans, running a hand through his hair.

"You're trouble," he mutters. Standing up, he shoots me a playful glare. But there's a smile on his face, and I can see the excitement flickering in his eyes even though he's trying to hide it.

I watch as he walks toward the stage, my heart racing for him. I know he'll be fine—he's always good at everything he does—but there's a thrill in seeing him like this, vulnerable in front of a crowd, even if it's just a handful of locals.

The opening chords of "Party in the USA" start, and Tristan shoots me a scathing look that makes me laugh. The crowd around cheers as they catch on to what song he's about to sing. Tristan shakes out his shoulders as he takes a deep breath before jumping in. His voice isn't perfect, but it's not terrible either, and the crowd seems to love it, clapping and rooting him on like he's a pro. I can't take my eyes off him, the way he loosens up as he sings, the way his confidence grows with each note. When he glances at me, eyes locking on to mine, I can't help but cheer through my laughter. Tossing my arms in the air, I shimmy to the beat as I fully embrace the buzz from the alcohol and the energy radiating around this bar.

When he finally makes his way back to the table, there's a wild grin on his face, and before I can say anything, he pulls me into a kiss, his lips warm and insistent against mine in a way that has me swooning.

"Payback, baby. Just wait," he murmurs against my mouth, and I smile, my heart pounding like it's reaching out to him.

"Bring it on, Golden Boy."

CHAPTER TWENTY-FOUR

TRISTAN

FUCKING KENNEDY, MY LITTLE firecracker.

I try to fight it, but the smile breaks free anyway, tugging at my lips before I can stop it. As soon as my lips met hers, I couldn't fight the desire to get her home and show her how crazy she drives me.

We left the bar a few minutes ago, laughter still echoing between us. I can't help but steal another glimpse of the red-headed wonder who consumes my every thought. Our shoes are long gone as the cool, silky sand spreads between our toes. We opted to walk the moonlit path of the beach rather than the sidewalk. Everything about the connection of her hand in mine feels natural, as if we've always done this.

Kennedy is different tonight—hell, on the island, in general. She's always magnetized my vision, but now my soul craves her. Which is fucking terrifying. The lightness in her nature leaves her free from the pressures of being perfect. The tension that always sits on her shoulder seems to have melted away as we drank, joked, and laughed at tonight's karaoke entertainment. I've seen the girl behind our "rivalry." And now that I've had a glimpse of the real Kennedy, I'm desperate for more.

Her hand slips from my grasp, and I'm immediately hit with an emptiness. With a smirk over her shoulder, Kennedy runs with a gracefulness that looks like she's floating on air as she makes her way to where the earth meets the sea. I stand there, mesmerized by her beauty, as she throws her arms out wide. With her head tilted toward the moon, she twirls in the tide. She's radiating, wild and carefree in a way that makes my chest ache.

"Isn't it beautiful?" Her soft voice snaps me from my trance. With slow steps, I move until I'm near her without interrupting her happiness. "The ocean, Trist. Isn't it just so peaceful?"

"Magical," I say, my voice cracking, and I clear the lust from it.

"No matter what happens with this project, I'm glad I was able to finally see the ocean in all of her glory."

Without thinking, I step closer, reaching out my hand. "Dance with me."

Her steps falter as her sparkling eyes find mine, and she smiles softly. "But there's no music."

"We don't need music, Firecracker," I murmur, taking her outstretched hand and pulling her closer.

She laughs, the sound swept away by the ocean breeze as she places her delicate hand in mine, her other landing on my shoulder.

Glancing down, I watch as the moonlight dances across her face, highlighting the curve of her lips, the way her eyes glimmer with the night sky reflecting in them.

Without thought, our bodies begin to sway to the soundtrack of the waves as if this is the most natural thing either one of us has done. The night air blankets us in our own bubble as we move slowly and unhurried. I'm not sure if it's the alcohol or Kennedy, but I can feel an energy pulsing through my system.

She wanted me to hate her. To fight with her. But all her efforts to push me away fueled me to fall for her more.

It's not long before her body is melting into mine, resting her head under my chin, and I can't help but notice the way her breath matches mine. Both of us enjoying this proximity.

Can she feel my heart beating and how it picks up when she's near?

A quiet sigh leaves her as her hand moves across my chest and slides beneath my shirt opening. A hiss leaves my lips as her fingers caress in gentle circles against my skin.

No words are said, both of us lost in the moment and our endless thoughts.

It's just the ocean, the wind, and the steady beats of our hearts.

·•••·•••··

The smell of fresh coffee fills the air as I stand in the kitchen, leaning against the counter, pajama pants low on my hips. Steam billows, slightly fogging the lenses of my glasses as I hold the warm mug in my hands. My mind drifts to last night. The sound of her laughter, the feel of her in my arms, and the relaxed expression she wore all night.

Soft footsteps sound on the tile floor, pulling me from my memory. Glancing up, my eyes collide with Kennedy's as she walks through the doorway. The morning light filters through the windows, cascading her in an angelic glow. My eyes trail from the copper curls piled messily on the top of her head, down her body, to the tight workout shorts hugging her curves and her sports bra leaving little to the imagination as it shows off her perky tits and toned arms and abs. Tennis shoes cover her feet instead of their usually barefoot nature.

Bringing my eyes back up to hers, it's when I realize she's doing the same to me. Heat flickers through my veins, causing my dick to stir in my thin pajama pants.

"You wear glasses." It's a statement, not a question, as she moves closer. Once she's near, Kennedy grabs the mug from my hands and brings the steamy coffee to her lips. She hums as she takes a sip.

I quirk an eyebrow when she returns the mug to my hand. "There's plenty in the pot."

"Yeah." She shrugs a shoulder. "I like yours better."

"Well, someone is in a good mood this morning."

Mischief sparkles in her emerald gaze. "Turns out, I can't get the image of this guy who sang 'Party in the USA' out of my head."

"That's weird." I smirk down at the little vixen. "I can't get the image of this girl dancing on the beach with me out of my head."

Kennedy flashes me a megawatt smile. "Speaking of the beach, I'm heading for a run."

"Want company?" I ask, setting the mug near the coffeepot to refill later.

"Only if you can keep up." With a wink and a twitch of her lips, Kennedy strides out of the kitchen. I can't help chuckling as I follow her. As she turns toward the living room, I reach out and land a playful slap to her ass. The sound cracks through the quiet space, and she jumps, spinning around with her mouth wide open.

"Did you just slap my ass?" she asks, half laughing and half surprised.

"Don't act like you don't like it," I say with a smug grin.

She gives me a teasing glare as she lands her hands on her hips. With a wink of my own, I move toward my bedroom to change into my workout clothes. I feel her gaze on my back the entire time I walk away. With a glance over my shoulder, I find her cheeks flushed as she averts her gaze.

·····•·•···

The earth moves beneath my feet as each step sucks me deeper into the soft sand, creating a resistance that forces my leg muscles to work harder. Running in the sand is no joke. Sucking in a lungful of salty air, I glance over my shoulder and find Kennedy half a step behind me. A look of determination is spread across her face, and I admire her tenacity. It's the same look she wears when she's fighting for her designs and her ideas.

Her gaze finds mine, eyebrow lifting, before darting past me. The sneaky woman was just biding her time.

"You going to race me, Golden Boy, or are you going to keep staring at my ass?" she shouts over her shoulder before taking off in a sprint.

"Oh, it's on," I mumble as I take off after her.

Wild curls break free from her bun as it bounces on the top of her head. Strong arms pump faster as her legs carry her farther down the beach. It doesn't take me long before I'm catching up to her. Kennedy looks over her shoulder and squeals as I gain speed.

We're nearing the end of the resort's property, but it doesn't stop Kennedy. As we approach the final cabana, she throws her arms in the air while shouting in victory. I can't help but chuckle at the spectacle in front of me. With her pace slowing, Kennedy leans over and places her hands on her knees as she fights to catch her breath.

"Nice race, Firecracker."

"Thanks," she says between gasps. "I didn't think you'd be that fast."

Placing my hands on top of my head, I smile down at her. "What, did you think I'd be too busy staring at your ass to catch up?"

"Honestly, yeah." Moving past me, she walks inside the cabana before collapsing on one of the beds. I watch in fascination as her chest heaves and her eyes close. Without much thought, I make my way over to the bed and plop down beside her. Only the cabana bed isn't very wide, and I land with half of my body on hers, which makes her laugh. Propping my head on my hand, I stare down at her, and almost instantly, there's a shift in the air.

Tension swirls as her emerald gaze flares with desire. Leaning forward, my lips find hers, relishing her gasp that turns into a sigh as her hands wrap around my neck. Plunging my tongue inside her mouth, our tongues graze as my hand smooths up her thigh to her hip. Gently, I roll her body toward me until our fronts are flush. As I glide my hand over her hip to the apex of her thighs, a low moan escapes Kennedy's lips.

"Trist," she murmurs against my lips as my fingers graze her center.

"Ken."

"I'm sweaty."

"I don't care." Trailing my fingertips to the waistband of her shorts, I slip my hand beneath the fabric. Fuck, she's not wearing any panties. My mouth finds hers again as my fingers slip between her slit. Back arching, she hums as I run my fingers back and forth through her pussy, causing her body to shudder. Kennedy's soft hand grips me tighter, causing me to pause.

"Is this okay?"

She nods. "Don't stop, Trist. Please don't stop." Her words turn breathy as her chest heaves.

Fuck.

I move my hand from her shorts, and Ken lets out a deep, frustrated sigh. Chuckling, I press a gentle kiss to her lips before mumbling, "These need to go." Her shoulders sag in relief as I snap the stretchy material against her skin, then trail my touch over the soft curve of her ass before I give her cheek a squeeze.

Rolling her over to her back, I leave a path of kisses and nips from her neck down to her sports-bra covered chest. Her body responds to every little sensation as I lick a path over the fabric of her bra. Flicking my tongue over the buttery material, she jolts at the friction against her stiff nipple. Sucking the peak into my mouth, I roll my tongue and feel it harden even more. With a pop, the material slips from my mouth as I slide down her stomach.

Gripping her waistband, I pull the tight shorts down her legs in one fluid motion, displaying her bare pussy.

"You're so fucking perfect."

Her cheeks pinken at the compliment.

"Let me see all of you," I rasp.

Turning her head to the side, she bites her bottom lip, embarrassment flooding her features. Slowly, she widens her legs as she trails her fingers down her body. My eyes track her movements, all the way down to where she stops between her spread thighs. Cock twitching in my shorts, I watch her openly touch herself. Her arousal glistens as she coats her fingers before she spreads her pussy lips, giving me the full view I'm desperate for.

Never, in all the years I've known her, would I have imagined Kennedy to be so free in her sexuality. Honestly, it's an even bigger turn-on. I'm fascinated as she draws circles around her clit, growing more aroused by the second. Unable to wait any longer, I kneel on the daybed between her spread legs and lean forward. Pushing her hands out of the way, I flick my tongue out and lick her from slit to clit. Both of us groan in relief.

"God, Ken," I mumble against her skin. "I can't get enough of you."

With one last taste, I'm lifting onto my elbows, my eyes finding hers.

"Why'd you stop?" she asks breathily.

"Because this isn't how I wanted our first time to be. You deserve better, Ken."

A smile spreads across her perfect lips as she shakes her head. Her fingers run through my hair, and with a gentle tug, she forces me to look into her eyes again.

"Get out of your head, Nelson." Her touch leaves my hair and trails down over my stubble before her delicate hand is cupping my jaw. "I don't need perfect. I just need you."

I just need you. My chest warms and my heart beats faster as I let those words sink in.

"Now," she starts before pushing against my shoulder. "Roll over."

Yes, ma'am.

With a hand wrapped around her waist, I switch our positions until I'm lying on my back against the canvas-covered mattress. Kennedy shifts her weight, her knees straddling my thighs and her bare pussy hovering over my lap.

"These need to go." She repeats my earlier line as she grips my elastic waistband. I wiggle my hips, and she moves the material down my thighs. Fingertips dance over the ink of my tattoo, and I watch as she admires the design. When my cock twitches, she lets out a soft giggle.

"Someone is impatient."

"Someone is leaking for you."

A shy smile brightens her pretty face as she eyes me.

"Inside my wallet, there's a condom."

She nods before reaching behind her and feeling around for the wallet that's in my back pocket. Removing the foil packet, she rips it open with her teeth before sliding the rubber down my aching dick.

Leaning forward, Kennedy grips my cock in her hand, and I swear her soft touch could have me coming right now. I'm embarrassed at how quickly this is going to be over. Hovering over my cock, she lines me up at her entrance before slowly sitting down.

"Goddamn, Ken. You feel so fucking good" I grit the words while gripping her hip and helping her take me. Inch by inch, her warm pussy swallows me. Her nails dig into my chest, breath catching, and the feeling is electric. I'd welcome that bite of pain any day as long as this is my view.

With her lip between her teeth, we both watch as she takes the rest of me with a roll of her hips.

"Oh god," she cries out, back arching. "You feel so good."

"Yeah, baby. So fucking good." I run my hands up and down her thighs as she uses her hands to anchor herself to my chest, writhing on top of me. We're both panting as we fight not to combust. She feels incredible, just like I knew she would.

Since arriving on this island, there's been a shift between us. It's become an easy routine to be in each other's company. Along the way, we stopped bickering and embraced our attraction. Our banter became foreplay, and while playing with Kennedy, I fell for her.

Kennedy's hands leave my chest as she pushes her sports bra up, exposing her perfect tits. As she rides my cock, she massages her breasts, tugging on her pebbled nipples. The sight is a goddamn dream. My grip tightens on her hips as she rocks back and forth, chasing her impending orgasm.

"Oh my god," she calls out. "This feels so good. You feel so good, Tristan."

"That's it, Firecracker. Ride my cock like the good girl you are."

My praise only spurs her on as her movements become sporadic. Her pussy clenches, her walls tightening around me. My thumb finds her clit as I circle the sensitive spot, applying pressure while she plays with her tits.

"I have never in my life been more turned on than I am right now, Ken. Watching you ride me, your perfect tits bouncing, your hair coming out of your hair tie. Everything about you is wild as you take what you need. You're so goddamn perfect, Kennedy Reed. You're so perfect and you're so *mine*."

She moans in response, riding me harder, and I continue encouraging her, even as I'm struggling to last. "That's it, baby. You feel so fucking good."

With my name on her lips, Kennedy's orgasm rips through her as she moans and trembles. Easing the circles, I draw out every last ounce of her orgasm while she rides out her release. It only takes a few moments before I'm spilling into the condom with a deep groan, feeling like I've just been sent to heaven. She collapses forward, our sweat soaked skin sliding together as our chests heave.

"I could get used to that," she says, sounding blissed out as we find a comfortable position.

"Coming on my dick?"

She shoves my chest and giggles. "No, well, I mean, yes, that too. But I mean waking up in paradise, working out on the beach together, and relaxing with the sounds of the waves as our soundtrack."

Nuzzling my nose behind her ear, I place a gentle kiss below her earlobe. "I could get used to it too."

"If you could live anywhere in the world, where would you live?" Her voice is soft, with a hint of exhaustion and curiosity as the random question comes out of nowhere. It's one of the things I'm starting to adore about her. She never lets an awkward silence fall over us—not that there are many. The questions allow us to continue getting to know each other better.

Without hesitation, I reply, "In the woods on a lake. What about you?"

She nibbles on her lip as she stares ahead as the tide meets the sand. "I love the hustle of the city—the lights, the sounds, the chaos—but this is pretty nice too."

It takes me a second to answer, my attention captivated by the beautiful woman lying in my arms. The words leave my mouth before I have a chance to second guess them. "We'll just have to have two houses. A place in the city and a vacation home on a beach," I say, as if it's the simplest thing in the world.

Her head whips upward, her eyes finding mine already watching her as she blinks at me. "We?" she whispers, almost as if she's afraid she misunderstood me.

A slow smile tips the corners of my mouth at the realization that I said *we*. Not *you*, not *I*. I can feel the weight of that two-letter word hanging in the air, but it doesn't feel heavy. It feels...right.

"Yes, 'we.'" I place a quick peck to her lips, that're still slightly parted from shock. "The city life suits you. We can work there and find a nice cabin on a quiet lake for when we need an escape."

Her gaze drops to where her fingers are lazily drawing shapes on my chest. "I didn't think you'd include me in your dream."

Slipping a finger under her chin, I tilt her head. "This isn't just a fling for me, Ken." My admission comes out low as my heart pounds hard. "Can't really imagine my dreams without you now."

Her eyes search mine, and I hope the sincerity of my words is reflected in them. For the briefest of moments, I'm worried I overstepped. After all, I am waiting for her to catch up to my feelings. But then her lips curl into the softest smile as she tucks a strand of hair behind her ear, snuggling herself closer in my arms.

"As long as you promise I can have a huge dock for my boat," I say, breaking the enchanted spell Kennedy seems to put me in.

"Oh, of course," she mocks. "Whatever Prince Nelson wants."

My fingers shift from where they were running up and down her back to skimming her side. Before she has a chance to see it coming, I find just the right spot to tickle her, pulling a squeal from her lips. Punishment for being such a smartass.

"Fine. Fine," she relents with breathless laughter. I pause my fingers as her giggles fill the space. "But only if you promise I can have a rooftop patio with an oversized lounger."

"Deal," I say, grinning. "I'm pretty sure I'll give you anything you want, Firecracker."

She hums in amusement, like she's pondering what else she could ask for. My fingers tickle her side again, her laugh bubbling out before I stop and stare down at her. When our eyes lock, they're full of warmth and happiness.

In this moment, the world seems quieter. Both of us dreaming of a future neither one of us thought possible.

CHAPTER TWENTY-FIVE

KENNEDY

"You're infuriating!" I practically shout, tossing my hands in the air. Long gone are the niceties.

"Me?" he asks, pointing to his chest. "How can you possibly think that when you're the problem."

It's Christmas Eve and Tristan and I have been in the conference room for the past hour, arguing over the internet with Dave, our IT Director, as we continue to sort out the delay in technology. I'm tired and frustrated on so many levels. Not only am I missing Christmas in the States with my friends and family, but I'm stuck in another battle with *Prince Nelson*. He's back on his high horse, expecting me to bow down to him, but he has another thing coming.

Yesterday was the deadline to have the smart technology system in the rooms up to date; however, Dave informed me that he needs more time. Time is not our friend. The villas are moving at a rapid pace, which means opening day is around the corner.

"Can't we just forget the smart systems?"

"Skip the smart systems?" Leaning forward and placing my weight on my elbows, which are resting on the table, I glare at him. "We've been working on this for weeks. I know we're close. We are close, right, Dave?"

Dave starts to answer my question, but Tristan cuts him off. "Close? It's crashed twice this week, and God knows how many times yesterday."

"We just need more time."

"Time. Time. Time. That's all you request. We don't have more time, Kennedy."

"And what are you suggesting, *Tristan*?" Disdain drips from my words. "Just scrap everything? We might not have time, but it's going to take us even longer to rip everything out that has already been installed."

"That's exactly what I'm suggesting. At least then we'll know things will work and be reliable."

An incredulous laugh erupts from my lips. "So you're suggesting that we go back to door-to-door service and handwritten orders. Yeah, that's going to speed things up."

Tristan leans forward, his mouth opening, but I shove my hand in the air to silence him. "Nelson Signature promised a luxurious resort, including high-end amenities and modern technology. Smart systems are those improvements. We're not going to paper menus and dumbing down the entire experience!"

"Enough with the dramatics, Kennedy. We're still promising high-end amenities, but instead of top-of-the-line technology, we'll have a reliable option, not a goddamn technological nightmare."

I'm taken aback, physically shocked at his outburst, and it's then that I know this isn't his doing. Someone in New York is pulling the strings and Tristan is just the puppet. It pisses me off even more that he's being controlled by the puppet master and not supporting the vision of this project.

Dave slams his notebook shut, startling me as my head whips in his direction. His eyes are wide as he bounces his head between the two of us. "Before you two kill each other, how about we take a deep breath? I'm sure we can all come up with a solution."

"A solution would be for this to have been resolved already." Tristan's glare toward Dave is glacial and has me cringing in my chair.

Spinning toward Dave, I give him my full attention as I wait to see what suggestion he has. But not before sending Tristan a pointed look.

For the next twenty minutes, the three of us hash out a variety of ideas in a somewhat professional manner. Dave has a front-row seat at the Tristan and Kennedy show, where we fight each other on everything. After talking ourselves into circles, we concluded that we need to continue with the smart systems—which I said—but implement them in a phased approach. The worst-case scenario has appeared, and the solution is to continue rewiring the resort. No one loves where we've landed, but it's better than scrapping the entire approach.

"I expect to see an updated timeline by tomorrow."

"Tomorrow is Christmas, Tristan."

"Kennedy," he grumbles beneath his breath.

"What? I think we can give him until the twenty-six. He deserves to have the holiday off too."

Dave gathers his items in his hands. "It's no problem, Miss Kennedy. I'll give you the new timeline by tomorrow. We'll find a way to salvage this without all the drama."

"Ha, there's already plenty of drama," Tristan adds as he stands from his chair and follows Dave to the conference room door. I watch the two exchange handshakes as I gather my items. I need to get the hell out of here and find some space away from Tristan.

The sound of the lock clicking sounds like a bomb going off in this tiny quiet space. "Where the hell do you think you're going?"

I scoff, refusing to look up at him. But I don't need to. Tristan's energy is palpable. I can feel him erasing the space between us as he moves to the side of the table I'm standing in front of.

The heat from his front meets my back as he reaches down, grabbing the outside of my legs. His rough hands trail up my dress and the material feels like silk against my smooth skin. "What do you think you're doing?" I ask, more breathily than I intended. I'm pissed off, and one touch already has me unraveling.

"Seeing you fight for what you want turns me on," he whispers against my ear.

"So you were pissing me off on purpose?"

I feel his head shake as he kisses the spot where my neck and shoulder meet. I'm such a slut for this man. I know exactly what he's talking about. It shouldn't turn me on to fight with him, but God, it so does. The push-and-pull fuels our banter and my need for him only grows.

What the hell is wrong with me?

"No, I wasn't trying to piss you off on purpose, but I love seeing that wild, firecracker side of you."

My back straightens at that.

"Wait." I spin around and place my hands on his chest. Confusion and concern line his features as he stares down at me.

"Did I hurt you?"

Shaking my head, I feel the crease deepen between my eyebrows. "What did you say about my firecracker side?"

"You know, your fiery side. The side that flares whenever you get passionate about something."

"So it was never about my hair color?"

"What? No–" His expression softens as the light bulb goes off in his head. "Did you think I was making fun of you when I was calling you firecracker?"

I nod, embarrassment flushing my cheeks.

"Oh, baby, I would never make fun of you for that. I love seeing your spark and your tenacity whenever you're passionate about something. All this time, I've been fighting and bantering with you because I love it when you finally snap. I know that sounds bad, but when you finally push aside your polite nature and fight for something, it's so fucking hot."

"All this time…" I pause, my eyes bouncing between his, "I thought you were making fun of me."

"I know I'm an asshole, but I'm not that much of a dick. I would never make fun of someone's appearance."

"I'm sorry I assumed that," I tell him quietly, swallowing past my suddenly dry throat.

"Turn around." His command is deep and gravelly as he gently grips my wrists and spins me back around. My hands land on the table to steady me as he pins me in place, making my stomach flutter. "Don't move your hands."

As badly as I want to ask him what he's doing, there's a part of me that wants to see how this is going to play out. Soft kisses tease behind my ear as Tristan sucks my earlobe in his mouth and bites down. My lobe pops free as he continues kisses down my neck, over my shoulder, and along the backs of my arms as he lowers himself to his knees. Shivering from the sensations, I suck in a deep breath as he gathers the material of my dress in his fists and glides it up to my hips. His nose trails the back of my thigh as a thrill races down my spine.

"Don't move those hands."

Glancing over my shoulder, I watch as Tristan leans forward and places gentle kisses across my turtle tattoo. The soft brush of his lips against my skin elicits goosebumps and has my body craving more. With one fist, he grips my dress while using his other hand to remove my panties. My core tingles when he places the material in the pocket of his slacks.

Searing eyes shoot up and meet mine. Desire swirls in his irises, and I'm needy to know what he has in store for me.

"Be a good girl and stay quiet." Leaning forward, Tristan licks me from front to back, and the moan I let out is guttural—the opposite of quiet. A smack echoes around the room and has my pussy clenching. I never thought I'd enjoy being spanked, but there's something in the way that Tristan smacks me but then rubs the pain away. It's deliciously arousing.

Standing to his full height, I feel his eyes roaming over my exposed skin. I'm completely vulnerable in this position, but I don't feel self-conscious in the way that I thought I would. Over the last few weeks, I've fallen into a place of comfort with him.

The sound of a wrapper ripping jerks my attention. Somehow, I missed Tristan freeing himself from his pants. He fists his erection and gives it a few tight pumps, then sheaths himself with the condom.

Our eyes lock with mutual desperation, our hunger for the other at the very surface. I'm so gone for this man, and there's no way to come back from it.

"This is going to be quick, Firecracker." His voice breaks the trance. "Battling it out with you was all the foreplay I needed."

"Then what are you waiting for, Golden Boy? Give it—" I'm cut off as Tristan plunges inside me. I hiss at the stretch of his thick cock as my walls relax around him.

"Fuuuuuck," he groans. "You're so fucking perfect, Ken. So"–thrust–"fucking"–thrust–"perfect."

"Oh my god," I moan as he hits the spot deep inside of me. He warned me this was going to be a quick fuck. The fact that anyone could unlock that door and walk in on us only excites me more.

One of his hands tightens around my hip, keeping him in place as he pumps in and out of me. The other hand trails up my spine before he's pushing down between my shoulder blades. Gasping, my chest crashes against the table and my ass rises in the air, allowing him to go deeper inside of me.

"Touch yourself, baby," he grits out. "I'm not going to last much longer, but I'm not coming until you do."

Before I do as he says, I angle my body until I can look at him without standing. Reaching up, I hold two fingers in the air. "Suck."

His eyes flare as he takes both fingers into his mouth. His hot tongue flicks at my digits, coating them in his saliva. When he pops my fingers free, I slip my hand between my body and the table as I find my aching center. My fingers rub my clit in circles as Tristan continues his powerful pace. It's not long before I feel the tension pooling in my belly.

"That's it, Kenny. Such a good fucking girl."

Yep, that does it. Praise kink unlocked. Tristan calling me a good girl again is the undoing I never knew I needed. My walls tighten against his cock, and I'm delirious with the desire to come.

"Fuck, that feels so good," I murmur into the back of my hand, which separates my head from the table. I'm trying like crazy not to be loud, but dammit, it's hard.

A loud crack pierces the room as a flash of pain hits my ass cheek, and it's all I need to fall over the edge. I continue circling my clit as I come hard, holding back a scream as my body shudders beneath him. Riding out every bit of pleasure I can, I'm desperate to close my eyes, but instead, I risk a glance and am so glad I did.

Standing behind me is the gorgeous specimen of a man I'm nearly bringing to his knees. Tristan's hands are on both of my hips as he thrusts unabashedly inside of me. His head tilts toward the ceiling, eyes closed, and the look of raw desire transforms his features.

"Your pussy is squeezing me so goddamn tight."

With a final pump and dragged-out moan, I feel him pulse inside of me. A thrill runs through me at the realization that I gave him that much pleasure.

Tristan collapses across my back, but not before he catches his weight with his arms. He peppers soft kisses across my neck before he stands up and slides out. Instantly, I feel empty and ready for him again.

"You're fucking perfect, Firecracker."

CHAPTER TWENTY-SIX

TRISTAN

IT HIT ME LIKE looking at a blueprint I'd been staring at for years.

I'm in love with Kennedy Reed.

As I stared at her blushed cheeks, it was like I was looking at the final piece of a project falling into place. She wasn't just a part of my life; she was the design I'd been looking for all along.

Now I can only hope she feels the same.

CHAPTER TWENTY-SEVEN

KENNEDY

ROLLING OVER, MY HAND connects with the cool side of a pillow. A pillow that's supposed to be occupied by Tristan. Blinking my eyes, I adjust to the morning light streaming in through the doors and find the other side of my bed empty. I'm hit with a brief sense of disappointment that I'm waking up alone on Christmas morning. The notion is silly, but I can't help feeling like I do. Somewhere over the last four weeks, my feelings have shifted drastically for Tristan.

I think I've fallen in love with him.

And clearly, I'm alone in that.

Tossing the covers aside, I roll out of bed and adjust my silk nightgown before padding across the floor to the bathroom. The smell of freshly brewed coffee wafts from the kitchen, letting me know where Tristan ran off to. After running through my morning routine and savoring the fresh, minty taste in my mouth, I grab my phone off my nightstand and head toward the caffeine.

I'm scrolling through the 'Merry Christmas' wishes and chuckle when I find my sister's.

> **Liv: Merry Christmas you little ho, ho, ho! I hope you're decking his halls and jingling his balls—I mean, bells—under that tropical sun. Don't forget to unwrap your 'present' slowly…**

> **Me: Ha. ha. Ha. Merry Christmas, Liv. Miss you! Love you!**

I realize how dark the space is when I close my screen—well, in comparison to how it should be. My eyes move over to the side of the room, where I notice all the blinds are drawn on the windows and doors. Continuing my perusal, I gasp at the small Christmas tree in the corner of the living area that glows with white lights. Moisture gathers in my eyes as I notice the simple winter wonderland scattered around the room. A few presents are wrapped underneath the tree in red-and-white plaid paper. *A Christmas Story* plays on the TV and large white candles are lit on the coffee table. It's simple and perfect.

"Trist," I whisper, moving closer to where he's sitting on the couch.

His back is against the armrest, which gives him the perfect view of my reaction. A sheepish smile curves the corner of his lips, and he's wearing those damn wide-rimmed black glasses again.

And, of course, he's not wearing a shirt.

If it weren't for the Christmas tree pulling my entire attention, I'd be drinking him in like a tall glass of water, because the man is fine. Especially bare chested with glasses.

He chews on his lower lip as he runs his fingers through his hair. Is Tristan nervous? "Do-do you like it?"

"Do I like it?" I walk around the edge of the couch until I'm standing above him. Bending down, I place a chaste kiss on his lips, tasting the coffee. "I love it."

His face breaks out in a beaming smile, one that would rival, well...a kid on Christmas. "I was nervous you wouldn't."

"Why wouldn't I like it?"

He shrugs as I step over his legs and sit in the space next to him. He's already reaching out his cup for me before I have the chance to take it from his hands. I find myself humming at the easy routine we've established. "How? When did you do all of this?"

"I had a little help from Destiny. Turns out, our general manager is incredible."

"Well, we knew that." I take a sip of the hot java and notice the perfectly tan color in the mug. Quirking an eyebrow, I look up and find Tristan watching me. My brows form a 'V' as I'm hit with a suspicious feeling. "You always drink your coffee black. Why is this the same tan shade that I make my coffee?"

"Maybe because I already drank mine while I was waiting for you, and when I heard you get up, I made a mug how you like it because I knew you'd steal mine."

Speechless, I snuggle deeper into the couch and his side. As his hand lands on the outside of my thigh, and I take in how festive the space looks once again, I can't get over how everything about this moment feels so domesticated. The thought has my heart palpitating.

Maybe I was wrong about Tristan. Maybe he feels the way I feel too.

With a slight pat to my butt that makes me smile, I glance up at him. "There's more, Firecracker."

"More? This is perfect. Can't we just sit here and watch Ralphie?"

His chuckle reverberates through my body. "It's on all day long. I think we'll be able to watch it any time we like. Besides, you have presents to open."

"But I didn't get you anything." My heart sinks at my carelessness. I cannot believe Tristan, of all people, planned this and even picked out gifts.

He stands, and I admire the way his ironically Christmas patterned pajama pants hang low on his hips. I take his outstretched hand as he bends down and kisses the spot below my ear. "I'll unwrap my present later."

The deep timber of his promise has my thighs clenching. We step around the coffee table and sit in front of the tree, but not before Tristan moves us closer together. He reaches into his pocket and pulls out his cell phone. Flipping through his homepage, he clicks on the camera app and angles it in the air. I smile up as he taps the screen.

My stomach flutters at Tristan wanting to document this moment. Of course, he's snapped a few pictures here and there, but this feels different. It feels like we could really give this a go and have a future together. One with our own Christmas morning traditions of late-night wrapping presents while our kids sleep. Of waking up to the sound of tiny pitter-patters across the floor as they rush to the tree. Watching our children unwrap a mountain of presents while we sit and drink coffee, smiles planted firmly on our faces.

"Here, open this one first." Tristan reaches behind me and pulls out a large, rectangular present wrapped in white-and-gold paper. I can't help but admire how perfectly minimalistic it looks. I wonder if he wrapped these gifts himself.

Tucking my finger beneath the seam, I gently pop open the tape. "You know you can just rip it."

"But it looks so pretty. I'd hate to ruin the work someone did."

He scoffs. "I'm wounded, Kenny. Do you think I had someone else wrap your present?"

Chewing on the corner of my lip, I look up at him with a one-shouldered shrug.

"Wounded. Deeply wounded." My body warms knowing he put the extra effort to wrap my gifts himself when he could have paid anyone to do it.

With the paper completely removed, I slide open the top of the white box and move the tissue paper. A soft gasp escapes my lips as I take in the gift in front of me. A large pack of Prismacolor colored pencils sits on top of a gorgeous leather-bound sketchbook. Reaching inside the box, I pull out the sketchbook and relish the buttery softness of the rich leather.

"Tristan, it's beautiful. You shouldn't have done this."

He doesn't say anything but reaches for the last present, and I hate that I didn't think about getting him a gift. When he places the gift in my lap, I glance up with an ornery smirk as I start to unwrap the gift slowly. I can see his eyes widening with impatience, and as he opens his mouth to tell me to, no doubt, hurry it up, a wide smile breaks across my lips. Gripping the paper, I rip it aggressively, and he shakes his head with a chuckle.

"Oh my gosh," I gasp as tears well in my eyes. My fingertips brush against the glass frame. Sitting in my lap is a large frame with a white mat around *my* rendering of this resort. There's a small plaque with the words: 'My first lead architectural project 2024.' Holding the framed rendering in my hand, I let the tears fall free, not concerned with Tristan seeing me cry.

"D-do you not like it?" Uncertainty laces his voice, and the last thing I want is for him to feel any ounce of self-consciousness when the gift was incredibly thoughtful.

Placing the box on the floor, I fling my legs over his outstretched ones as I toss my arms around his neck. My lips find his, and I capture his gasp as my tongue dips inside his mouth. With a flick across his, I feel him growing hard beneath me—his pajama pants aren't hiding anything. As much as I want to prolong this moment, now is not the time.

Leaning backward, Tristan groans at our loss of connection. My smile widens as I stare into his darkened hazel eyes.

"That was the most thoughtful gift anyone has ever given me. I love them... I-I love you."

I'm hit with nerves as shock flares across his sharp features. But any uncertainty is gone just as quickly, feeling warm from the inside out as he smiles. Reaching up, he brushes a loose strand of hair behind my ear, but he doesn't remove his hand. Instead, he grips the side of my face, his thumb rubbing across my cheek as he pulls my head toward his. His forehead leans against mine and he inhales deeply. A comfortable silence falls over the room, the only sound the lit flames of the candle and my heartbeat, which I'm sure he can hear.

"I never allowed myself to think about my future outside of the company. It's been a guarantee in my life that I would work in the family business and, eventually, I'd get married, but I never put much thought into the type of wife I'd want. That was, until you came back into my life. I love you, too, Kennedy."

His lips find mine, and instead of a hurried kiss, this one is languid. It's passionate and filled with so much longing and adoration; I feel his love being poured into me.

Tristan Nelson was supposed to be the enemy, but when I thought I was building walls around my heart, he was busy taking them apart, brick by brick.

Chapter Twenty-Eight

Tristan

"There was this time when I was five or six and we had finished opening presents..." Kennedy tells a story from her childhood, her hands flying in all different directions. "But when I went into the kitchen a few hours later—I mean, I think it was a few hours later, I was young with no concept of time. Anyway, there was this huge package inside our kitchen. I remember running to my mom, telling her there was another gift."

"Santa," I say with air quotes, "must've forgotten a present."

"That's exactly what I said."

Since opening presents this morning, the two of us have fallen into a tropical hibernation. Instead of watching it snow, like we would if we were at home, we've been watching the palms blowing in the breeze. *A Christmas Story* is still playing in the background; however, I don't think we've watched it chronologically all the way through yet.

We've been wrapped up together on this oversized couch, exchanging childhood Christmas stories and enjoying the quiet. The silent moments never feel awkward, which I'm taking as a sign that we're finally fully comfortable with each other. Neither of us feels the need to keep the conversation going.

Sitting here, listening to her tell stories from her childhood, I can't help but wonder how the hell I got so lucky. She might have said she didn't get me anything for Christmas, but her telling me she loves me is the best gift I've ever received.

I'm on cloud nine that we are both on the same page. Kennedy Reed loves me. The Golden Boy in her story who got everything he ever wanted. The guy who banters with her whenever he has the chance. The guy who has shown her for the past month how much she means to him. She's everything I never knew I wanted.

Kennedy shifts slightly, and my arm around her tightens as I savor the warmth of her body against me. The Christmas movie fades into the background as I watch her watch the movie. Her soft giggle fills the air as Ralphie makes his grand appearance in his pink bunny suit.

"No matter how many times I watch this movie, it never gets old."

I press a kiss to the top of her head. "I never watched a lot of Christmas movies. Mom would have the black-and-white classics on, and when I was younger, I imagine I watched them, but once I hit my teens, Christmas never felt as magical."

I'm afraid my dark cloud puts a damper on the day when she's silent for a moment. I mentally curse myself and try to think of a way to fix the mood.

"Well, that sucks," she says bluntly, in such a sweet tone that it makes me chuckle. Pressing a kiss to my cheek, she lazily draws circles on my arm. "What was your best childhood Christmas, then?"

"Easy." A rumbling laugh in my chest breaks free at the memory flooding my mind.

"This is going to be good." Amusement dances in her emerald eyes.

"When I was ten, I wanted a kayak to use on Lake Michigan when I visited my cousin. It was the same year my mom decided to host this giant Christmas Eve dinner. I'm pretty sure she invited everyone we knew, including our doorman."

Kennedy moves away and sits up straighter as she gives me her full attention. I immediately miss her warmth, but I love how she's hanging on to every word.

"Anyway, she told us this story about how Santa heard we were having a big Christmas Eve dinner, so he convinced his elves to drop off our gifts early. Being the naive boy I was, I believed her and thought it was the coolest thing."

She coos an "awww," and I shake my head as my lips turn up. "Any ten-year-old would have loved that."

I nod, my smile growing wider. "She told all of the kids to go to the media room—"

She rolls her eyes, and I chuckle as she interrupts me. "Typical rich kid with a media room... How stereotypical."

"While we were in the room, they organized the gifts. Now, I don't know if I've told you this, but my mom loves to host. She's the 'hostess with mostess' down to every last detail. From planning the menu to decorating our house until it feels magazine worthy. So you can only imagine how perfect our tree was."

Smiling brightly, she nods. "Your mom sounds a lot like mine."

"All of us kids came back to the living room and gathered around the tree, patiently waiting for our presents. I noticed the bright orange kayak behind the tree and couldn't help but bounce in my seat."

"Oh no, is this going where I think it's going?" When she cringes, it's too cute. I can't resist leaning forward and placing a light kiss on the tip of her nose.

"Oh, it is." I pause as the images play on a loop, and it's as if I'm that ten-year-old boy watching it happen again. I can hear the chaos that filled the room. "The kayak shifts and the tree starts to fall. All of us kids started screaming and scurrying out of the way while some of the adults rushed to save the tree from falling, but it was no use. Down went the twelve-foot tree. Thank God for shatterproof ornaments or it would have been a real mess."

"Your poor mom." Kennedy grips her chest. "She must have been devastated."

"She was for a second, and then suddenly, she burst into hysterical laughter. Everyone was caught off guard, and we were waiting for her to snap, but she never did. Instead, she threw her hands out wide and shouted, 'It's a memory.' And she was right."

"What did your dad do?"

My body relaxes deeper into the couch. "He didn't say much that I remember. He probably stood by with a scotch in his hand as he let everyone pick up the pieces."

Her brow furrows and creates an adorable crease between them. With my thumb, I massage it away. "Don't think too much about it. Dad was always a little distant with family functions. He was never mean about it, but he was definitely cold when it came to the holidays. Mostly just uninterested. Mom was the one to shower us with love and try to make our childhood memorable."

The grip of her hand on mine tightens, and I glance down at our connection. She pulls herself closer to me and peppers gentle kisses along my scruff-covered jawline. Turning my head, I kiss her, smiling across her lips. I love how she knew I didn't need words of sympathy, just a few kisses instead.

"What about you, Firecracker? Any special Christmases?"

Her head tilts, as if she's recalling her memories. "Honestly, there aren't too many that stand out. Mom worked hard at always making sure each Christmas was memorable, and Dad was there leading a supporting role."

Just when I think she's going to let the conversation end, her eyes widen, and a glow radiates around her. "Oh my gosh, I can't believe I almost forgot about this story!"

She turns, tucking her legs underneath her as she faces me. "It's also a Christmas Eve one."

"Seems like Christmas Eve is full of excitement for both of us."

With a nod, her lips quirk. "Every Christmas Eve, Mom would prepare a nice dinner in our dining room, which she would have decorated like a magazine too." Her eyes sparkle as she recalls the memory. "We'd be dressed up in our church clothes for the Christmas Eve service that we went to after dinner. Anyway, dinner was halfway over when either Olivia or my dad said something. I can't remember what, but all I know is that it was something hilarious. I had just taken a big drink of milk but didn't have a chance to swallow."

My eyes widen in anticipation. "I spewed milk all over my plate and part of the table. My ham loaf was floating on a plate full of milk. Now every year, there's a running joke about it every time I'm served ham."

I can't help but erupt in a fit of laughter as I imagine the scene she's just described. She shrugs but laughs along with me. "There you have it, my embarrassing Christmas Eve dinner."

"Remind me to watch my plate next time I eat with you, Firecracker."

"Ha. Ha." She smacks my chest, and I quickly grab her hand, pulling her closer. She lands across my front and moves until she's in a comfortable position resting over my body. The credits of the movie play, and I reach for the remote on the armrest.

"Mind if I put football on?"

"Nope," she says as she cuddles against me. I click through the channels until I find the Colorado Colts game, smiling at the TV as the announcers discuss the Colts's star running back, Quinton Boyd, who happens to be married to a friend of mine.

"No promises if I'll stay awake. Turns out, you're pretty comfortable." We fall into a peaceful silence with the only sound coming from the game, and I know it's likely we'll both be napping soon.

The warm glow of the Christmas tree flickers, a reminder that this Christmas I'm getting more than I ever thought possible. Everything I need is right here in my arms.

I love her and she loves me. I could live through thousands of Christmases and never tire of the way loving her makes me feel.

My thumb traces up and down her soft skin, and I feel her sigh, content in this moment. Glancing down, I find her already staring up at me.

Leaning down, I brush a loose strand of hair off her neck and place a gentle kiss on the flesh beneath her ear, where I can feel her pulse speed up. "I love you," I whisper. Smiling, her eyes sparkle like the damn Christmas tree.

"I love you too." Her words are quiet, barely above a whisper. It feels like the whole world slows, just enough for me to savor the moment of her in my arms.

This right here is the Christmas I'll remember most. The one where I didn't need anything but Kennedy Reed.

Chapter Twenty-Nine

Kennedy

"Well, if it isn't my long-lost office bestie. I'm surprised you remember my number."

"It's a good thing you're saved in my contacts."

Zoe laughs lightly. "But seriously, how are things going? I'm surprised I haven't received any death notifications."

"It's going...surprisingly well."

"I bet it is." Innuendo drips from her lips, and I bite my own to keep a smile from breaking free. Thankfully, we're on a call and not a FaceTime or my expression would have totally given away all my secrets.

"It's New Year's Eve, and I'm on the beach in my bikini, sipping a cocktail. It doesn't get much better than that."

"You could be getting railed by your hot boss on the beach."

"Zoe!" I gasp, scolding my friend, who better not be in the office repeating that for all our co-workers to hear. As much as I love this newfound relationship with Tristan, I'm not sure if I'm ready for the office to know about it.

"Relax, I'm down the block getting coffee. The days are a bore without you."

Rolling my eyes, I shield my face as I stare out at the ocean. There's a large vessel moving way out near the horizon. "Have you seen any updated pictures of the resort?"

"Oh my gosh, yes! You've been the talk of the office. Everyone is so impressed by how the resort is turning out." She pauses, and my chest warms at the compliment. "Not to mention, that soft launch on Tristan's social media."

My stomach drops. I don't follow Tristan on social media because, not too long ago, the sight of his smug face would make me irrationally angry. "Wh-what do you mean?"

"Girl, you seriously need to follow him back."

"Hold on. I'm going to right now." Placing the call on speaker, I pull open my Instagram app and search for his name. "What's new with you?"

Zoe updates me on things in the office, how she and her husband are trying for a baby, and the stress with that. I nod—not that she can see it—and respond when appropriate, but my mind completely freezes when I stumble upon Tristan's Instagram account.

The nine-photo grid is filled with pictures from our time in St. Lucia. A photo of the sunset across the horizon from the resort's beach. A selfie of him relaxed on a lounge chair, shirtless and wearing sunglasses.

But it's the three pictures sprinkled throughout his feed that cause my heart to bounce to my throat. There's one of the beach, but in the background is me wearing a bikini, toes in the sand as the water meets the shore, and my head is thrown back toward the sky. Another is us in the hot tub, clinking bottles of beer after a long day of chaos. But it's the last one that has a small gasp leaving my lips.

"You found it." The words aren't a question as Zoe's voice softens; they're a statement.

"I can't believe he posted that." The photo is of the two of us in bed together. My head is laying in the crook between his arm and shoulder, eyes closed, while my hand rests on his bare chest.

"Did you read the caption?"

"No," I say on a shaky exhale as I tap the image. Tears well in my eyes as I read the caption under the intimate photo.

The greatest gift I could ask for. Merry Christmas, everyone.

If I thought my heart swelled the moment I saw the post, it's nothing in comparison to reading those words. I'm the greatest gift he could ask for. Me? My lungs seize as a tear slips free and trails down my cheek. The hand gripping my phone trembles as my pulse speeds up.

Warmth spreads through my body, and there's no doubt in my mind that I love Tristan. I know I told him on Christmas Day, but seeing this, there's no hesitation in my mind that we are destined for one another. The thought of building a future together feels like seeing the perfect blueprint come to life—strong, deliberate, and meant to last forever.

He isn't just a part of my life now.

He's my future.

"I'm glad you two finally put aside your past and accepted what we've all been seeing since you started working at Nelson Signature." Zoe's voice cuts through my thoughts.

At the mention of work again, my swooning heartbeat from the post transforms into dread that causes my stomach to drop. What if people at work have seen this? Who am I kidding? Half of New York has probably seen the post. Tristan Nelson, the Golden Boy of New York, has been on everyone's radar. Girls all over the city—hell, the world—want to take him off the market, and here he is, posting that he's taken.

"Oh my god," I gasp, hand flying to my mouth as I use my thumb to scroll through the comments.

"Don't read the comments!" Zoe practically shouts.

"Do you have a video feed of this beach?"

She chuckles. "No, but I know you're spiraling. For what it's worth, everyone at the office is happy. I mean that. Hell, Victoria is over the moon, and even Xander has commented about how much he likes seeing his brother like this."

"If you so say," I grumble, unable to stop reading the comments. There're a mixture of congratulations and well wishes. But there are also frustrations from his followers that he's no longer a bachelor.

When I decided to pursue things with Tristan, never once did I think about the ramifications. The limelight that follows him around and the events we'll have to attend. Nelson Signature isn't just a small architectural firm, it's nearly the top real estate development in the world. His dad is a mogul in the industry.

"Can I do this?" Insecurity pours from my question, and I find myself sitting up, bending my legs, and tucking my knees under my chin as I stare out at the blue water.

"Of course you can. You're Kennedy fucking Reed, a baddie who deserves to be the top architect in modern times and who deserves to be loved." I hear the smile in her voice, which causes the corners of my mouth to tip up.

"Thanks, Zoe."

"Anytime, babe. Now go soak up the bliss of being newly in love."

"See you soon."

We end the call, and I flop back down in my chair. Chewing on my lip, I stare at Tristan's social media feed. My thumb hovers over the 'follow' button, and I hesitate for a moment before clicking it. I watch as the blue button turns white.

Instantly, as if he was waiting for it to happen, a text message pops up.

> **Tristan: Took you long enough. How hard was it to hit follow?**

> **Me: I just wanted to make sure you were worth it…still on the fence.**

> **Tristan: Still on the fence? You weren't on the fence last night. Need I remind you where you were sitting?**

My cheeks flame at the reminder of last night. The two of us were lying side-by-side on one of the outdoor daybeds, enjoying a beer, and watching the stars since the sun sets so early. Next thing I knew, I was no longer on my back. My legs were straddling his face as he enjoyed his second dessert.

> **Tristan: I bet those cute cheeks of yours are warm and in the prettiest shade of pink.**

> **Me: Shut up.**

Tristan: I love you, Firecracker. See you in our room whenever you're done bronzing like a goddess.

Me: OMG, what is with you today?

Tristan: It's New Year's Eve and I'm excited to ring in the new year with you.

CHAPTER THIRTY

TRISTAN

From: alexandernelson@nelsonsignature.com
To: tristannelson@nelsonsignature.com
Date: January 3, 2025
Subject: Grand Opening

Tristan,
     Congrats on surviving this renovation
with Kennedy. I thought for sure she would
have killed you by now. I guess it's safe to
assume the two of you have… "patched things
up."

     With the grand opening being in a week,
the board, including myself, Dad, and Victoria
will be flying in tomorrow to observe the
final stages of completion.

     Dad wanted me to pass on that Kennedy's
services will no longer be needed and she will
be returning on the jet tomorrow evening once
our debrief is complete.

     Way to not fuck up this project, little
brother.

     Proud of you.

-X
Alexander Nelson, Development Manager
Nelson Signature Hotels & Resorts
New York, New York

CLOSING OUT OF MY emails, I'm instantly on edge. How can my father be so cold in not allowing Kennedy to oversee the grand opening of *her* project? Everything was her idea, down to the last detail; I was merely a spectator.

Sliding my phone out of my pocket, I scroll through my messages until I find Xander's name.

> **Me: What the fuck?**

No surprise, he messages back immediately. He must've been anticipating my response.

> **Xander: Don't shoot the messenger.**

> **Me: That's exactly what I'm doing.**

> **Xander: I have no control over the matter. Throw me under the bus if you have to, but Dad is planning a new project and he wants her back here.**

> **Me: Why would I throw you under the bus?**

> **Xander: Come off it, I know you two are more than what you're letting on. I saw the Instagram picture.**

In a moment of weakness—or a lust-filled haze—I posted a photo of her hand on my bare chest. Should I have done it? No, but there's no way in hell I regret it. It's not the first time I posted images of her. Over the last week, I've captured a few candid moments. Some I've sent and she's posted on her socials, while others I've kept on my camera roll.

Kennedy may be following me now, but at the time she wasn't, and I wasn't afraid to drop a comment or two.

> **Xander: She's brought a new side out of you. Can't say I hate it.**

> **Me: Save the sentiments. How am I going to explain that she's not going to get the accolades she deserves?**

> **Xander: I don't know, brother. That one is up to you to figure out. Like I said, I'll be the scapegoat. Tell her while we appreciate everything she has done, I need her back in New York for her next assignment.**

I huff out a breath and lock my phone before walking through the resort. It's hard to believe that six weeks ago, we arrived to total chaos. Now the new entrance is complete, providing a warm and welcoming atmosphere. The oversized columns that broke up the line of sight are gone, and in their place are beautiful wood support beams. Spread throughout the lobby are white fabric chairs and couches, with pops of coral and orange, which Victoria designed.

The resort feels like it's finally come together, and now I have to tell the woman I love that she won't be featured in the photos during the grand opening. As much as she needs to know, I want one more night with her before this blissful moment is broken.

"Hi, Destiny," I greet our general manager, who is behind the front desk.

Her welcoming smile spreads brightly across her dark features. The woman is a huge asset to this location, and I'll be speaking with HR as soon as I return to New York to give her a raise.

"Good afternoon, Mr. Nelson. Is there anything I can do for you?"

Rapping my knuckles against the cool counter, I say, "As a matter of fact, there is. Have you seen Kennedy?"

"Miss Kennedy is in the guest wings, helping out Mario and his team with making the beds." Mario is one of our housekeeping managers. With all the furniture delivered and the rooms set up, I'm not surprised that Kennedy volunteered to help make beds. Although, I've seen her bed-making ability, and I hope she isn't causing Mario more work.

"Thank you, Destiny. Have a great evening."

"You too, Mr. Nelson. Will you and Miss Kennedy be dining at Lullaby Lagoon this evening?"

"We will."

"Great, I'll make sure they have your table ready." We exchange a few more pleasantries before I head off in my search for Kennedy.

After ten minutes, I finally found her on the second floor halfway down the hall. She's bent over a king-sized bed, her dress clinging to her perfect hips. I lean against the wall, arms folded across my chest, as I admire the woman before me. I'm not looking forward to her leaving and me spending the next however many days alone without her in my bed.

Kennedy is in the middle of wrestling a fitted sheet. Every time she tries to tuck it under the mattress, the other side pops off. Grumbles and curses leave her sweet lips as she lets out a deep sigh.

"You could help instead of standing there watching me struggle," she sasses.

I huff a laugh as she blows a piece of hair that has fallen free from her claw clip. The curly red tendril refuses to leave her face, no matter how hard she blows it. With another exasperated sigh, she stands up and tucks it back into place.

"Having a bad day?"

She plants her hands on her hips as she shakes her head before she strides across the room. Our toes touch as she looks up at me. Even with the humidity causing the baby hairs around the top of her head to frizz out and the bead of sweat that has gathered on her upper lip, Kennedy Reed is the most beautiful woman I've laid eyes on.

Bending down, I kiss her. She relaxes into my touch and flicks her tongue against my lips. When I grant her the access she's searching for, she lets out a low moan. Her hands slide up my chest, eliciting a chill down my spine, before landing behind my head. Kennedy toys with the soft hairs on my neck, making me hum into her mouth. If she's not careful, I'm going to toss her on this bed and have my way with her.

Footsteps sound and Kennedy breaks free, her eyes wild and her cheeks a pretty shade of pink.

"Oh, Miss Kennedy, Mr. Nelson, I'm sorry to interrupt," one of our housekeepers addresses us. Kennedy ducks her head, and I take the opportunity to push her embarrassment.

"Allow me to be the one to apologize. It turns out Kennedy can't keep her hands off me."

With a flick of her wrist, Kennedy lands a soft smack to my stomach, and I watch both women's cheeks flare with a matching deep blush. "Ah, young love. Enjoy it, you two."

Tucking that same loose strand behind her ear, Kennedy smiles at the older woman. "I tried really hard to make the beds, but it turns out, I'm terrible at it."

I knew she would be. But Kennedy's big heart wouldn't let her sit around while the staff were busy working to get the rooms ready.

"Nonsense. Thank you for offering to help."

We bid the woman farewell and step out of the room, hand-in-hand.

"I can't believe you said that." Shock laces her words as I smirk down at her.

"What? It's true."

I push the button to call the elevator as I take in a new angle of the resort from the third-floor window. Purple flowers blow in the wind next to the sidewalk, which leads to the private pools. The property has four pools on the ground—the main one, two smaller ones for the first-level rooms, and a medium-sized pool for guests who don't want to be near the crowded main pool.

A ding has my attention turning toward the elevator as the door slides open. Kennedy steps in, with me on her heels. She hits the button for the main floor, and as soon as the doors close, I'm pressing her against the wall.

"Tristan." My name leaves her lips on a gasp, her eyes locking onto mine with hunger I already feel.

"Fuck, Kennedy, I can't get enough of you." Our tongues dance their sweet rhythm. Gliding. Tangling. Tasting. Peppermint from her gum hits my tastebuds, and I deepen the kiss even more, wanting to feel all of her that I can. Her hands slide over my hips, down my thigh, before cupping my growing erection. As she palms my dick, squeezing it just right, I let out a strangled noise.

A light chuckle leaves her lips, and we separate when the doors notify us that our ride is over. Reaching for her hand, I pull her behind me as we exit the guest quarters.

"C'mon, Firecracker, it's time for dinner."

She raises an eyebrow. "Is this like a legit dinner, or am I the dinner?"

Stopping in my tracks, Kennedy's front runs into my shoulder as I take in her blazing eyes. "Are you offering yourself?"

She rolls her eyes, and I want to be rolling them for a whole different reason. "No, Golden Boy, take me to dinner." She glances down at her Smartwatch, brow pinched. "Trist, it's not even five o'clock and we're having dinner?"

"I have a whole night planned with you." I tug her closer to me as I place an arm over her shoulder. "And I was planning on ordering cheesecake and snagging a bottle of champagne for later."

"Now I can get behind that plan."

· · · ● · ● · · · ·

Dinner at Lullaby Lagoon was delicious, just like it has been every time we've dined there. I need to make sure the marketing team reaches out to a few food bloggers to get them to sample the food. There's no way they'll leave here without feeling satisfied and writing us a raving review.

As we move through the dimly lit resort, I revel in the feel of her soft hand in mine. I'm captivated by Kennedy Reed, and I hope that at the end of this, she doesn't hate me. I don't know how I'll go back to a world where Kennedy views me as her enemy.

Call me selfish, but I'm not ready for our time to end—not tonight, and not on this island. Tightening my grip on her hand, I glance down and find Kennedy already smiling up at me.

With my free hand, I place a finger under her chin and tilt her face. Her green eyes sparkle in the night light.

"You're beautiful," I whisper as I lower my face to hers. Before I know it, I'm groaning into her parted mouth as she grips the hair at the nape of my neck. Forever the impatient girl, Kennedy has pulled me down to hers as our lips collide in a heated kiss.

Bodies relaxing, our hips meet, and I feel her subtly grinding against me. Blood pumps powerfully through my veins as I deepen our connection, stroking her tongue as she seeks friction. My girl is turned on. She's starved for my touch, and that thought alone has me wanting to take her right here on this vacant sidewalk.

I invade her mouth like I'll never kiss her again, consuming, taking everything she throws my way.

I crave her, and no amount of tasting will satisfy my hunger.

She's everything I've been searching for, even when I didn't know what I was looking for.

The crack in my heart becomes a gaping hole as I pour my love into her. I pray that love gets us through what's to come.

Her chest rises and falls as her breathing intensifies. Trailing a hand down her side, over the curve of her hip, I feel for the slit in her dress, the same slit that has given me brief glimpses of her leg I can't stop imagining wrapped around me as I thrust inside of her.

My touch travels over her exposed skin, to her inner thigh, and toward her center. With a gentle caress, I can feel her arousal coating the thin scrap of fabric, and I barely hold back my groan. Gripping her lace thong, I drag it up and down, up and down, building the friction she craves as I let the material graze her swollen clit.

Unabashedly, she moans, never stopping kissing me, and my dick twitches in my shorts. I need her. As she sucks on my tongue, I'm desperate to feel her tight pussy grip my cock. I'm seconds away from taking her right here when I become aware that anyone could walk up on us. I ease my fingers away from where she's eager for my touch as a soft whimper escapes her lips.

"Not here, baby," I say as my eyes scan the area. A few feet away, a cream-covered cabana catches my attention. A sly smirk spreads across my lips as I gently pull her in the direction of the beach.

Her sweet giggles fuel our jog through the sand, but she struggles in her wedged sandals. Reaching down, I scoop my arms behind her knees as I sweep her off her feet in a fireman's carry.

"Oh my gosh," she gasps as she wraps her arms around my neck, gripping on for dear life. One hand playfully slaps my chest before she clasps her hands together. "Put me down."

"Why?" I ask, pausing to look at her. Pink tinges her cheeks, giving her a rosy glow. "Afraid I might drop you?" I playfully pretend to drop her before bouncing her higher into my arms. She lets out a shriek, and I laugh.

"You're such a jerk," she says through a sweet laugh.

"The jerk you looooove."

"Yeah, I do." Lust coats her voice, which pushes my feet to carry us faster through the sand.

Stepping foot inside the private cabana, I gently set her down on the daybed as I move around the sides of the cabana and loosen the ties holding the curtains back. I keep the side open that faces the ocean.

As I stand at the edge of the bed, I stare down at the angelic woman beneath me. Her hair is spread around her head in a halo effect. Her swollen lips are parted and emerald eyes blaze with desire as her gaze roams over my body.

She's perfect. Flawless. Breathtaking.

But best of all, *she's mine.*

Slowly, I begin undoing the buttons on my tropical printed short sleeve. Kennedy watches raptly, and I decide to milk the moment. She huffs a breath, which has me quirking an eyebrow at her.

"Impatient, are we?"

"Aching."

"Desperate."

Her eyes roll, but then she says all-too-seductively. "For you, Tristan."

I groan as I slip the shirt down my arms and toss it aside. Before I have a chance to unbutton my shorts, Kennedy's slender fingers are reaching for my waist. I watch as she sits up and works my shorts free.

Her warm hand slides inside my boxers and grips my aching cock. I moan long and deep at the contact and tilt my head to the sky, thanking the almighty.

How did I get so fucking lucky?

Leaning forward, Kennedy's pink tongue slips past her lips as she licks me from root to tip. My hands smooth over her shoulders as she sucks me into her mouth. Groaning, I work the clasp of her cropped top until it falls open. Her perfect tits spill free, and I reach out to cup them in my hands. I play with them while she bobs her head up and down, the feel of her and the way she's pleasuring me already pushing me to the edge.

Shoving the material of my shorts and boxers down my legs, I move my hips backward as I pop free from her mouth. Her swollen lips glisten from saliva as she looks up at me, then reaches behind her to unbutton her skirt. Moving backward up the bed, she lowers the material, and I remove it the rest of the way. Sprawled out on the bed, the only thing she's wearing now is a scrap of lace between her thighs that I'm quick to remove.

I pepper kisses up her neck as I lower myself on top of her until I find her waiting lips. My cock brushes her wet center, and we both call out as lust overtakes us.

"Fuck, Kennedy," I hiss.

"Yes, Tristan," she whimpers as her hips seek me out. "Fuck me, please."

"Condom," I say as I start to move away from her.

"Don't, Trist."

My eyes snap down to hers, and I see how positive she is.

"I love you," I tell her, overcome by how safe she feels with me.

"I love you, too."

It feels like an eternity passes as the two of us stare at each other. In those moments, it's as if our souls are coming home, tangling themselves in one another with silent words that don't need to be spoken.

As if someone cut the string tethering us together, I fall forward, crushing my lips to hers. Tongues duel and teeth gnash as our bodies vibrate with need. The thrust of my tongue against hers has her hips driving forward. I place carnal kisses down her jaw, her neck, and her chest as I suck a breast into my mouth. Flicking her pebbled nipple with my tongue, I bite down gently, which has her crying out.

Her hands find the nape of my neck as she holds me to her. Sucking and nibbling, I kiss her wholly while my hand finds her wet pussy. I thrust two fingers inside her, feeling her walls clench. She cries out again as I continue pumping deep inside her, bringing her closer and closer to her release.

"Tristan—" she pleads. "I'm so close."

My thumb lands on her swollen clit, and as I press down, continuing to pump inside her until she's screaming my name.

"Fuck," I breathe out as my hooded gaze stares down at her. My cock aches as pre-cum oozes from my tip. I need to be inside her, and now. I'll never grow tired of the sight of Kennedy Reed coming from my touch. It's the sexiest fucking thing—her flushed cheeks, parted lips, heaving chest.

Sliding my fingers from her pulsing pussy, I grip my cock with my wet fingers.

"Roll over, Firecracker."

She does as I say and moves until she's on her knees, away from me. Bending down on her elbows, she lifts her ass in the air, and I admire this angle. With a few quick pumps, I line up to her entrance and thrust inside. She gasps as I fill her completely, and I pause for a second to let her adjust to my size.

"Move, Tristan. For the love of God, move."

I smack my hand against her ass and feel her clenching around my dick. From this position, I watch the skin of her cheek pinken with my handprint. Thrusting forward, my hips meet her backside.

"Hold on, baby." Gripping her hips, I begin moving faster, and she matches my pace. Both of us are desperate to find more pleasure.

Her moans fuel me as I continue to thrust deeper. Reaching forward, I pinch her clit and feel her orgasm building once again. She plays with her tits as I continue pumping inside of her and working her swollen clit. Within seconds, she's moaning as waves and waves of euphoria roll through her. I watch in fascination as I draw every ounce of her orgasm before quickening my pace.

My balls tighten, and I'm on the brink of coming. Thrusts grow more erratic as I roll my hips and hit her deeper and deeper. Watching her come unleashes a beast within me as I frantically fuck her.

The grip on her hips tightens, and I hope I'm not hurting her, but the idea of marking her, showing she's mine, spurs me on. With one final thrust, I'm coming with a roar. Once I spill every last drop, I start to pull out of her and watch as our orgasms start to drip. With two fingers, I plunge our cum back inside her, pulling another whimper from her lips, before dropping my forehead to her lower back. Trailing kisses up her spine, I feel her panting against my head.

Lying beside her, I pull her into my arms. "You're fucking perfect, Firecracker."

"You're not so bad yourself, Golden Boy."

We stay there in silence, the only sounds our breaths and the lapping of the waves on the shore. Stars sparkle in the sky as shadows of a passing ship flick across the horizon. It's calm and peaceful with her in my arms, her head on my chest.

I place a small kiss on her forehead as I whisper, "I love you." In this moment, it's only her and I. I'm not sure how much time passes before I slip my shirt over her naked body and carry her back to our room.

I just hope she forgives me.

Chapter Thirty-One

Kennedy

Tristan's alarm wakes me from a peaceful rest. His hand trails up my bare thigh, over my hip, and across my stomach before pulling me closer. Our warm skin meets, and I melt into his embrace. Nuzzling my hair with his nose, he peppers tiny kisses down my neck before nipping at my shoulder.

"Morning, beautiful." His voice is rough with sleep.

Tristan's fingers trace lazy circles across my waist as goosebumps break over my skin, and desire pools between my thighs. My hand finds his, and I intertwine our fingers.

"Morning." Shifting closer, I enjoy a few more moments of blissful serenity before the day's chaos begins.

"As much as I want to lay in bed with you all day, we've got to get up."

I groan as Tristan leans over me and kisses my cheek. Rolling over in his arms, I toss a leg over his hip. He grumbles at the contact.

"Are you sure?" My hips thrust forward, and I feel his morning wood.

"Firecracker," he warns.

"Fine. Fine." I untangle myself from our connection as I fling off the covers. Swinging my legs over the edge of the bed, I press my bare feet against the cool floor.

"Shower?" I ask over my shoulder, and I already know his answer before I see the heat flare in his hazel eyes.

As I move past him in the connected bathroom, he reaches out. With a gentle tug, my hands land on his chest while his lands on each side of my face.

"You're not getting away that easy."

"I wasn't running away. I was racing you to get to the shower spray first."

A huff of laughter leaves his lips before he lowers his mouth to mine. Tristan presses a gentle, lingering kiss, which leaves us both smiling. When he pulls back, a lopsided grin spreads over his swollen lips as if he's proud of the reaction he's caused.

With a smack to my bare ass, I gasp at the slight burn and watch as he retreats to the bathroom.

"Hey, you distracted me."

Only his deep timber can be heard as I chase after him.

The morning continues with a comfortable silence and quiet conversation. That is, once Tristan finally let me out of the shower, which he said he wouldn't do until I came twice.

As we move through our routine, we both brush our teeth together, shoulders bumping as we share foam-covered smiles in the mirror. I apply my makeup while he shaves his neck. Slipping a shirt off a hanger, his nimble fingers work each button while I add the finishing spray to my hair.

There's no rush in our moments, just the two of us, and it's when I'm realizing I feel at ease, like this could be our future.

• • • •••• • • • •

The two of us walked into the lobby, hand-in-hand, much like we've done for the last couple of weeks, but today feels different. After pouring us each a mug of coffee, Tristan handed me mine before taking a seat farther away.

Something feels off, and I can't help but feel the shift of energy among us as we wait for his family and additional executives to arrive. My eyes float around the lobby, and even if I don't feel totally at ease, I still smile around my mug.

Everything looks amazing. It's hard to believe this is the same resort we stepped foot in almost five weeks ago. The lobby is a beautiful representation of all the hard work and the perfect depiction of my renderings. Sleek, modern lines blend effortlessly with the island's natural charm. The floor-to-ceiling windows let in the dancing sunlight from outside. And I will admit, Tristan's idea of moving the entrance was a good decision.

Even the subtle details from local makers and island colors are exactly how we planned it. I should be proud. Hell, I am proud. But my focus keeps drifting to the broody man near me—his body is tight with a stiffness that hasn't been here since before we arrived.

A slight salty breeze drifts through the open doors, and my gaze slides to him as I try to read what is going on behind his stormy eyes. A crease forms between his eyebrows as he stares intently at his phone, fingers flying over his screen.

With his dad arriving back on the island, is he feeling the pressure again? He shouldn't be. Tristan did an incredible job on this project, and he should be so proud. I know I'm proud of him. For once, I was able to see past the persona he puts on for everyone else and see the real Tristan Nelson. The guy who wants to be accepted for who he really is. It's what made me fall in love with him.

My stomach twists as uncertainty washes over me. Or is it because he soft-launched us on social media? There's no plan for how we continue our relationship. Am I going to lose my job for sleeping with my boss? Oh my gosh, what if he regrets us?

He must feel me observing him because his eyes bounce up to meet mine. I flash him a look, which he reads. Only, instead of answering me, he flashes me a wink that does little to comfort me. It only leaves me more confused.

Maybe I'm reading too much into his mood shift? Maybe he's nervous about the grand opening? He turns back to his phone, as if nothing is wrong, and I'm left to stew in silence with a nagging feeling I can't quite shake.

Before I can dwell any longer, the sound of voices filters through the open doors of the lobby. Mr. Nelson, Xander, Victoria, and the rest of the team of executives enter with an air of authority and confidence.

I move to my feet, smoothing my sleeveless dress with shaky hands, suddenly feeling too exposed. Too raw. Too...small. Insecurity hits me like a tidal wave, and I fight with all of my strength not to cower in my heels. The group takes their time walking toward us, their gazes taking in the changes.

"Good morning," I greet, working overtime to keep the shakiness from my voice.

Mr. Nelson gives me a tight-lipped smile and a terse nod. Xander flashes me a wink, but it's Victoria who gives me the warmest welcome. Her smile is blinding as her eyes glimmer with excitement. This is her doing too. Her designs have brought this space to life.

It's so good to see her again.

Tristan steps up next to me, and a gentle touch caresses my lower back. It feels like a silent reassurance, almost as if he's grounding me.

"The space looks incredible." Victoria's voice is full of awe as she moves deeper into the room. I smile as she grazes her fingers over the coral-colored pillows.

Mr. Nelson observes like he's cataloguing each new detail, his critical gaze scanning every inch of the renovation. Soft murmurs from the others can be heard behind me, but their opinions don't matter, only Mr. Nelson's. His silence makes my heart race as I wait for his reaction.

Everything is riding on this moment. My design. My vision for the resort. My future in this company. He's the owner of this development, and what he says next will either validate everything or...destroy it. No matter if Tristan, Xander, and Victoria all love the property.

Xander breaks the silence first by throwing me a lifeline. "The lobby flows well with the island theme. I love the modernization with the soft beiges rather than the darker browns."

"It feels more natural," I explain, defending my vision. Xander smiles and gives me a small, approving nod as he mouths, *breathe*. I do as he says and take a deep breath, trying to calm my nerves. When Mr. Nelson doesn't say anything, the room falls into an awkward silence.

My chest tightens, and I search for Tristan for support. He's standing stiffly, with his hands in his pockets, an unreadable expression plastered on his face. I notice he's standing a little farther away from me than I would like. But I'm not the kind of girl who needs a man at her side. No, I'm Kennedy Reed. I'm confident, hardworking, and can stand up for myself.

Mr. Nelson lets out a heavy breath as he turns his attention back to the group. "What's the status of the villas?"

Steeling my shoulders, I find his gaze. "We are still three to four weeks out. However, the exterior construction is complete and only the interior finishes need to be finished."

"I see."

"The interior construction shouldn't hinder the guests' experiences," I add.

Mr. Nelson crosses his arms as he watches me intently. "I would hope not. We don't need any complaints about noise, not on top of everything else."

Tristan starts to interject, but I beat him to it. I refuse to let him talk over me, as if I can't handle the scrutiny from his father. "We've installed sound barriers for the construction zones, and we've worked with the crews to ensure that working hours won't be during peak guest hours. Each room will also receive a complimentary basket with ear plugs, champagne, and a few other local specialties."

Mr. Nelson huffs in response as he mills over my words.

"We're working around the clock, and like Kennedy said, we've thought it through, and the guests won't experience anything negative that we can't combat with a solution."

"A lot is riding on this opening," Mr. Nelson says as his eyes meet mine. "Thank you for your hard work. The jet will be departing in two hours to take you back to New York."

My stomach drops to my feet. "Wait, what? I'm leaving?"

You could hear a pin drop. Mr. Nelson turns his attention from me to Tristan. "Your work here is done, Miss Reed. We'll handle the rest here."

I blink, feeling completely blindsided as nausea rolls through me. How can I be dismissed so easily? The amount of press that will be here and I won't be featured at all. I designed this renovation, I've seen it through from sketches to reality, and now I'm being told I won't even be there to witness the benefits of all that hard work.

A burning sensation fills my eyes, but I refuse to show weakness. I shift my weight, glancing at Tristan, searching for some sign that he's as frustrated as I am. But all I get is that distance again. That *wall*.

And that's when the sinking feeling intensifies.

He knew.

It all makes sense now.

My mind flashes back to the last twenty-four hours. Last night's perfect date. How he worshiped my body. The gentle way we woke up this morning. To fucking me one last time in the shower. And then the distance he was showing me afterward. I knew there was something wrong with him, and it wasn't all in my head.

It was all his way of saying goodbye. He refused to be a good person and give me the heads-up.

My heart clenches as pain erupts throughout my body, taking my breath away. I feel my heart break in half, and it has me wanting to physically curl in on myself. But I won't. He won't get that satisfaction.

"I guess that's it, then."

"Yes," Mr. Nelson says. "A car will take you to the airport."

He turns to Tristan, focusing his attention on him and not me, the person who just had the rug ripped from underneath her. His deep timbered voice demands, "Show me the rest of the resort."

As some of the executives start to follow Mr. Nelson, I look up at a stoic-faced Tristan.

"We're done," I say sharply before spinning on my heel, not allowing him a chance to say anything back. Today, I'm having the last word. I storm off to the penthouse to gather my things as anger takes the place of my broken heart.

CHAPTER THIRTY-TWO

TRISTAN

MOISTURE GATHERS, CLOUDING THE whites of her eyes, but she never lets the tears fall. "We're done."

I feel my face fall in shock.

Two words I never wanted to hear come out of Kennedy's mouth. *"We're done."* I wanted to run after her. To beg her to listen to me. To apologize for letting this blindside her and to let her know that I don't agree with the decision. But I don't. I choose to be the cowardly version of myself. Feet frozen, I watch as she storms out of the lobby.

Please turn around. Please look over your shoulder.

She never does.

"Did she just quit on us?" I hear Xander ask.

Glancing at my older brother, I shake my head. "No, she didn't quit on us." I pause, swallowing past the thick emotion in my throat. "She quit on me."

Fuck. What have I done?

I thought she'd be angry. I thought she'd be upset. But I never thought she'd end it all.

Running my hands through my hair, I try to think of how I can fix this. I've got to go after her. I can't let her leave the island like this.

Not after everything we've been through. I go to take a step, when my brother's hand clamps down on my shoulder.

"Let her go, Tristan."

I shrug out of his touch and turn my glare at him. But it's Victoria's voice that has me pausing my attack. "He's right, Trist. Let her cool down. This is your moment, big brother. This is your time to show Dad how serious you are about the company. Talk to Kennedy when we get back to New York."

Torn between what to do, I let my brain win out, rather than my heart. I let Kennedy go and pray to God she'll let me explain when I get back to the city. That she'll believe me when I say that what we have is deeper than this.

. . . ● . ● . . .

For the next three days, I drown myself in work...and alcohol. Although I never let the alcohol affect my work, I use it to cope as soon as I'm off the clock. I've moved from the penthouse to a small suite. I couldn't be in that space without her, and I knew my dad wouldn't stay anywhere else.

Xander and Victoria have tried to drag me out of my room, but I refuse. The only place I've gone is the boardroom, where Dad has had me sitting in back-to-back meetings, and to my balcony, where I stare out at the horizon, wishing I was anywhere but here.

I fucked up. I know I did, but I honestly didn't think my dad would dismiss her so quickly. Nothing like him arriving, taking one look around, and sending her on her way. The least he could have done was include her in the sit-down luncheon he had thirty minutes later or have her complete the tour with me. A whole thirty minutes after I watched Jayden load her luggage in the back of the sedan, she never looked behind her.

But that's what I fell in love with. Kennedy's ability to wear her confidence like a shield. The entire time I watched—from a distance—her shoulders were back, head held high, sunglasses firmly in place.

I've tried calling her, texting her, hell, even sending her emails from work with bullshit questions. She hasn't returned my calls or texts and the emails she did return were so professional, HR would gladly use them as examples of how to communicate between departments.

There were no quips, no sass, none of the banter she'd been throwing my way for the past six years of knowing her. Her firecracker personality has been distinguished, and I'm the one holding the hose.

A soft knock on the door pulls my attention from where I'm moping on the balcony. With my beer dangling between my fingers, I move through the room until I'm pulling open the door. My younger sister stares up at me, her eyes widening in shock as she takes in my appearance.

I know I look rough; I don't even think I've showered today, and if the crinkle in her nose is any indication, I'd say I smell a bit too. My beard is no longer neatly trimmed, my hair is a tousled mess from my hands running through it a thousand times, and the bags under my eyes are taking over my face.

"You look like shit," she says as she pushes her way through my door.

"Well, fuck you very much, Tori."

She shrugs as she moves farther into the room, and I'm on her heels. "I'm just calling it like I see it."

"As much as I appreciate the critique, what are you doing here?"

Spinning around, she holds up the ice bucket, which is full of local bottled beer. "I thought we could have a sibs' night."

"I'm not really up for company."

"And I'm family, not company."

Rolling my eyes, I follow her onto the balcony, where I take my place in a chair, while she sets the bucket down and fishes us each out a bottle. Popping the top, I take a long gulp of the light beer as silence washes over us.

Victoria props her feet on the railing in front of her, mindlessly picking at the label on her bottle.

"Remember growing up, you were always the one I would go to when I needed something fixed? Whether I broke a toy or had some kind of issue at school, I'd always go to you for help."

"Of course, I remember." I nod as I turn toward her, wondering where she's going, which is exactly what I ask.

"Well, it's my turn to offer my advice."

"I'm not really interested in your advice, Tori. I already know I fucked up."

"Yeah, I know you did."

I scoff, but she continues.

"Look, I'm not here to sugarcoat things, Trist. I'm going to lay it out there and tell you how to fix it."

Bringing my beer to my lips, I take another sip. "I don't know if it can be fixed."

"It can. I know we didn't talk as often as we usually do while you were here, but when we did, I noticed a change in you."

I quirk my eyebrow, curious.

"You're happier, lighter. It's like she sparked something that you've kept hidden for a long time. Hell, it might even be since Asher died."

I bristle at the mention of my cousin's name. He was my best friend, the one I dreamed all my dreams with. When he died, my dreams died with him. My future was forced to be Nelson Signature, and while I don't mind it, it's never been my passion.

"I know it's hard to hear his name. The two of you had such a deep connection, but when you were with him, you were free. It's the same freedom I saw when you were here...with Kennedy. You both are miserable."

My head whips in her direction. "You've talked to her?"

"Well, yeah. She's my friend, and I had to apologize to her for my dad. *And* my idiot brother."

"Way to pour salt in the wound."

"Oh stop, you know I love you." She waves me off.

"I might love you, but Kennedy and I are done. She won't even take my calls or answer my texts."

"She has every right to be upset, Tristan. You blindsided her, and you know it. But don't give up, not yet. When we get back to New York, you need to apologize to her in person."

"I don't think there's any room for forgiveness. I've fucked this up real good. It's not like I've always given her a reason to trust me."

Her head lulls toward me with a subtle smirk. "Oh, sweet, naive brother. Women are...well, we're easier to forgive than you might think, especially when we know the guy's heart. And deep down,

Kennedy knows your heart. She knows you, Trist, the *real* you. Don't give up on her."

"How do I do that?"

"Don't treat her like a project, treat her like your partner. Tell her how you feel about her and prove to her that you're worthy. Take a leap and fight for something you love. I've seen how she's changed you—or, not necessarily changed, but brought out the old Tristan. Give her a reason to take him back."

I let her words linger. Kennedy is the only person who knows my deepest secrets and how my vision for my future was completely different than what it is now. Of course, Victoria knows some things, but Kennedy got to see the real me. The side of me I haven't shown anyone and far too long. I'd give up the company if it meant I could have Kennedy Reed in my life.

Sitting up taller in my seat, I feel hope for the first time in days.

"There he is."

"Who?"

"My big brother. Who would have thought that getting stuck on an island with your *enemy* would be the beginning of your happily ever after? You both bring out each other's best parts. Not only that, but you're not the same guy who came to this island, Trist. You've grown. I've seen it. And I know she has too. You just need to be honest with her."

"When did you become such a romantic?" I ask her with a chuckle.

"Oh, please, I've always been a romantic." She nudges my shoulder, and I refuse to touch that with a ten-foot pole. "What you have might not be perfect now, but nothing worth having ever is. Love isn't immediate—it's a paradise in progress."

A paradise in progress? I like the sound of that. Clinking my bottle against hers, I lean back in my chair as we fall into silence. She came and said her peace, and now my brain is spinning with how I win back the girl.

My girl.

Nelson Signature has once again raised the bar on luxury resorts with their grand opening of Paradise at Piton Peaks. This breathtaking resort is nestled near St. Lucia's iconic Piton Mountains. The resort has opened its doors to eager guests looking for a one-of-a-kind island escape. The grand opening revealed a seamless blend of luxury and nature while allowing St Lucia's tropical beauty to shine while merging with modern elegance.

With the recent opening, guests were able to experience fine dining options, including an entertaining hibachi dinner and private beachside dining. With eleven unique restaurants ranging from local cuisine, French crepes, authentic Italian cuisine, and American gastropub options, guests are bound to find something they enjoy and support a variety of dietary restrictions. Other standout features include multiple resort pools, in-house spa treatments inspired by the island's natural volcanic mud baths, and private over-the-water villas coming Spring 2025. Guests are treated to an array of activities, from scuba diving to sunset cruises to horseback riding to mountain climbing. There's an activity for everyone.

Spearheading the project is Mr. Nelson's middle son, Tristan Nelson, an emerging star in the real estate industry. His forward-thinking approach has added a modern charm to the resort while keeping with the island's natural beauty. His unique eye has set the resort apart from others, especially with the technological advances made throughout the property. Paradise at Piton Peaks has positioned itself as the top destination for those seeking a serene yet luxurious getaway.

Though the architectural team played a pivotal role in transforming the space, the Nelson family remains the face of the brand. Guests can expect unforgettable experiences at this new St. Lucia destination. With its perfect combination of luxury and adventure, the resort promises white sandy beaches, stunning sunsets, gorgeous views of the Pitons, and an unforgettable stay for guests looking for comfort in a five-star experience.

CHAPTER THIRTY-THREE

KENNEDY

IT'S BEEN ALMOST A week since my sudden departure from St. Lucia, even though it feels like yesterday. The wounds are still raw, and I've been licking them since I left. My heart physically aches. I'm so angry at the way things ended.

The first few days were a blur. No, seriously, I couldn't see clearly from all the tears I shed. I might have kept my composure the entire time I packed as I waited for Tristan to chase after me but, like a coward, he never did. The minute I climbed into the car, I lost it. I don't know what I would've done if Tristan had come after me. Right now, I like to think I would have heard him out, given him a chance to explain why he didn't have the decency to give me a heads-up. But at that moment, I was so completely devastated that I'm not sure I would've listened.

One thing I know is that I'm grateful this happened on a Friday, and I had the entire weekend to prepare for the office on Monday. The anxiety of how my coworkers would react kept me paralyzed with fear. Not only did I not want to deal with their looks and whispers, but I didn't want to have to answer their questions, especially since there is no me and Tristan. *Us* was a fragment of my imagination, a fairytale ending to rivalry.

I spent the whole weekend tossing and turning, sleepless night after sleepless night. Turns out, my body didn't get the memo that she has to sleep alone now. No more cuddles with a sexy guy named Tristan. I dodged every call and text, only answering work-related emails. Long gone is the playfulness, and in its place are only the utmost professional responses. Mom always said to kill people with kindness, and that's exactly what I plan to do.

He's nothing more than my boss.

Oh, hell, who am I kidding? Even with this massive ache in my chest and the constant way I feel—mopey, miserable, and heartbroken—I still miss him.

God, I miss him so much.

Tomorrow is his first day back in the office, and I have no idea how I'm going to handle being in the same room as him again. The grand opening was Tuesday, and I was notified by email that he would be back in the office Friday for a debriefing meeting with the entire team. I wonder if it's too late to call in sick...

As I'm lying on the couch, a romantic comedy plays in the background, because even if I can't keep love, I can watch other people chase after their happily ever afters. My phone vibrates on the cushion underneath me, and I bring the screen to my face. A flash of excitement courses through my body at what I see. It's the first time I've felt a positive emotion since I returned.

There on my screen is the news notification on Paradise at Piton Peaks' grand opening. Sitting up in my seat, my blanket falls to the ground as my heart pounds while I swipe open the article. My stomach churns with nerves as I skim over the article. It's full of praise for the resort, giving it a glowing review for the grand opening. The article mentions the modern renovations, state-of-the-art technology, lavish guest experiences, and delicious food. *My* renovations. *My* ideas. They loved everything I put together. Tears flood my eyes as I'm hit with an overwhelming burst of pride.

As the article comes to an end, that pride quickly morphs into something else. Pain, disappointment, utter shock. Not once is my name mentioned. Nowhere in the article is it known that I had anything to do with this project. The only name mentioned over and over again is Mr. Nelson's prodigal son, Tristan Nelson.

Rationally, I know it's not Tristan's fault his name is splashed throughout the article, but the irrational voice inside my head sure can blame him. Tossing my phone aside, I melt back into the couch. Add another tally to why I'm dreading tomorrow.

How could they not mention my name? Sure, they mention the team, but when does the lead architect not get any acknowledgment? I poured so much into this project, and nowhere will I receive the recognition I deserve. While I know it's not that big of a deal at the end of the day, it was important to me. This project was everything to me. It was a steppingstone in my career.

Everything about it feels so...wrong.

"Don't read the article! Don't read the article!" Lana comes running out of her room in pure panic. Coming to an abrupt stop in front of the couch, my facial expression must say it all, because her shoulders deflate.

"Too late."

"Dammit." She moves around the coffee table and sits beside me, curling her body into mine as she wraps her arms around me. "Talk about a shitty week."

"You can say that again," I grumble, placing my head on her shoulder.

"Talk about a shi—" My hand covering her mouth cuts her off.

"I didn't mean that literally." She shrugs and tightens her hold.

"Zoe will be here any minute. We're having a girls' night in."

"Lan, I'm really not in the mood."

"That's precisely why we are having it. It's time for Kennedy to get her groove back."

"Wasn't her name Stella?"

Lana rolls her eyes as she moves to the opposite side of the couch. "Stop being so literal."

Before I have a chance to respond, there's a knock at the door. Lana jumps from the couch and practically hurdles through our townhouse to answer. I hear hushed voices coming from my two closest friends, and I know they are discussing me. I hate feeling like this. I'm giving myself one more night to wallow, then I'm putting on my big girl panties and striding through that office like that bad bitch I am.

"Hey, babes," Zoe's soft voice greets. "I brought Chinese takeout and wine."

"Zo, I'm not a scared animal. You don't have to use that sugary voice with me. I promise not to pounce on you or take off and hide."

"Well, I wasn't sure where your headspace was at."

Lana comes back into our tiny living room with wineglasses and forks in her hand, while Zoe is busy unpacking the boxes of food from the brown paper bag onto the coffee table. The familiar smell of Chinese food wafts through the air as Zoe opens each box, and my mouth instantly waters at the sight. Boxes of orange chicken, beef and broccoli, chow mein, egg rolls, crab rangoon, and fried rice cover my table.

"Hungry, Zoe?" I chuckle as I stare at the piles of food—enough to feed a small army.

"I wasn't sure what you wanted, and I wasn't sure if you were eating enough."

Grabbing a fork from Lana's outstretched hand, I stab my fork into the box and pull out an egg roll. "Lucky for you, I'm starving."

The three of us fall into silence as we squeeze onto the couch, taking turns passing the cartons of food as we stuff our faces. Best friends, the real ones, don't care if you eat after each other. They avoid dirtying up dishes and share cartons of food, especially when one needs it the most.

As the opening credits of *10 Things I Hate About You* begin, Zoe interrupts our feast. "So are we ready to talk about the elephant in the room?"

"Which one?" I ask around a mouthful of chow mein. "The fact I was left out of the article, I get to see my ex-slash-tropical fling-slash-boss tomorrow, or the fact that Heath Ledger was fine as hell in this movie?"

Lana clinks her fork against her wineglass, almost as if she's signaling a winning sound. "Heath Ledger, RIP."

Zoe rolls her eyes as she digs into the orange chicken. "I was referring to your Golden Boy."

"First of all, he's not *my* Golden Boy. He's not my anything."

"That's my girl," Lana agrees. "I say you keep him at arm's length tomorrow, but wear something that makes you look hot—hotter than usual—just to flaunt it in his face."

"Wait," Zoe interrupts. "Are you not on Team Tristan?"

"First of all, there are no teams."

The girls snap their heads in my direction as their eyebrows furrow, but it's Zoe who jumps in first. "Yes, there are teams, and while we are all Team Kenny, we're also Team Whoever makes you happy."

"And that's why I think she needs to move on from *hewhoshallnotbenamed*."

"Tristan. We can say his name." I rip off a piece of crab rangoon and pop the warm cream cheese mixture into my mouth.

"How are you going to handle tomorrow when you see him? Honesty."

"I have no idea, Zo. I won't be the girl to avoid him and cower in the corner, but I also don't know how I'm supposed to be professional when my heart aches for him. I miss him, even though I shouldn't."

"Why do you think you shouldn't?" Lana asks. I stare at her quizzically. She's been team whoever makes me happy, and this question is throwing me for a loop.

"Because he hurt me."

"Ken, I think in some weird way, Tristan wasn't trying to hurt you. Yes, he didn't tell you that you would be leaving, and I know that blindsided you, but we saw how the two of you were. Each time you FaceTimed us, there were stars in your eyes, a glow that wasn't there before."

"It was the sun," I murmur.

Zoe nudges me in the ribs with her elbow. Her expression tells me she's not buying that for a second.

"No, I've been on vacation with you many times, and I know that wasn't the case. That was the Tristan Nelson effect."

"And I saw that same look on his face when he'd call in for work meetings," Zoe adds.

"Ken, you're my best friend, and I will always fight for you and whatever makes you happy. And while Tristan isn't my favorite right now because he hurt you, I also saw him bring out fun Kennedy. The girl who wasn't afraid to let her hair down and leave work in the office."

"That's true. You definitely seemed more at ease around him."

"So what do you think I should do?" Tears well in my eyes, my throat clogging with emotions. "Simply forgive and forget. I'm not wired that way. I wish I were. It'd make life a lot easier, but I carry shit. I pack it up in bins and store it forever."

"I don't think that's what Lana is saying." Zoe turns to Lana, who nods in agreement. "But I think she's saying you should give him a chance to explain himself. Maybe there's a perfectly good reason why he let the news blindside you. Maybe he was scared of you turning against him."

"Which happened anyway."

Zoe shrugs. "Do you still love him?"

Turning my attention back to the movie, I think about her question. I don't believe love can simply be turned on and off with a flip of a switch. Love is complex and multidimensional. While it takes layers to build and to fall in love, one swing of a wrecking ball can shatter the love that you know. And while I feel like I was hit with a wrecking ball, there are still pieces of those layers stuck together.

"I think she found her answer," Lana says as she sips from her wineglass.

"We don't need you to tell us; the important thing is that you know. Now you need to decide how you are going to handle tomorrow. Are you going to put up a professional front? Or give him a chance to explain himself?"

"What if...what if I choose to be professional?"

"Then that's your decision. Take the time to continue healing, but establish boundaries from the beginning. Make him see that you're not ready to discuss what happened in St. Lucia, but you are ready to continue your working relationship."

"Is that what you guys think I should do?"

"Honey, we're here to pick you up, and tell you how wonderful you are, but we can't make that decision for you." Zoe stretches her arms over my shoulders before pulling me in tight.

"I think you need to do whatever is best for you right now," Lana adds, offering me a reassuring smile. "But if your heart is giving you any indication that there's something still brewing between you and Tristan, I think you need to listen to it."

Half-eaten boxes of food gather on the coffee table with empty glasses of wine as we finish watching the movie. As much as I love the romance between Kat and Patrick, my mind is busy spinning around all the scenarios for tomorrow.

Deep down, I know they're both right. Too bad my heart and my mind won't get on the same page.

Turns out, tomorrow is going to be more difficult than I imagined.

Do I give him one last chance?

Or do I establish a professional relationship with a man I love deeply?

CHAPTER THIRTY-FOUR

TRISTAN

IT'S BEEN A WEEK without her.

Without her addicting smile.

Without her hypnotizing eyes.

Without her captivating touch.

I always swore I didn't want to be like my dad, and here I chose the company over her. If it came down to me or her, I would've—should've—quit on the spot. Working for Nelson Signature was never my dream, but it's always been hers. If there's one thing I've learned from my father, it's how not to be a husband. For as long as I can remember, he's prioritized his work over his wife and children. That's not the type of man I want to be.

I might have been her "boss," but every renovation idea came from her. I should have pushed harder to ensure Kennedy was included in the final stages of the opening. I know that, but hindsight is 20/20. Instead, I kept my mouth shut to appease my father, and look at where that got me.

Today everything changes. For the first time in seven days, I get the opportunity to be in the same room as her. To smell her sweet scent that drives me wild. Today, I will fight for her. I only pray I'm not too late.

Walking through the lobby of our building, I'm hit with a wave of emotions buzzing beneath my skin. People hustle around me as they move toward their offices. Seven weeks out of this environment has me wishing for the simplicity of the island again.

"Mr. Nelson," one of our security guards greets. And with a welcoming nod, I realize I've never taken the time to learn the names of the people who work for us, not like I did in St. Lucia.

Maybe Kennedy had a point. Maybe I was a self-absorbed prick who walked around as if I was better than everyone.

Deciding to be better, I step around people and make my way toward the security officer.

He stands up straighter as he watches me approach. "Is everything okay, Mr. Nelson?"

I nod as embarrassment floods my system. "Everything is fine; however, I do want to apologize to you."

"What on earth for, sir?"

"For never taking the time to ask you for your name."

"It's Todd, sir."

Reaching my hand out, I wait for him to take it. Todd's eyes lower to my hand before he grips it. "It's nice to meet you, Todd. Please call me Tristan, and thank you for all that you do for our building."

"Of course. Have a great day, Tristan."

With a satisfied smile, I turn and weave my way to the elevators. Stepping inside the waiting car, I join a group of people going to various floors. I adjust the cuffs on my lavender dress shirt before doing the same with the collar of my wool coat. Being thrust back into New York's bitter January air has taken quite a toll on me. I can feel my sinuses closing with the temperature shock.

The doors open with a ding, and I adjust my collar again. Nerves have me fidgeting with anxiety about seeing Kennedy again. As stupid as it is, I want to look good for her, impress her. Even though I know no expensive suit is going to fix anything.

Sounds of chatter, ringing phones, and keyboards clicking signify the familiar hum of the office. It feels foreign being back here. As my eyes scan the floor, I immediately latch onto her bright red hair. At the far end of the space, Kennedy stands with her back to me, talking with her friend, Zoe.

I take a moment to check her out blatantly. Her legs look sky-high from the tall black heels she's wearing, and the black skintight long-sleeved dress hugs her delicious curves. Curves I'm desperate to trace under my gentle caress as she's sprawled out beneath me. Her long hair is curled in big waves and hangs down her back. She looks powerful and confident, like she always does.

Zoe's gaze catches mine. Her lips move as she nods in my direction. Kennedy looks over her shoulder, and those green eyes bore into mine instantly. My breath catches in my throat as I take in her sullen features and the dark circles beneath her eyes, bags she's trying to hide with layers of concealer. Even still, she's devastatingly gorgeous.

She lifts her chin, giving me a terse nod as the corner of her lips lifts slightly. Her eyes are cold and distant, not showing any warmth at all. It's the same greeting she'd give to a passing colleague, not someone you've spent countless hours with, tangled in sheets, and sharing "I love yous."

Shock has me moving on autopilot as I make my way toward my office. Placing my bag on my spare chair, I round my desk. The dull, empty desk lacks any signs of personality—no framed photos, special trinkets, or any signs of actual life. Although, there is a to-go cup with a sticky note next to it.

Fuel up and get your girl. – V

She's as subtle as a freight train, but I appreciate my sister's support.

Glancing at my watch, I notice I have an hour until the debriefing meeting.

Time to formulate my plan.

· · · ●·●·● · ·

The conference room is a hive of energy as I step inside. Conversation flows as I take my place at the head of the table, glancing around the room with a new appreciation of the team I work with. Victoria is to my left with her design team, and Kennedy is at the far end of the table on my right with her team. She keeps her gaze locked on her iPad, completely ignoring my presence.

Tapping my fingers on the table, I resist the urge to shout across the room that I love her and miss her. Once the final person enters the room and the door is shut, I stand from my seat, ready to begin the meeting. From my place at the head of the conference room, I can feel the weight of everyone's attention locked on me—everyone except for the one person I'm most desperate to have it from.

Clearing the emotion from my throat, I'm about to speak when the sound of the door creaking open has me pausing. I glance to the side and watch as my father enters the room. A surprise to everyone, including myself. Shuffling sounds as everyone sits up straighter, and the temperature in the room drops. I can practically feel the tension growing as everyone internally panics at the owner of the company joining our causal team meeting.

My father strides deeper into the room, and my heart sinks with each step he takes. With his suit jacket draped over his arm, his presence alone commands attention. A lone chair sits opposite Kennedy, and that's the one he has his eyes set on. With his tall stature, broad shoulders, and stern expression, my father exudes authority. Even with his stoic expression not giving away his thoughts, I can tell what his motives are.

He's here to take charge, as usual. With my father in his seat, I glance at Kennedy. Her posture is rigid, her hands white knuckling her iPad, as if it's her safety vessel. While she's fighting to not show her cards, I've spent too much time watching her, learning her quirks. I can tell she's angry and full of resentment.

This is the man who overlooked her. Who dismissed her as if she wasn't a huge part of this project. He didn't give her the recognition she deserved. Now he's sitting in her space and not in his office, away from the day-to-day.

And I was the fucker who went along with it. But that stops right now. I'm giving her the acknowledgement she deserves.

With a final glance at my father, I turn my attention back to my team. "Before we get started with today's brief, I want to acknowledge someone who has gone above and beyond during this entire project."

From the corner of my eye, I notice Kennedy look up at me. Her expression is a mixture of surprise and anger, but she's quick to mask it.

"Kennedy's designs, her creativity, her work ethic—she's been a driving force behind every vision we had for this resort coming to life." I don't spare my father a glance as I continue to stand up for the woman I love. "Without her, Paradise at Piton Peaks wouldn't be what it is today."

I can feel my father's glare boring into the side of my face. He wanted this project to be the one to make his son as well-known as he is. Dropping my name over and over again was a publicity stunt to make the dynasty of Nelson Signature stand out even more in a prominent field.

And while I did have a part in this project, Kennedy had everything to do with it.

"Thank you, Kennedy." My words are soft and sincere as I let the people in the room drift away. It's just her and me. "You deserve all the credit for everything that has been accomplished on this project."

With a beat of silence, Kennedy gives a small, appreciative nod with a tight-lipped smile. Looking around the room, I watch as the team exchanges looks of surprise. But I don't care. I don't care if my father is pissed, or if the team is wondering why I'm making such a big deal about this.

I'm choosing her.

Victoria is the first person to make a move, breaking the silence as she claps slowly. The rest of the team catches on, giving Kennedy a deserving round of applause. Kennedy's cheeks flush a deep pink as she shifts uncomfortably in her seat, not wanting to be the center of attention. Her eyes move around the room, lips pressed into an unsure smile, before her gaze lands on me. The moment is fleeting, but I tip my head in a subtle nod, hoping my expression carries with it everything I'm trying to say.

I see you.

You deserve the world.

I'm sorry.

Please forgive me.

With a deep breath, I turn back to the agenda in front of me and begin the meeting. "It looks like the only thing we are waiting on is the completion of the over-the-water villas and the finalization of the smart systems throughout the rooms. Any updates?"

"As I've mentioned previously," Kennedy begins, squaring her shoulders, as if the last few minutes never happened. "The villas will be completed in roughly two weeks. The only items left unfinished are the interior details, which shouldn't affect guests' experiences."

"Right," I choke out before clearing my throat. "Thank you, Kennedy."

She offers another tight-lipped smile, and I feel the temperature drop into the negatives. It's icy in this room.

As the meeting wraps up and chairs slide away from the table, it's Kennedy who rises first. Bolting toward the door, I'm quick on her heels, ignoring the murmurs and my father in the process.

If she won't talk to me, I'm going to hope she'll at least listen. The two of us leave the room together, only she doesn't spare me a glance. It's like she's determined to keep me at arm's length, and I can't say I blame her, but I also hate it.

She stays quiet, her eyes focused ahead, and I can feel everyone's attention on us as we move together. I'm building the courage to talk to her. I feel like a junior high boy who has his first crush.

"You're really not going to talk to me?"

"We're talking right now," she quips, glancing at me while her expression remains neutral. Professional. I smile softly as I see the slightest hint of my firecracker.

I snort a self-deprecating chuckle. "It's not like how we used…" I let the words trail off, and her nostrils flare, knowing what I was going to say. There's no sense in rehashing the past, as it's behind us now. All that matters is this moment and building a future with Kennedy by my side.

Her eyes roll as she quickens her pace. I can't let her get away, not again.

"Wait." I reach out for her, only she's too far away. My hand falls to my side with a smack, and she pauses. Even with her back still to me, I take it as a win that she stopped.

"I can't do this," I say, louder than I intended, and her shoulders stiffen. My raised voice has people turning to watch our interaction. This isn't how or where I wanted to do this. But fuck it. I can't take this animosity. Not when I'm one second away from needing to feel her skin against mine.

"You can't do what?" I barely hear the question in her hushed voice.

With a tentative step forward, I start to close the gap between us. "I can't pretend that what we shared didn't happen. That it didn't matter. That I didn't fall head over heels in love with you. That I don't crave your touch, your attention, your presence. You might think I'm fine with how we ended, but I'm far from it. I'm fucked up without you."

Kennedy turns to me, moisture seeping from her tired eyes as her cheeks turn a light shade of pink. Her gaze bounces around the room as she takes in the crowd that's gathered. Those from the meeting are frozen behind me, while others who were at their desks are now standing, their heads peeking over their cubicles. Shock has her hoping I'll stop my declaration, but I've fully committed now.

"I love you," I say as my voice cracks. "I'm in love with you, Kennedy Reed. I screwed up by letting you walk away. I should've fought harder for you, and that's a regret I have to live with. I was hoping that the decision would be reversed. And I was trying to prevent this." I gesture between us.

"I was blindsided," she says with a shaky exhale. There's a mix of emotions there—hurt, betrayal, anger, and something softer. I hope it's love. If there's an ounce of love left in her soul for me, I can work with that. I can prove to her what she means to me. I'll water that love and nurture it while it grows.

"I messed up." I take another step forward. "I let the insecure boy seep into the conversation when he should have been buried a long time ago. You helped show me that it was okay to be myself, to let go of the desire to please and to find what I'm passionate about again. You helped heal me, Ken, and I don't even think you realize that. Instead of fighting for myself, I made decisions to appease my dad, to keep the peace in our relationship. You peeled back my layers and showed me it's okay to fight for what I want. And that's you, Kennedy."

Tears pour openly down her cheeks, and even though we are in a crowded office with people staring at us, it feels like it's just her and I. I wait on bated breath as I wait for her to respond. Her mouth opens and closes, but nothing comes out. My chest tightens more and more as each second passes.

"You hurt me," is all she whispers, and it's filled with pain.

"I know, baby. I'm so sorry." It's as if there's a cosmic pull that forces us to erase the space between us until her heels hit the toes of my dress shoes.

Tentatively, I reach up and cup her cheek, wiping her tears in the process. "You and me, we're a paradise in progress. I'll fight like hell until our foundation is strong and stable."

She chokes on a sob as she melts into my touch. "Don't push me aside again, Tristan. My heart can't handle being ripped away from yours."

Her delicate fingers trail up my jacket's lapels until she's gripping the material. She pulls me toward her while reaching up on her feet, and as our lips finally meet, fireworks shoot from behind my eyes with both elation and relief. Cheers fill the office floor, and I'm reminded that all our co-workers are watching us.

With much reluctance, our lips fall away, and I rest my forehead against hers. "I love you, Firecracker."

"I love you, too."

Chapter Thirty-Five

Kennedy

It's been two weeks since Tristan and I had our movie moment in the middle of the office floor. The entire thing felt like a scene from one of the rom-coms Olivia and I grew up watching. We've been working on mending our relationship and taking things slow, but we're still together. St. Lucia forced us to have real conversations, but living together escalated our relationship. Now that we're back in New York, we've been dating at a much slower pace.

When I accepted his speech about getting back together, I was still angry at him. But, I mean, there was no way I was saying no in front of our entire floor of co-workers. It's like those people who propose in front of everyone you know. You say yes, and then call it off in private. Only I have no intention of breaking things off with Tristan. In fact, I hope to keep him forever, but we'll cross that bridge when we get to it.

Today, I'm meeting his family during their weekly Sunday dinner. My nerves have my stomach aching. I've met most of his family, everyone except his mom, formally, but that was at the office, and this is inside their home for a dinner that she prepared for us. It's terrifying. Especially being outside the office with Mr. Nelson.

"You look beautiful," Tristan murmurs in my ear as he kisses my pulse point. The two of us walk hand-in-hand down the sidewalk toward his parents' brownstone. The air is still crisp, but the sun shines high in the sky. After weeks of gloom, walking in the sunshine is everything I didn't know I needed. The rays warm my skin, slightly easing the anxiousness swirling inside me.

The Nelsons' brownstone comes into view. With Tristan's hand on my lower back, he guides me up the stairs. "Relax, Firecracker."

Glancing up at him, I try to paste on a reassuring smile, but his small chuckle tells me it looks more like a grimace. Wiping my hands on my leopard print skirt for what feels like the tenth time, I hope the sweat is removed before I have to shake his mother's hand.

He doesn't even get the chance to knock—or push open the door—before it's being opened for us. Standing in the doorway is his mother. Her bright hazel eyes match her son's as they stare at me with a welcoming warmth. She wears her brunette hair pulled back and secured behind her head, smile blinding as it lights up her face.

"You're here!" she shouts, pulling Tristan into a hug as I stand still beside him, watching their interaction.

He wraps his arms around her back and pulls her in tight. As she rocks them back and forth, I can't help grinning. It's too cute.

Tristan grumbles some unintelligible, and she lets him go as her gaze slides over to me.

"Mom, I'd like you to meet Kennedy Reed."

Reaching my hand out, I pray it isn't sweaty. "Mrs. Nelson, it's a pleasure—"

My words are cut off as she flicks her wrist in my direction before embracing me. The connection is full of love, hope, and excitement.

It almost makes me forget how nervous I am. "Nonsense, sweetie. The first girl Tristan brings home can call me Krista."

The only girl? Quirking an eyebrow, I look over her shoulder and meet her son's gaze. He lifts one shoulder and shrugs, as if he's answering my unspoken question.

As she pulls away, she reaches down and squeezes my hand. "Come on in. Food's almost ready."

With her back to us, I take the opportunity to admire the beautiful home. As we step inside, the grand entryway features a large, dark, wooden staircase that contrasts against the warm beige walls and light-colored carpet. Even before I'm instructed to, I step aside and begin slipping out of my booties.

"You don't have to do that," Tristan whispers.

"It's no problem," I say. My shoes aren't filthy, but there's no way I'm risking a black mark against this carpet. Not when this house is worth more money than I'll ever see in my entire life.

Krista pauses in the doorway. "Oh, sweetie, you don't need to remove your shoes."

"No, really, I don't mind," I insist.

"Tristan, up in the guest bedroom, there are a few pairs of new slippers. See if any are Kennedy's size."

"You really don't..." my words trail off as she flashes me a wink, and before I know it, Tristan is running up the stairs I was admiring. If I thought there was going to be this much fuss, I would have kept my shoes on. Who am I kidding? I probably still would have taken them off because...anxiety.

"I'll take you on a small tour. Everyone is waiting in the parlor."

With one last glance up the stairs, I follow his mom into the next room. The living area is a mix of classic and modern elements, which has my jaw dropping. Cream couches face a stunningly intricate carved fireplace. It's breathtaking.

"Your home is beautiful."

"Thank you. We've had this home since the kids were little, and I have no idea how some pieces survived toddlerhood."

That's when I notice the bookshelves lined with vases and antiques.

"You did an excellent job with Paradise. I was so angry on your behalf that they didn't include your name."

Sheepishly, I tuck a strand of hair behind my ear, unsure how to respond, but I settle on a simple thank you.

We move into the oversized white marble kitchen, where pots line the stove as their smells mingle together. My stomach grumbles at the fragrance. Xander walks in from the opposite direction and smiles brightly.

"Ready for your first Nelson family dinner?" He smirks, and my eyes widen.

"Xander, don't scare the poor girl."

"Nah, Kennedy can hold her own." Moving over to the fruit bowl, he pops a few grapes into his mouth.

"I don't doubt that for one second," Krista adds. "If she finally put Tristan out of his misery, she can handle anything."

Conversation flows between the two, and I stand back and observe. A few minutes later, Tristan comes back into the room, carrying a pair of white slippers. He places a gentle kiss on my cheek before bending down to situate the shoes at my feet. I slide into the soft material, and when my feet feel like they're standing on clouds, I'm instantly grateful for the slippers.

"I hope Mom wasn't overwhelming you too much."

Xander looks over at us from where he's leaning against the counter. "I rescued her just in time. Mom was giving her the fifth degree and listing all the responsibilities that come with the Nelson name."

"Mom." Tristan's eyes widen, but Krista ignores his chastising.

"Your brother was the one scaring the poor girl."

"The poor girl is standing right in front of us and looks like she could use a glass of wine." Victoria steps into the kitchen and wraps her arms around my shoulder. "Come, Kenny, I'll show you where Mom keeps the good wine...and baby pictures."

"Don't you dare." Tristan squints at his sister, almost as if he is daring her.

We both chuckle as Victoria leads me out of the kitchen and toward what I assume is the parlor.

It's not long before Krista is calling everyone into the dining room. I admire the ornate woodworking, which is original to the home as my eyes trail over the large rectangular table. A neutral table runner sits in the center of the table, where dishes of food wait—roasted chicken with vegetables, mashed potatoes, and a garden salad.

Mr. Nelson waits at the head of the table. It's the first time I've seen him since arriving in his home. He's as intimidating as ever, and I fight the urge to hide behind Tristan. As we all fill the empty seats, I'm instructed to sit next to Tristan and across from Victoria, while Krista and Xander sit on each side of Mr. Nelson.

"Thank you for inviting me." The statement is open to anyone, but I'm hoping Mr. Nelson implies it's directed at him.

Mr. Nelson glances up, meeting my eyes for the first time. "Of course. Any friend of Tristan's is welcome."

"Girlfriend," Tristan corrects and my cheeks heat. I'll never tire of hearing him claim me, especially in front of his father.

The sounds of silverware clinking against plates are the only sounds in the room as the food platters are passed around. It's not an awkward silence, but a relaxed one, as if this is just a normal day. I guess to them, it is.

A few moments pass when Mr. Nelson clears his throat. "Are the villas completed at Paradise? What's the update?"

"Dennis," Krista chastises beneath her breath. "I thought we promised to keep business away from the table."

He doesn't respond, but I can feel his stare in our direction. My heartbeat picks up as the air starts to feel heavy. These damn villas are going to haunt me forever.

Wiping the corners of my mouth with the fabric napkin, I turn my attention to him. Tristan's hand lands on my thigh in a reassuring touch. "The villas should be completed this coming week."

A hum comes from the head of the table as my only reassurance that he heard me.

"Kennedy and I fly back down tomorrow morning for the final walk-through," Tristan is quick to add.

"These villas seem to be more trouble than they're worth," Mr. Nelson grumbles.

"They have been a pain, but the reward will be worth it." I smile sheepishly at my boss.

"I agree with Kennedy," Xander chimes in, setting his fork on his plate. "There's a lot of hype around them, with reservations booked through the year starting at the end of the month."

"Please, no more work talk. Today is about getting to know Kennedy." Krista sips from her wineglass as she stares down her husband. As intimidated as I am by my boss, it seems he's just as intimidated by his wife.

The conversation moves away from work as Victoria, Xander, and Tristan all razz on each other. As I'm about to take the last bite of mashed potatoes, Krista's voice has me pausing with my fork in the air.

"It wasn't that long ago when the kids were giving Tristan hell about a pretty girl in the office who was giving him a run for his money." She pauses, her eyes filling with moisture. "I begged them to tell me all about this girl, because I already knew she was special. Especially if she was bringing out the boy he used to be."

Tristan shifts in his chair uncomfortably, and it's my turn to place a reassuring hand on his thigh. He uses his opposite hand to weave our fingers together, giving them a quick squeeze.

"Tristan's road hasn't always been easy, and along the way, we lost a bit of him, but since the two of you have been together, I've seen the old Tristan again. The one that jokes, laughs, and walks through life for himself. We have you to thank for that, Kennedy."

It's my turn for tears to well in my eyes. I cast a glance at Tristan, who leans in and kisses my forehead.

"All that to say," Krista pauses, picking up her glass and everyone follows suit, "welcome to the family, Kennedy."

Cheers ring out around the table, and the warmth that surrounds me has me feeling complete.

We no longer stand on opposite sides of a blueprint, sketching rough straps from varying ideas as we try to outdo the other. Our paradise in progress is now complete.

In the wake is a solid skyscraper, built brick by brick from each moment we've shared—good, bad, and ugly. Our past supported our future, and together we'll walk solid and unwavering.

Epilogue

Four Years Later

It's funny how one place can hold so many memories. St. Lucia isn't just an island anymore—it's part of our history, woven into every major change in our lives.

Almost four years ago, this island was just another dot on the map. A location for a project with a hard-to-hit deadline, long hours, and more than a little tension between me and Kennedy. Now it's a living scrapbook holding every milestone, every turning point, and every new chapter of my life.

The private jet jolts as turbulence shakes us mid-descent, and I glance out the window to see the island's familiar coastline coming into view. Turquoise waters glisten in the sunlight as a wave of nostalgia hits me. Years later, this sight still affects me the same way with a mix of excitement and curiosity for what's to come. But the subtle dip of the plane drags my focus from the ocean back to the woman sitting beside me.

My wife's fingers are white-knuckling the armrest as if that's the only thing holding us in the air. Her face is calm, but her body betrays her.

"Still?" I tease, keeping my voice low as I fight the grin desperate to break free. "After all this time, I thought you'd be used to flying."

Her eyes dart to me, narrowing slightly, though her lips twitch like she wants to smile. "Oh, shut up," she murmurs, nodding toward my lap, where something—someone—sleeps soundly, completely unaware of the world around her. "This time, it's different. Now I have more to lose."

I let her words hang in the air for a moment, the weight of them sinking in as I look down at the tiny form curled up in my lap. My heart skips a beat.

There she is. Our daughter.

Lucy.

She's only a year old, but already she's got the kind of presence that demands attention. The soft curve of her face and her bright red curls just like her mother's. Lucy's little hand is nestled against my chest, her fist gripping my shirt as she rests peacefully in my arms.

The island below us stretches into the distance, but I can't help but focus on her, my daughter, the tiny miracle that changed everything.

We come back to this island for so many reasons—romantic, professional, nostalgic. But it's never been more meaningful than it is right now. Lucy is named after this place, a quiet homage to the island that brought Kennedy and me together to work out our issues and embrace the chemistry that had been swirling around us all those years ago. It feels fitting, almost like fate.

Looking down at Lucy, I can't help but marvel at how much life has shifted.

The last few years have been a blur—engaged just six months after we started dating, married a year later in a ceremony that felt like it could've been plucked from a dream. Our honeymoon here, followed by the shocking, incredible news that Kennedy was pregnant, something neither of us expected, but both of us embraced wholeheartedly.

Then the birth of our daughter. The sleepless nights and endless days, but also the overwhelming joy that came with it all. Watching Kennedy step into her new role as a mother, all the while continuing to lead as the head architect at our firm, made me fall even more in love with her.

Now, here we are again, four years later, returning to where it all began—with Lucy in tow.

I glance at Kennedy again, her eyes soft but focused on the island below us. As the turbulence settles, I see the small smile on her face. For all the changes, for all the growth and challenges we've faced together, she's still my Firecracker, the one I've always loved, and now, the mother of our daughter.

I kiss the top of Lucy's head, then look out the window again, at the island waiting for us. And as the plane begins its final descent, I know one thing for sure: there's no place I'd rather be.

• • • •●•●• • • •

As we pull into the resort's circle drive, the car slows, and I watch as the familiar entrance of the resort comes into view. The lush greenery and towering palms are as beautiful as ever, and the soft hum of the ocean breeze carries with it a sense of calm that never quite fades when we're here.

We park, the tires making a soft sound as we stop in front of the grand entrance. The moment the car door opens, the warm, tropical air rushes in, wrapping around us like a familiar embrace. I take a deep breath, the salty sea air filling my lungs, and I can't help but smile. Moving around the car to the opposite side, I remove Lucy from her car seat.

The newly appointed assistant manager is already walking toward us, his wide grin as inviting as the sunshine overhead. It's been a few years since we've seen Jayden, but his enthusiasm is as contagious as ever. After our time on the island, it was a no-brainer to promote our favorite driver to the assistant manager position he deserved. Jayden's the kind of person you can't help but be happy to see.

"Mr. and Mrs. Nelson." Jayden's beaming smile greets us before stretching his hand out.

"Jayden," I say while Kennedy takes Lucy from my arms, allowing me to take his hand to shake. "Assistant manager looks good on you."

He smiles before turning his attention to my wife and daughter. Kennedy lights up. "It's so good to see you again!"

"Always a pleasure," he replies, beaming. "And this little one. I can't believe Lucy's finally here! You've got to be excited to share this place with her."

Kennedy's smile softens as she cradles Lucy against her chest. "We are. She's already making the most of the air here."

I nod, unable to take my eyes off the way Kennedy looks at our daughter, the glow of the sun casting a golden halo around them both. It takes my breath away.

How did I get so lucky?

Jayden claps his hands together, clearly eager to help us settle in. "I'll have your bags waiting in the presidential suite. Feel free to take your time and enjoy the resort. The new restaurant is incredible."

We exchange a glance, both Kennedy and me eager to try out the new Italian restaurant that Michelin star chef, Scott Mariano, wanted to open at our resort after vacationing here a few years ago. While we haven't had a chance to try out his cuisine, we've heard so many incredible things about the menu.

The resort may have changed a bit, but the core of it—the magic that first brought us here—has remained the same.

We thank him, and he heads inside as we begin our stroll toward the beach, bypassing the main entrance. The entrance I remember suggesting and Kennedy glared at me for even daring to question her design. Golden light from the setting sun shines down on us, and I glance down to find Lucy gazing out over the water, her bright hazel eyes wide with wonder.

She squirms in Kennedy's arms, eager to explore, and Kennedy asks, "What do you think, Luce? Should we let you take your first steps on this sand?"

I chuckle as Kennedy lowers her to the ground. The tiny soles of her feet sink into the warm sand as she looks up at us with that familiar look of curiosity, as if she's just beginning to realize how big the world around her is.

The ocean, sparkling in the soft light of the afternoon, calls to her. She reaches out toward the waves, and Kennedy carefully helps her take her first steps into the surf.

I pull out my phone, capturing the moment—a memory that feels as sacred as the first time I saw Kennedy take those steps into the ocean. There's beauty in this shared experience, one that connects us, not just to this island, but to each other, and now to our daughter.

Watching Lucy take her first steps into the ocean, I can't help but reflect on how far we've come. This island, our oasis, has been a place of new beginnings, but it's also become a constant reminder of everything we've built together, everything we've overcome, and the love that has only deepened over time.

The golden hour fades, but the warmth of the moment lingers as I snap another picture. This is the start of a new chapter for us, and as much as this island will always be our past, it will continue to be our paradise in progress.

The End

• • • ● • ● ● • • •

Want more?

Thank you for reading *Paradise in Progress*! Something new is brewing, get ready for **a brand-new series is coming in 2025**, unlike anything I've written before.

Want to be the first to catch a glimpse of what's next? Sign up for my **newsletter** to receive exclusive updates, sneak peeks, and behind-the-scenes fun before anyone else:

https://authoralexisbuxton.myflodesk.com/lq9goai3y4

While you wait, don't miss my **CTU Eagles** series—a collection of interconnected standalones following a group of college students who've formed their own family as they navigate studies, sports, and falling in love.

https://mybook.to/ctuseries

Big things are on the horizon, and I can't wait to share them with you!

ACKNOWLEDGEMENTS

Paradise in Progress was such a joy to write. Most of this story came to life surrounded by the sounds of my children's laughter and splashes from our pool, the heat of the sun and Ohio humidity, and the refreshing taste of lime sparkling water. From playful banter to daydreaming about tropical vacations, I had endless fun creating these characters. It also brought back cherished memories of my own honeymoon in St. Lucia with my husband in 2012.

If you've read my other books, you know *Paradise in Progress* is a departure from my usual emotional sports romances. Stepping out of my comfort zone to write something so lighthearted and comedic was terrifying, to say the least. Thankfully, I had an amazing team cheering me on, helping shape this story into something I'm so proud of.

First, I want to thank my **BookstaBabes Reading Group**. What started during COVID as a buddy-reading space grew into beautiful friendships. Last January, when we discussed books we wanted to read, the need for a good workplace romance came up. Someone suggested I write one—and so I did. Aileen, Alexa, Brook, Jess, Lauren, and Lindsay: thank you from the bottom of my heart for being my biggest hype girls. Your support means more than words can express.

To my husband, Brad, and my kids: I love you with my whole heart. Thank you for holding down the fort and always encouraging me to keep going.

To my family and friends: Thank you for your endless support, in all its forms: *big or small.*

To Jenn McMahon: I can't imagine doing this author journey without you. Thank you for your endless words of wisdom, for sharing the latest piece of advice, and for your love and support. You truly are such a light in this industry and I'm so grateful to call you one of my closest friends.

To Krista: What started as one beta read on a different project has quickly grown into a friendship I treasure. I love your voice messages filled with random thoughts, perfect song suggestions, and your endless patience as I ramble on for minutes. You always respond with enthusiasm when I throw out random ideas for future stories, and your insights have made this book so much better. Naming a character after you was the least I could do—thank you for everything!

To My Alpha & Beta Readers (Alex, Aly, Carlene, Hollie, Libby, and Kari): Thank you for helping me make this one of my best books yet. Your feedback and reactions made me laugh, cry, and swoon. And smack my forehead at time or two at the obvious mistakes. I'm so grateful for each of you.

To Brittni at The Romance Doctor: Thank you for always picking out the plot holes and the inconsistencies, especially when pants are taken off multiple times.

To my incredible editor, Mackenzie at NiceGirlNaughtyEdits: I cannot thank you enough for shaping this rough manuscript into a beautiful story. I have had the absolute pleasure of working with you.

I am beyond excited to continue working with you on future projects. You are an absolute gem!

To Ashlee: You turned my simple cover vision into something beautiful. Thank you for creating the cover of my dreams. I am beyond obsessed with every little detail. Your talent is remarkable!

To my incredible ARC/Street Team members: Thank you for sharing my stories with the world. So many of you have been with me since day one and I can't tell you how much I appreciate your unwavering support. It might not seem like a lot to you, but to me it means the world.

Finally, to my readers and the entire Bookstagram community: thank you for picking up my books when there are millions to choose from. Your support lets me keep following my dreams, and I couldn't do this without you.

With all of my love,

Alexis

About the Author

Alexis Buxton is an avid reader turned author. A lover of all things love, Alexis enjoys reading all varieties of romance novels – the steamier, the better. Writing has always been a passion of hers and with the encouragement of friends and family, Alexis decided it was time to follow a childhood dream. She enjoys writing romance novels with damaged characters who need a little extra love and leave you *feeling all the feels*.

Born and raised in Ohio, Alexis currently resides in a small, lake town in Ohio with her husband and two small kiddos.

An avid sports fan, when she doesn't have a book in her hand, you can find Alexis watching sports. She prides herself on being a Cleveland Browns fan, even on the hardest days (or years). She also enjoys adventures with her family, visiting breweries, attending races at her local dirt track, and supporting local businesses and restaurants.

Alexis runs on caffeine and chaos, but she wouldn't have it any other way.

STAY IN TOUCH

facebook.com/authoralexisbuxton

instagram.com/author_alexisbuxton

goodreads.com/alexisbuxton

tiktok.com/@authoralexisbuxton

9 798988 822649